# The

# DARK

## *End of*

# TOWN

# The
# DARK
# End of
# TOWN

## JULIA POMEROY

CARROLL & GRAF PUBLISHERS
NEW YORK

THE DARK END OF TOWN

Carroll & Graf Publishers
An Imprint of Avalon Publishing Group, Inc.
245 West 17th Street
11th Floor
New York, NY 10011

AVALON
publishing group incorporated

Library of Congress Cataloging-in-Publication Data is available.

ISBN-10: 0-78671-720-3
ISBN-13: 978-0-78671-720-0

9 8 7 6 5 4 3 2 1

Design by Maria Elias

Printed in the United States of America
Distributed by Publishers Group West

*Dedicated to my first love, my mother,*
*Miggs Pomeroy*

# Acknowledgments

Special thanks to my editor, Will Balliett, for taking a shine to Abby; to my agent, Richard Parks, for his patience and hard work, and to Dale Davis for introducing me to him. Thanks to Aven Kerr for her thoughtful readings; thanks and love to Anne Beaty for endless moral support and much more; to my father, Liv, for raising us in interesting places; to my brothers, Eugene and Raif, for their humor and friendship; to my children, Jarrett and Algy, for being my role models; to my husband, John Gregory, for believing in me and pushing me on. And last but never least, thanks to my friend Phyllis Stoller, for reading and rereading this book, for being picky, demanding, and always encouraging.

Many thanks to the village of C., for being such an inspiration—I have taken liberties all over the place—moved buildings, changed stores, renamed streets, and borrowed surnames I love from the phonebook. Any resemblance to people living or dead is purely coincidental—except for some of the staff of the old B.P., and that wasn't my fault, I told them to go away, but they forced themselves onto the page.

# CHAPTER ONE

By some strange coincidence, it was exactly two years after Jonah killed himself in the flatbed of his father's old pickup, that Abby got the call about the missing minivan.

At that moment, Abby was also in a truck, an enormous truck, trying to get up her own driveway. She knew it was her driveway, but it was different—darker and steeper. And while she knew the house at the top of the hill was home, it wasn't her trailer—diarrhea-brown and patchy with age—it was a sweet white farmhouse, with a long, deep porch along the side facing the slope. More than anything, Abby had to reach the house. The reason why wasn't clear to her—she might have left something burning on the stove and smoke was filling the kitchen. Or maybe she had forgotten to turn off an upstairs faucet, and water was seeping under the door. Whatever the reason, she knew that every second she delayed, something was getting worse.

The truck struggled, its tires spinning then catching. She glanced up at the house and saw, with growing panic, that it had grown two new additions, one barely visible behind the house, the other a lean-to on its left side. The new structures were dirty, the paint peeling, the clapboard hanging off the framing. She pushed down on the accelerator, but the vehicle burrowed down, deeper into the mud. The pitch of the engine's whine went up an octave but she kept pressing down on the accelerator, unable to lift her foot. Finally, with a jolt, the wheels stopped moving.

As soon as she stepped out of the truck, she sank to mid-calf. Her boots were held down by suction and at her first step, one foot slid out and down into the cold, wet clay. She heard herself whimper. She looked up at the house: it had grown to twice its original size, rooms and add-ons stuck to it like fungus. The original building was hardly visible.

Both feet bare now, she pushed her legs through the viscous, dark substance. She tried to grip it with her hands, but it squeezed out between her fingers. With each step the mud was thicker, deeper. Her whimpering turned to a dry, painful sobbing, each breath raking painfully down her constricted throat.

At first, the sound was nothing more than a pale echo in her head. Then it became a rusty knife cutting into the nightmare. Finally it sharpened, gaining strength, slicing the dream away and disgorging her into the real world. She lay in bed, covered in sweat, still shuddering with unshed tears. She became aware of her surroundings. Her legs were weighted down by her two dogs. Her thin trailer walls were all that was keeping the dark night outside and she lay as still as she could, her chest rising and falling. The phone kept ringing. Her breathing began to quiet. Slowly, she turned on the bedside light.

"Hello?" Her voice was ragged, sounding strange even to herself.

"Abby?" The woman's voice at the other end sounded unsure.

"Who's this?"

The voice gained confidence. "It's Dulcie. What took you so long?"

"A dream. Nightmare." Abby tried to clear her throat. "What time is it?"

"Two-fifteen. Someone's taken my car."

Abby was having trouble understanding her. "Your car?"

"My car, they've taken it."

"Where?"

Dulcie's voice rose. "I don't know where. It's gone. Come over?"

Abby sat up in bed, trying to clear the mud from her brain. "Stolen?"

"No. I think they'll bring it back."

"Nobody stole it?"

"I think they borrowed it."

Oh, yeah. "One of the kids?"

"No, not one the kids!"

"Dulcie, call the police."

The small, double-hung window in her trailer bedroom was open and a breeze rustled the pages of a calendar hanging on the wall above the dresser. It was the only decoration in the drab, boxy room, a freebie from Hudson River Bank. For the month of May they had a color photograph of an old farmhouse with a wraparound porch, the painted boards dappled with sunlight. Corny, but you'd live there in a second.

"Abby, I'm scared—"

"Oh, shit, Dulcie, come on, I—"

"Please, Abby."

"Are the kids home?"

"I'll check. But it's not the kids. They have a car. Better than mine." She sounded pathetic.

Abby forced herself to pay attention. She cleared her throat again. "Lock the door and call the police. Or go to bed. We'll talk in the morning, okay?"

"Abby, please, I need you."

"Why me, Dulcie—"

"You'll think of something, please, I can't be here alone—"

The panic in Dulcie's voice sounded genuine. Resigned, Abby let out a slow, deep breath. "Okay. Check on the kids then lock the doors, front and back, Dulcie. I'll be over soon."

"Great, great. Thanks, Abby."

Abby hung up. She moved the small poodle mix, Rick, and his eyes stayed closed, though his tail gave a wag of acknowledgement. Delilah, the pit bull, watched her with doting eyes, her powerful tail drumming on the bed. Slowly, Abby put her feet on the floor and stood up. Like a hangover, her dream was still with her. She moved to the bathroom cautiously, so as not to shake it loose again. In the tiny bathroom, she looked at herself in the mirror over the sink. Muddy circles under her eyes, skin with a waxy, restaurant pallor. Nothing new. As she brushed her teeth, she thought with resignation of Dulcie, who somehow managed to look after her children and the people who worked for her all at the same time. It wasn't a big deal to go keep her company for an hour or so. The least she could do.

By the time Abby was ready to go, Delilah had taken over her warm spot, and Rick was on her pillow. She didn't have the heart to move him, and as if reading her mind, he snuggled in deeper.

# CHAPTER TWO

It was a flat, moonless night. On Abby's hill, it was so dark it felt as if black curtains were hanging over the night sky. In Bantam, the small, crooked village was a ghost town in the cold glare of the streetlights, the houses closed and sleeping. A cat scuttled across the road in front of Abby's old Ford Bronco, turning to look at her with yellow, suspicious eyes.

Around the village circle, she passed the darkened restaurant where she worked for Dulcie at least four nights a week. She turned up a long, steep side street, drove slowly for two blocks, and parked. She put the hand brake on, because High Street was named in the days before developers, when a street had to earn its title. She had no desire to find her Bronco back down on Main Street.

Dulcie's house was a shabby but solid Victorian, painted a faded green, with a tilting front porch. It looked black in the darkness. A faint light showed from behind the curtains of the front windows. She knew that the original brass doorbell, a twist handle in the middle of the oak door, would send a peal throughout the house. Not wanting to wake anyone, Abby knocked softly on the heavy door.

When Dulcie opened up, Abby noticed that she looked pale, with bluish smudges under her eyes. She looked as if she hadn't slept at all, but then she usually looked tired. A single mother of three with a restaurant—some people might call that burning the candle at both ends. Dulcie was a large woman, tall, with thick arms and legs rightly called limbs. Her looks, combined with the long flowered skirt she was wearing, gave her the appearance of an exhibit at a country fair. Dulcie was originally from the Midwest, of good Scandinavian farmer stock. When she was twenty, she signed up for a package tour to New York City, her first trip east. She fell in love with the city, and within a year she was back, living in a fifth-floor walk-up on East Thirty-third Street and working as a waitress in an Irish pub. Two years later, she married the owner. Eleven years after that, tired of his girlfriends, she took her three kids and moved upstate.

After looking up and down the dark street, Dulcie took Abby's arm and pulled her into the house. When she turned away, Abby noticed that her pale blond hair was tied back with a garbage tie.

The house had never been renovated and had a Victorian gloom to it, a lot of dark wood and dark brown wallpaper. A sobersides of a house, at war with the few bright belongings scattered about by Dulcie's three teenagers: pink and purple notebooks, an electric blue windbreaker, and a pair of frayed yellow hightops at the bottom of the stairs. A skateboard leaned on the banisters, its bright underside worn from curbside contact. Abby had been to the house before when the hip-hop was so loud it gave the old house a heartbeat, but tonight the only sound was the creak of the loose parquet as they crossed the hall. On the left was the dining room, now Dulcie's office. The table was lit by a gooseneck lamp and covered in papers, a computer, and an adding machine. They went into the dark kitchen behind the dining room. It, too, had a nineteenth-century feel to it, as if you might find a servant girl with a name like Colleen scrubbing iron pots in the sink. However, when they walked into the kitchen the only visible dishwasher was a chrome and white anachronism. It was open and empty, as though Dulcie had just finished unloading it. Abby could smell fresh coffee.

Normally Dulcie had a big, dimpled smile, but tonight she was too pre-occupied. She took two cups out of the cupboard, and without asking Abby, started pouring.

Abby pulled out a chair from under the scarred wooden table, and sat down. She yawned, her jaw cracking.

"I think they've done it before," Dulcie said intensely.

"Taken your car?"

"I've been putting on so many miles, and the car has been smelling funny—"

"Funny?"

"Like a strange perfume, or aftershave." Dulcie brought the two cups to the table and sat down. "You know where I park my car?"

"No."

"Up here, at the end of High Street. There's a dirt turnaround. I usually leave it there."

"How come?" Abby was surprised Dulcie didn't use her own little driveway, or park on the street in front of the house.

"When I park in the driveway, someone always blocks me in, one of the kids or a friend of theirs. This way, I'm free to go. Also, I hate to parallel park, okay?" She looked at Abby defiantly, daring her to comment.

"Okay, okay. So what happened?"

"Normally, I leave work at about midnight, park the car in the round-about, come home, unwind for a while, then go to bed. I sleep until maybe eight-thirty or nine, do a few chores, work at my desk, bookkeeping, stuff like that. If I have errands, I drive to Pittsfield or Albany. I'm usually back at the restaurant by four in the afternoon. I'm pretty dependable. The thing is, I think this creep has been taking my car while I'm sleeping."

"I don't know, Dulcie—"

Dulcie waved her to silence. "I've noticed things, but I didn't put it together before. Then tonight, I couldn't sleep, I was worried about the steaks we've been getting, have you seen how fatty they are? Big streaks of fat and gristle, it's dis—"

"Dulcie, not now—"

"Right, right. Anyway, I was in the living room, going over some invoices from the supplier. When I heard a car start up nearby, I didn't think much of it. Even though, this *is* a quiet neighborhood, nobody's out late. But for some reason, when the car drove by, I looked up. It was my blue minivan! I ran to the window, and saw part of the license plate as it turned the corner. It was mine! I was so freaked out, I didn't know what to do. So I called you."

"Did you go out to make sure?"

Dulcie shook her head. "No. I was afraid. I didn't want to go alone."

"Why didn't you take one of the boys with you?"

"Are you kidding? And put one of my kids in danger? What if someone's waiting out there? With a gun?"

"Great, so put me in danger. Anyway, if they took the car they're not waiting out there. You're sure they've done this before?"

Dulcie nodded. "Looking back on it I'm sure."

"So this smell in the car—"

"Yeah, a sort of lemony perfume smell."

"Cologne, or aftershave?" If Dulcie could answer this question, they could cut the suspects down by half the population. Maybe.

"I couldn't tell. It was just citrusy, you know. But good. And another thing—I've been getting incredible mileage. I've kept track, I know." She stood up, reached in the pocket of her skirt, and pulled out a crumpled piece of paper. She flipped the piece of paper onto the table and sat back down.

Abby looked at the paper, which was covered in numbers. Given the time of night, it meant nothing to her. "Why would you get good mileage if someone were stealing your car? It shouldn't make any difference."

Dulcie looked at her as if she were simpleminded. "You would, if the thief replaces the gas he uses. You'd read the odometer, and come to the conclusion that you're driving all these extra miles without having to fill it. I even called *Car Talk* to boast about it. They said, only a hybrid can get fifty miles to the gallon. Not a minivan. They had a good laugh." Dulcie rubbed her face with her hands. "Seriously, Abby, it gives me the creeps. I feel as if someone's watching me."

Abby nodded. "They probably are. So who else has a key?"

Dulcie shook her head. "No one. I mean, I have my key, and I have a spare. I've never given it to anyone."

"Where do you keep it, in the house?"

Dulcie snorted. "That wouldn't do me any good. I keep it in one of those magnetic key boxes, you know, hidden in the fender."

"Does anyone know you keep it there? The kids? Anyone at the restaurant?"

Dulcie shrugged. "I don't know. Maybe. I've probably told the kids. And why would I tell anyone at the restaurant?"

Abby thought. "Have you used it recently?"

Dulcie shook her head, as if at her own failings. "At least twice since Christmas. And maybe once in the fall. I'm always locking my key inside the car. I'd be up a creek without that spare."

"Where did you do it? At the restaurant, at night?"

"Oh, I've done it at the drugstore, once at the restaurant—I even locked myself out of the car when I went to church. I only go twice a year, Christmas and Easter, so this was Easter. There I am, in front of everyone, scrabbling around under the car, on my knees. Father Gary came over and offered me a cushion. Funny guy."

Abby nodded. "So that's most likely how they did it. You've got to go to the cops."

"I don't want the police involved. What if it's a friend of one of the kids, or someone I know?"

"But what if it's a stalker, or some psycho?"

Dulcie thought about it then shook her head. She spoke gently. "I'm sure it's someone who needs a car. A perfectly normal person, just ashamed to ask. You know, doesn't have enough money to buy a car. Just got a job in Albany, or something." A shadow seemed to pass over her. "Goddamn it, they should take out a fucking loan. You're right, it's probably a psycho, trying to freak me out. Some crazy person, who hates me. But a psycho, wouldn't he have done more to scare me?"

"Like maybe leaving something weird in the car? A photograph of you, or a pile of shit, or something?"

9

"Oh, my God. That's really disgusting. Should I warn the kids? What am I going to do?"

"Okay, okay." Abby looked into her coffee cup, then up at Dulcie's expectant face. "Let's go. We've gotta wait for Psycho to bring it back." When Dulcie looked at her blankly, she added: "The car?"

Dulcie paused, then stood up. "You're right! We should be sitting in the living room now. Bring your tea."

Abby shook her head. "No. We've got to wait outside, right where they park the car, so we can see them. If you know him, you can talk to him—I hope there's just one of them—and that'll end it."

"I can't do that, I can't talk to a thief! You do it, please. You could wait outside, not too close to the car, I have night-vision glasses and blankets, and I'll give you my cell phone, and when they park the car and get out, dial my pager. I'll be sitting in the living room, and I'll look carefully, see if I recognize him, and neither of us has to deal with him directly. It's much safer for both of us. And the timing's perfect, I don't have anything going on too early so I can sleep in."

It sounded to Abby as if she had been set up. Dulcie must have considered waiting for the car. It didn't matter, she wasn't going to argue about it. She much preferred watching a parking lot than going back to bed with her nightmares. "Okay. But I need something waterproof to sit on. The grass'll be wet."

# CHAPTER THREE

S uspiciously fast, Dulcie found her a ragged blanket, a flashlight, an anti-quated pair of night-vision glasses her son had found on an army sur-plus web site, and a vinyl-covered boat cushion. Her arms full, Abby trudged up the road to the turnaround, which was nothing more than a clearing in the trees where the asphalt gave way to a dirt circle. The village officially ended with the tarmac. To the right were scrubby woods, and to the left open pastures sloped up the hill, separated from the turnaround by a hedgerow.

Abby stood for a minute, trying to visualize exactly where Dulcie would park her car so she could position herself to get a good view. She decided the field was the best place to be, as long as she was hidden behind the hedge. She worked herself in behind the bushes, put the slippery vinyl cushion down on the damp grass, and sat. The blue glow of her watch told her it was three-thirty. She wrapped the blanket around her shoulders, and settled in.

She should have brought a book, some Pepperidge Farm cookies, and a kerosene lantern, she thought to herself. Or built a fire and roasted some marshmallows. The night still seemed particularly black, and she sat, waiting for her eyes to adjust to the dark. Eventually, she started to make out the outline of the hedge, and if she turned and faced the field, she could see the difference in blackness between the gently curving field that rose behind her, and the sky. The stars were hidden by clouds. Curious, she put the night-vision glasses over her head, and switched them on. They were too big for her and felt heavy and awkward. It took her a moment to adjust to the strangeness of them.

The turnaround was now awash in a green glow. She thought about those times when she and Jonah had taken a sleeping bag up their hill and laid down, staring up at the stars, listening for the rustle of a possum and watching the bats feather across the bright yellow moon. And now, here she was, squatting behind a hedge, in all likelihood in grave danger of being pissed on by someone's Doberman, with this Peeping Tom contraption on her head. She was disappointed in herself: thirty-two years old, a widow, no children, no career, living in a trailer. An old, ugly trailer, to boot. As the weight of the goggles gradually bowed her neck and back, she thought back to Jonah.

The first time she met him, she was living in New York in a grubby little walk-up on East Fifteenth Street. When she wasn't working for a temp agency, she was a struggling model. As a girl she had stood out at Bantam High, with her long legs, clear, bright skin, chestnut brown hair, and green eyes. So after high school she told herself college could wait, but New York couldn't.

However, in the big city she was just one of the vast armada of pretty girls, portfolios under their arms, whose major source of encouragement came from the construction crews that blocked downtown streets most days of the year. The big agencies told her that at 5'8" she wasn't tall enough; the backroom agencies wanted a fee. She finally found a small office that agreed to send her out on a trial basis.

That Thanksgiving, Abby went home to Goose Creek. Before she got the train back to the city, her mother gave her a duffel bag to give to the son of a woman she had met at the farmer's market. He was a junior at NYU and Abby would be doing her mother's friend a big favor, and anyway, she and the boy were bound to get along, they came from the same school district.

Resentfully, Abby carried the heavy duffel bag back to the city with her. She knew what was inside, because she had poked through it. A fleece-lined jacket, textbooks, some homemade jam, sneakers, other odds and ends. Surely he could have done without it all until his next trip home. When she got back to her apartment, after trudging up the dark staircase carrying both her own bag and the duffel, the jam jars clinking heavily inside, she called the number her mother had given her. He had one of those messages on his answering machine that was the ultimate in terse: "Speak now," surrounded by acres of loud, gravelly heavy metal. She left her name and phone number and put the duffel bag in her closet.

Two days later, she booked her first catalogue job for a discount clothing chain out of Boston, and decided to celebrate. She asked her roommate, Mary, to go out for a drink with her. She'd found Mary on a bulletin board at NYU; she was a shy English major who sniffed everything she touched. She'd pick up an orange and sniff it before peeling it; she'd sniff her fingertips before typing; she'd sniff her brush before putting it to her head. Mary, the Sniffer. Mary turned her down. She was busy.

On Friday, Abby met up with some people she barely knew at a bar on McDougal Street. At the end of the evening one of the guys offered to walk her home. He was interesting, or relatively so—the sound level in the bar was so high their conversation had never progressed past small talk and a good deal of nodding, so she didn't really know. But he looked interesting. When they got to her apartment, she unlocked the door, and there, sitting on the floor, looking through the upstate duffel bag, was a stranger with long, stringy dark blond hair. Mary the Sniffer was standing nearby, watching him.

Her first impression of him was of energy. He jumped to his feet. His voice was too loud in the small apartment. "Look, this bag—it's a voodoo ritual of motherly love—each item is meant to protect a different part of the body." He held up a jar of jam—"stomach," he said, then grabbed the warm jacket, "—torso," he pushed a book with his foot, "—head," and picked up a shoe, "—foot. See? I'm safe, I could walk in front of a bus, nothing would happen to me!" He looked intently at Abby, waiting for her to say something.

Abby couldn't come up with anything. She stared at him. The guy from the bar broke the silence by giggling. Jonah pushed everything back in the bag, zipped it up, and was gone.

The chemistry between her and the guy from the bar had barely survived the walk home and now it dissipated, like cigarette smoke on a windy day. Within ten minutes Abby told him she was tired, and he said he had a paper to finish. He'd been gone less than five minutes when the intercom buzzed. She stood in the hallway, listening to footsteps echoing up the stairwell. It was Jonah. He stopped when he reached six steps from her floor. He was still carrying the duffel bag.

Suspiciously, Abby wondered if there was something wrong with him. "What is it?" she asked.

He held out a hand to her. In it was a pot of jam. "It's good stuff. Take it. Thanks for bringing this down from Bantam." He smiled at her. It was a true smile, and in the harsh light from the stairwell she thought he looked beautiful. His scruffy hair made a halo of yellow around his face, framing a stubble of beard on his pale cheeks, a gently curved chin and pale eyes, their color hard to see in the overhead glare.

When she and Jonah first moved up to Bantam, after his father's death, they had so many plans. They were going to turn the barn into a sound stage, build a recording studio, and transform the farm into a place where artists would come to create, a haven for young, exciting filmmakers. Abby worked at the restaurant, and Jonah wrote grants and made endless phone calls, encouraging people he knew from the city to come up and be part of something important. But the whole thing never quite worked out. The grants didn't come in, and Jonah's friends would come for a few weeks or a month, but when they realized how much physical labor was involved, they left.

Sometimes apologetically, other times after a row, usually on the trail of steady work and a paycheck. Jonah was deeply disappointed they didn't see what he saw and weren't prepared to work with him toward it.

But Abby thought he scared them off. One day he would get up at dawn and work until there was no light left to see his tools, never stopping to eat, and expecting his volunteer labor force to do the same. The next day he would sit in his and Abby's bedroom, writing on his old Toshiba laptop. Without him, the construction would dwindle to a halt. There was no rhythm or pleasure to the work, and Abby understood why everyone eventually found somewhere else they had to be.

She quit her waitressing job so she could work alongside him but, if anything, that made matters worse. They quickly burned through the little money Jonah's father had left them, and though they lived on peanut butter sandwiches, the bills began to pile up. In hindsight, it was all an inevitable progression—they should have gotten out while they still could. But at the time there seemed no way out. To Abby, the farmhouse became a prison. When she was there, she felt she was a prisoner inside Jonah's head. The very space seemed to side with him during their raging arguments that began out of nowhere and ended only when one of them drove off.

After Jonah's death, she had gone back to work at the InnBetween. One of the things she treasured, after those noisy, intense days, was a measure of peace and quiet. *Well,* she thought as she crouched in the bushes, *there is plenty of that here, waiting for a car thief who may never show up.* A picture of where her life was going started to materialize out of the dense night air, gripping her. She saw her future, entangled in a swamp of failed dreams and loneliness, her only human contact squeezed out of dinner shifts at the Inn-Between. The dark night that surrounded her only added to her feeling of isolation. The glasses she was wearing turned the world into a cold moonscape, and she started to panic. Her heart banged in her chest, and she swayed on her haunches.

Maybe it was the blood pounding in her ears, but she didn't hear the footsteps moving quickly toward her up High Street. When she finally did, she raised her eyes and looked in their direction, forgetting the heavy goggles strapped to her head. Whoever it was suddenly turned on a flashlight and pointed it directly at her. The bright white light exploded onto her retinas, knocking her over.

She lay still.

Then, a whisper:

"Abby, you there?"

It was Dulcie. Relief flooded through Abby, followed by anger. She ripped the glasses off her head, and slowly sat up, her eyes still closed. "What are you doing, I'm blind, go away—"

"Sorry, but you forgot the cell phone—" Dulcie leaned over the hedge and dropped the small phone into her lap. Then footsteps on the tarmac, getting quieter and quieter. More silence.

Finally, the white glare behind her lids faded. Abby was relieved to hold the phone. A lifeline to the world outside her head. She sat up a little straighter. This time, no mind wandering. No poor me. She listened, actively. Crickets. A dog barking. The shrill voices of a TV, probably from High Street. The horn of a car. Burst of laughter. Another dog. She checked her watch. Twenty minutes had passed since Dulcie had brought her the phone. An owl hooted. A distant whine of an engine. Yes, an engine, distant, but getting closer. Abby realized it was slowing at the intersection, then turning onto High Street. She fumbled with the cell phone. When she opened it, it seemed dangerously bright, visible to anyone. The car was moving slowly up High Street. She pushed the numbers so that she could leave a message on the pager. She imagined it vibrating in Dulcie's hand as she sat tensely by the darkened window. Luckily, the clouds that had been shielding the moon had drifted away, allowing it to cast a sudden, strange brightness upon the street. She could see the car moving slowly up the street. It reached the edge of the turnaround. The high beams were directed straight at her, and for a moment Abby thought she was going to be run down. She felt completely exposed. Then just as quickly, the vehicle turned into the circle and stopped. The engine was turned off and the headlights doused. The interior light came on. Abby peered through the spiny branches of the hedge.

Sitting alone in the minivan was a young woman. The dashboard lights gave her a greenish glow and maybe it was a trick of the lights, but she seemed to be smiling. Pleased with herself. She rested her forehead on the steering wheel. Or maybe she was just picking up something from the floor. A sideways motion made her hair swing in her face and she opened the door and climbed out.

She bent over the car door and Abby guessed she was locking it. Then, like any shopper at the mall, she hitched a purse over her shoulder, turned and walked away. Abby listened to the sharp sounds of her heels on the tarmac. She walked in the middle of the street. Abby raised her head over the bushes to try to see her fully, and at that moment, the woman stopped and turned, as if she sensed someone there. Abby froze. The woman's head moved slowly, as if she were scanning the end of the street where Abby was only partially hidden. Finally, she turned away and walked briskly down High Street.

Slowly, Abby stood up straight, her knees stiff and painful. She picked up her possessions, limped out of the bushes and down the street in the direction the girl had taken. Within moments she was at Dulcie's front door, letting herself in quietly so she wouldn't wake the kids. She stood in the darkened front hall. No greeting from Dulcie, which surprised her. Abby put the cushion, blanket, and commando glasses down by the door, and went softly into the dark living room. An armchair was pulled up to the window, as planned. She couldn't tell if anyone was in the chair and felt a flicker of worry. Afraid to look in the chair, she pushed aside her anxiety and peered around the high back. Dulcie was curled up, her feet tucked under her, her mouth slightly open. She looked bloodless in the stark light from the street. Suddenly, she breathed heavily and turned her head, nestling into the armchair. She was fast asleep. Abby noticed that she had covered her lap in a thick, oversized, creamy angora blanket. The pager was resting on the blanket.

"Hey." She shook Dulcie's shoulder.

Dulcie started awake, staring at Abby blindly for a second. Recognition appeared in her eyes, followed by the partial memory and, finally, dismay. "Oh, shit. I was sleeping."

"So I see."

Dulcie sat up and rubbed her eyes like a child. "Oh. Did you see who it was?"

"Sort of," Abby said.

"What do you mean?"

"Well, it's a girl, but I don't know who she is. I was hoping you'd recognize her."

"Shit. Does she have her own key?"

"Looks like it." Dulcie had been no use at all.

"She works in the restaurant?"

"I don't think so, but it was dark and I was hiding in the fucking bushes."

"Come on, Abby. Don't be a jerk. I'm sorry I slept, okay? I've been on my feet all night, being nice to people. It's tiring."

Abby relented. Dulcie did work hard. "Okay."

After a pause, Dulcie threw off her blanket. "I'm hungry. You hungry? Let me make you some tea and toast."

Abby was cold and tired. Tea and toast sounded good. They went into the kitchen; Dulcie put the kettle on the stove and turned on the gas. Abby sat down at the table. The kettle was a black and white cow, with a head and mouth for the spout. She wondered if one of the children had given it to their mother, or if Dulcie had picked it out herself. Dulcie found some tea bags and put slices of white bread in the toaster. She put out butter and jam. After a few minutes, the cow whistled, and the toast popped.

"Well, that's that." Dulcie poured milk into her tea.

Abby bit into her slice of toast. "We know it's a she—and she didn't look dangerous, so my feeling is, we wait for her again tomorrow before she takes the car and we nail her ass."

Dulcie groaned. "Forget it. I'm going to change the locks first thing. Throw away that key box. I can't do this again tomorrow."

Abby shook her head. "I want to know who she is. We're waiting, okay?" She held Dulcie's gaze until her boss looked away, defeated.

Dulcie sighed heavily. "Okay. When do we start?"

Abby took a last bite of toast, savoring the sharp sweet taste of the strawberry jam. "As soon as we get off work. And this time, you sit *outside* with me. It was lonely out there in the dark."

The sun was rising as Abby drove home. She snaked up River Street, past where the asphalt ended and the dirt began. Nestled on the left side of the road, hidden by three huge maples, was the old Silvernale farmhouse. Abby's farm. When Jonah died, she inherited it. In the old days, when his father was alive, it was a dairy farm that spread out over more than 250 acres. Along the road, and on either side of the old clapboard house, were the rusted-out cars, pickups, and farm vehicles that her father-in-law used up during his tenure. Some of them might have been older than that. She and Jonah had never gotten around to doing anything about them, so they sat where he left them. She had found her two-toned blue and white 1975 Bronco in the yard, a snowplow weighing down the front end. She took the plow off, put in a new air filter, and changed the oil and the spark plugs. The shocks weren't great, but with a full tank of gas, there was no looking back.

In his last years, her father-in-law sold off a good deal of the land to pay his wife's medical bills, but Abby still owned the farmhouse, two barns, and seventy acres. She leased the farm for a modest amount to a young couple, Lloyd and Noreen. They had cows, so they kept the pastures baled or chewed, and they maintained the farmhouse. Abby got a tax break, which she couldn't use. But as long as she never had to set foot in the house, she was satisfied.

To get home, Abby turned into the farm driveway, but rather than make the final loop into the yard, she kept going straight on a rough track that wound up the hill behind the house. Past the crest of the hill, hidden from view, was her double-wide trailer, its mustard-brown siding peeking through the honeysuckle. An antique, she found it for $320 in Copake, and had it trucked up. She had to dig a well, and she still hadn't finished paying off the septic tank, but it was worth it. It was beautiful on her hilltop. She could see as far as the Catskill Mountains in one direction and the Berkshires in another.

When Abby got home she let the dogs out, pulled off her shoes, and crawled into bed. She lay there, but she was so tired sleep wouldn't come. Like faulty wiring, her nervous system kept firing, keeping her awake and agitated. Her gaze went back to the calendar. She looked at the date. The perfect farmhouse in the photograph seemed to glow. She pictured the Silvernale porch light that morning, two years earlier. How the light was still on, though the sun was shining. You could only tell it was on if you looked straight at the bulb. A little Y of light inside the thin glass.

Two years ago, she had pulled up in front of the house and sat in the car, engine running, grateful that everything looked normal. The boots she had left on the porch were still there, and one of the upstairs windows was open, just the way she had left it the day before. Nothing to worry about. She turned off the ignition, climbed out, and walked up to the porch. And then she noticed that light bulb. A flush of dread rolled over her like a deep, hot blush, making her ears burn. Afterwards she thought it wasn't so much intuition, as it was her unconscious processing faster than reason. She pulled at the screen door, her heart hammering so hard she could feel it in her neck. She stood in the front hall trying to listen to the house over the pounding of her own blood.

# Chapter Four

Five hours later, Abby woke up to an overcast sky and sharp, intermittent barks from Rick. Not surprising, because her smaller dog always found something worth barking at—chipmunks, crows, an occasional leaf. She lay in bed, thinking about living alone. She didn't mind it. True, sometimes if she was alone for too long she heard her own voice echo inside her. At those times her vision was a little glassy and her ears felt as if they had water in them. Like having a bad cold. Ironic, because living with Jonah had been so relentless that she had often longed to be alone and still; now she had enough quiet to make her ears ring. Sometimes she had to sing or talk out loud to pierce the silence. She welcomed the sharp yap of her small dog.

She got up and looked out the living room window. The dogs were watching the road. Waiting. For what, anyway? She looked at her Bronco. One day she was going to have some bodywork done, fix the rust, knock out a few dents, but that day seemed to have slipped into the blue distance, like the Catskills.

She showered and, in sweatpants with her hair wrapped in a towel, sat outside the front door on her white metal porch chair, sipping coffee. From where she sat, she could see Lloyd's cows grazing on the opposite slope. The day was clearing. Sun was breaking through the cloud cover in a cone-shaped beam, like the precursor to a holy event. The view was like the layering of scenery in a children's play, starting far away with the soft blue hills and getting brighter and greener as it grew closer, ending with the emerald green of each blade of grass in her own field.

She wondered about the dark-haired girl. Where had she come from? Had she gone to meet someone? Maybe she really did have a job in Albany and couldn't afford her own car. While Abby drank her coffee, the glorious view stretching in front of her, she thought how strange it was to dress up in nice clothes, and take someone else's car. Without asking. And with a smile on your face.

By day, Bantam was a very different town. It bustled. There were cars on the traffic circle and pedestrians on the sidewalks. As usual, Main Street looked charming and deceptively placid. Most of the buildings were turn-of-the-last century brick, the tallest one three stories high. There was the Clocktower at one end, and next to it the old vaudeville house with its long, graceful windows. Along the same side, Joe the Barber had his shop, with used golf balls for sale in the window; next to Joe was the health food store, and next to that the Bantam Bookstore. The liquor store was further down, before you reached the Dollar Store. Across the street was the Kipling Movie Theater, For Dog's Sake Grooming Salon, and the old Carlson building, still holding onto its name from the days when it was a family-owned department store, carrying everything from shovels to silk stockings.

It was a peaceful town until the train thundered through, right behind and along the Clocktower side of Main Street. It swayed and screamed and whistled. All traffic stopped. They said the bricks of the buildings on that side of the street were being shaken loose. The year after Jonah died, the train plowed through town and derailed over River Street, throwing massive freight cars off the tracks. Amazingly, no one was hurt, but the accident seemed to prove a point about Bantam. Like its namesake, the small rooster, it was not to be taken lightly. Abby knew this for a fact.

Dulcie's restaurant, where Abby had worked since she first moved back to the area, was called the InnBetween. It was in an old brick building on the Circle, stuck in the V between Route 46 and Findlay Street. Hence the name. It looked bigger than it was, because of the ornate wraparound porches on each floor. If you stood facing the building, Route 46, on your right, headed steeply downhill; on that side of the building the basement had an entrance onto the street.

In the late eighties, a Boston couple bought it, did extensive renovation, and named it Chez Nous. But the business was not as lucrative as they expected: the locals wouldn't come and the weekenders didn't like the food. They had spent too much on the renovation and after four years they were bankrupt. A year later, Dulcie bought the building at auction from the bank, paying for it with her divorce settlement. She found the original sign in the attic, hung it over the front door, and applied for a liquor license. She was a good boss, and Abby respected her. She was as close to family as Abby had in town.

That night, it was about a quarter to twelve by the time Abby gave Dulcie the high sign. They left the restaurant together. Abby walked briskly along the dark street, while Dulcie trailed behind like a child on her way to the dentist. They had agreed not to mention to anyone what they were doing, in case the person taking Dulcie's car was connected to one of the staff. The plan was simple. Abby would drive her car to Dulcie's house and park. Dulcie would drive directly to the turnaround. She had already stashed two sleeping bags in the back of the minivan. Quickly and quietly, she was to hide herself and the sleeping bags behind the hedge. Abby would join her. With luck, no one would see either of them doing all this.

Everything went according to plan, and they met behind the hedgerow, on the same patch of ground Abby had occupied the night before. They each climbed into a sleeping bag and sat down. They had nothing to lean on, so they propped themselves up against each other.

"What do we say if someone finds us here?" Dulcie whispered, once they had settled in.

"We say we're on a Vision Quest, and this is the second of three nights we have to spend in the wild."

Dulcie giggled. "No one's going to believe that. Not when they find us sitting behind a hedge. With cookies."

"You brought cookies? Good idea."

"Who knows how long we'll be out here?"

"So we tell them we've run away from home."

They stopped talking, and let the night lull them. It was comforting having Dulcie's warm body next to hers. Eventually, Abby dozed off with her head on Dulcie's shoulder. When Dulcie moved, she adjusted by lying down on the ground, the sleeping bag pulled up around her.

She awoke to Dulcie shaking her.

"Is she here?" she whispered, looking around in confusion.

Dulcie's had her sleeping bag over her shoulder. "It's four A.M. The car's still here. She's not coming."

Abby stood up and sure enough, the blue minivan was right where Dulcie had parked it hours before. She went over to the car and put her hand on the hood. As cold and damp as the seat of her jeans. She wondered if, after all, the woman had spotted her the night before.

"That's it, I'm changing the locks in the morning," Dulcie said, her voice hoarse from lack of sleep. They walked past the car and down High Street. They didn't bother saying goodnight when Dulcie climbed her crooked porch steps and Abby unlocked the door of the cold Bronco.

# CHAPTER FIVE

L ater that day, Abby arrived at the restaurant a few minutes before her shift began at 4:00 P.M. Dulcie had a school event, and wouldn't be in until later. The afternoon had turned muggy and hot. The floor staff hadn't arrived yet, but the kitchen staff had been working since noon. They were taking a break, drinking espresso on the second-floor porch. They called it "going to church," and no one was allowed to discuss work with them while they were there. As long as you kept it social, however, you were always welcome: they were especially partial to gossip about other restaurants, regular customers, or townsfolk. Abby dropped in, said hello, then went back downstairs to supervise the dining rooms. The upstairs room felt warm, so she checked the air-conditioning. It was set at sixty-eight degrees, but the thermostat read seventy-two. She put her hand to the vents, and felt nothing coming out. She went back upstairs.

"George, when did you turn on the air?" George Bellomino, the chef, grew up working in his father's luncheonette, and the business was in his blood and in his gut. Bull-necked, with a huge, round belly that was as hard as a bell, he had a sweet smile and a stubborn, overshot jaw. When he worked he wore balloon-like pants busily patterned with fruits, and a red or yellow bandanna tied around his large head.

"What d'ya think, Sandy, about, say, two?" Sandy, his second-in-command, was George's opposite. He was pale next to George's ruddiness. A slight man, he was fastidious, with curly brown hair and a soft, high-pitched voice. In the kitchen, he and George could be overheard having long discussions about plate presentation, and different schools of thought on puff pastry. Goodfella meets the Mikado.

"Quarter to two, I had just taken out the profiteroles," Sandy said with his usual precision.

"Not cold enough out there?" George did not look sympathetic. The cold air didn't run in the kitchen. They had to make do with fans even during the summer. "Come on, Sanford, back to the salt mines." They clomped down the wooden stairs.

Abby went into the upstairs office, looking for the phone number of the repair people. She finally found it listed under P for Plumber. Mike Testarossa. He seemed to repair everything—heating, air, and refrigeration. She called and left a message.

Downstairs, the staff had begun to arrive. When they complained about the heat, Abby turned on both ceiling fans and told them to open the windows, though there was no breeze and the air from outside was hot and stale, indistinguishable from the air inside. She tried the air-conditioning controls again. She checked her watch. Four-twenty, and they were scheduled to open the dining room in forty minutes. Abby left a new message for the plumber, this time begging him to call her.

Slowly the place filled with familiar faces, some local, some New York City weekenders stealing a little extra time away. Occasionally, Abby found herself scanning the crowd, looking for the dark-haired car thief. The night dragged on. The plumber didn't return Abby's call, even though she left two more messages. Strangely enough, the customers seemed to be having a good time. Maybe they were pretending to have stumbled into a hangout for hard-drinking expatriates on some forsaken tropical island, because the staff could barely keep up with the orders for Mexican beer and gin and tonics. The women sat holding their hair up so the fans could cool off their necks. Abby wondered if they were taking consolation from knowing that their waiters, shiny with sweat, were far hotter that they were.

Only one person complained, and it wasn't about the heat. A regular customer, with a name something like Alaria, privately known to the staff as Malaria. A woman in her early forties, she was eating alone. She stopped Abby on her way to the kitchen.

"Abby." She smiled apologetically. "I need a huge favor."

"Sure. What can I do?"

She pointed to the ceiling. "This awful music—I can barely swallow my food, my stomach's in knots."

Abby listened, but had trouble distinguishing the music from the clatter of dishes and noise of fifty-some people, eating, laughing, and talking.

"I'll take care of it." She smiled at Malaria, and continued on to the kitchen. After putting in her order, she went down the back stairs to the bar. Henry was mixing up martinis. Henry was twenty-four years old and claimed to be of Aztec descent. He had an aquiline nose that broadened at the nostrils, a wide generous smile, and thick black hair that he wore in a high ponytail, the lower half of his scalp shaved. He was loyal, hardworking, and had a crude sense of humor.

"Henry, Malaria says—" she began.

Henry sneered. "Tell her to go fuck herself. All she does is complain."

"She says, 'your choice of music is making her gag.' "

Henry let out a bark of laughter. "You tell Malaria that I've got a better way to make her gag, okay?"

Abby shook her head. Tsk, tsk.

Cyrus Leighton and his wife, Paula, sat at a fourtop on the porch. He was an old toad, round and slow and squashy. He befriended Abby when he found out about her fledgling career as a model, and that she had worked briefly on a soap opera when she and Jonah were first married. He discovered that he could tell her long stories about his peculiar history as a New York theatrical producer, and then as a Hollywood screenwriter, and she would listen. A few vodkas, however, and he became mean and caustic. Most evenings he would call her over and try to get her to sit down. On a quiet night she usually would. Sometimes he would tell her a joke, or order Paula to tell one. Abby enjoyed some of the dirty ones, but didn't understand the "insider" ones, often about screenwriters in Hollywood. He and Paula would tell them, then laugh until their eyes filled with tears.

The crowd was thinning out by the time Cyrus Leighton caught her eye and called her over. He insisted on kissing her cheek. She tried to avoid it, since he was still eating. Of all their customers, he was the most disgusting eater. One waitress said he once asked her for a scotch and soda, and on the final ess he spat a glob of food onto her arm. She still shivered when anyone mentioned it. Abby's response was, they should be grateful he was usually a vodka drinker. When the waitress looked puzzled, Abby had to explain, as if to a simpleminded child: "No ess—you know?"

"Hello, Cyrus. Paula. How's your meal?"

As usual, Cyrus talked with his mouth full. "This is the best roast chicken. We can't find chicken like this, even in the city." Abby could see a good deal of that same bird as he spoke.

"I'm glad. You up for the whole summer?"

Cyrus Leighton swallowed noisily. Tenderly, Paula reached across the table and plucked a morsel of his dinner off his chin.

"Darling," he said, in a gravelly voice, "I hate it, but I have to go to Hollywood. They're starting work on my new picture. I'll be there for a few weeks, then they'll throw me off the set, and I'll be home. Isn't that right, Paula? Ask Paula, she knows."

Paula nodded cynically. "It's true. He's a big mouth, they don't like having him around. He tells them what they're doing wrong."

"They wanna kill me, but I'm a damn good writer. Fuck 'em. Which reminds me. Sweetheart, I got a job for you. You wanna make some money?"

"Of course she does, Cyrus. She's working here, isn't she?"

"I'm actually doing this for fun." Abby was leery of a job offer from Cyrus Leighton.

"Don't worry. I'm not offering you an acting job. Though you could probably still do it. A little tuck under the chin, though, maybe an eye lift." He was looking at her appraisingly.

She tried not to lose her temper. "I've got to get back to work, Cyrus." She started to walk away.

"Leave her alone, Cyrus." Paula shook her head.

"Wait, wait, don't go. Transposing! Transposing!" Reluctantly, Abby walked back to their table.

"Explain better, Cyrus. She's confused."

Abby sighed. "Explain better, Cyrus."

"You know I write longhand. Number 2 pencil, legal-size pads."

She shook her head. "Believe it or not, I didn't know."

"Anyway, Paula usually types up my stuff." Paula rolled her eyes at Abby. The reluctant saint.

Cyrus continued: "But she's coming to California with me, and I need the work transposed. So, I give you the keys, and you do it."

"You trust me in your house? Why don't you just give me the originals, I'll do them at home, give you a disc?"

"I can't let the originals leave my house. Twenty bucks an hour."

"Twenty-five, and I do as much as I can, when I can."

"Twenty-five and you finish it. There's only about thirty pages. Deal?"

Abby wondered if she was getting into something she would regret. "Deal."

"Terrific. You won't be sorry. Will you water the plants?"

That was it. The thin end of the wedge. Next she'd be doing their laundry. "You're pushing your luck. Okay, but no special trips, okay? Just when I'm there."

"Yeah, yeah. What d'ya think I am? Tell me, that bald guy over there, sitting at the round table, that the famous artist, whatshisname?"

"Yup."

"That stuff he does, it's a scam."

Abby shook her head at him. "He says the same thing about your work."

Paula smiled. "He would, Cyrus darling, if he knew who you were."

Cyrus barked with laughter. "Okay, okay. You got me. Bitches. Hey, Abby, you wanna come home and have a threesome? Or get that beautiful waiter of yours, Henry, and bring him with you. I like to fuck a young guy once in a while."

With some people one should not go past the hello and good-bye stage. "I'm going back to work. Goodnight, Paula."

Abby walked to the cash register, her legs feeling like cement. The heat and humidity were finally catching up with her. She felt a surge of sadness. She and Jonah would have laughed about Cyrus Leighton. The famous artist, who had recently had a retrospective at the Guggenheim, was getting ready to leave. He and his family were standing up, putting down napkins, gathering up purses and jackets, laughing, talking. He caught Abby's eye and saluted. Abby smiled back and watched them file out the front door. She went through the swing door into the service area of the kitchen and helped herself to a cup of coffee. It was like tar, but it woke her up.

The intercom buzzed. When Dulcie hung up, she turned to Abby: "Henry says Bailey is getting mean. He's been doing shots of V.O. Would you, please? I can't face him."

The Chez Nous couple had made a lot of changes to the old InnBetween. Originally, the basement was where the kegs were kept. It had a dirt floor and low ceilings. They dug it out and poured a cement floor, laying a carpet the color of dried blood. They tore out the weathered, dark wood bar on the street level, and put a smaller yellow oak bar down in the basement. They were after an intimate English publike feeling. Instead, what they achieved was a rather claustrophobic bar-in-a-basement, popular primarily with the adulterer crowd, those customers looking for a dark secluded place where the drinks are strong and your spouse can't see you from the window.

Originally, there was only one narrow staircase running up the back of the building between the basement and first floor. To make the new bar accessible to customers, the Chez Nous people added a second staircase in the dining room. It was this staircase that Abby took to go down to the bar.

Below ground, the bar ran at right angles to the staircase, along one wall, and the rest of the room was given over to more tables. At the moment they were all empty, and there was only one person at the bar. He had his back to Abby so she couldn't see his face, but Henry looked up as she came down the stairs, and rolled his eyes.

She stopped on the last step of the staircase, as far as possible from the solitary customer who was slouched in his barstool, his chin a few inches off the top of the bar. She kept her distance just in case he decided to make a lunge, or even if his breath was bad. From this angle she could see his reflection in the back bar mirror. Not good. Bailey, the wife-beater. Or so people said, and Abby for one believed them.

Henry, with a sarcastic smile, said: "Bailey was just leaving."

"Like hell I was. Gimme another V.O." The deep voice seemed to come from under the bar.

Bailey was a huge man, probably six-foot four, his powerful frame beginning to run to fat. Word was he fell off a steel girder at a construction site and shattered his leg. He walked with a decided limp, and Dan the dishwasher said he had a foot-long iron pin in his leg. Abby would've thought his leg was hollow.

"You're finished. I'm cutting you off," Henry said firmly.

Bailey looked at Henry as if he was going to reach across the bar and squeeze his neck. Henry leaned on the back bar, and crossed his arms. Abby thought of herself as a physical coward—any violence or threat of violence and her instinct was to run. True, she kept hoping to stumble across her inner warrior, but so far, not a trace. Nevertheless, she could see that Henry was bracing himself, and Bailey was slowly rising from his barstool. They were staring at each other. Enough was enough. Time to speak up. "Henry! Shut down the bar, okay? We've got inventory to do—"

A distracted Bailey swiveled his head in her direction. His eyes were bloodshot marbles. Their color reminded her of the red wine she wanted with her dinner.

"Henry, let's hurry it up—"

"Who the fuck are you?" Bailey interrupted.

What a pig. "I'm the owner," she lied. "You've seen me plenty. It's my place, and it's closing time. By the way, Henry, I'm not getting any more V.O. They won't deliver."

"I won't come back to this fuckin' place if you don't get V.O."

Hah. Makeshift plan working. Until Bailey churned over the information and came up with a solution. "Nah, I'll bring my own bottle. Cheaper. You bet your fuckin' ass." Plan backfiring. Mayday.

Abby gripped the railing tighter. She spoke sternly. "Bailey, would you follow me? I have to show you something. Come on, let's go."

Oddly enough, he slowly stood up.

"Did you settle up with Henry?" she asked reprovingly. He gave her a dirty look, and threw a few singles on the bar. "Come on, let's go."

"We gonna fuck?" he asked. *Oh, yeah, can't wait*, she thought to herself. *I haven't had sex since way before my husband died, so I'm going to break the fast by screwing you.* She backed up the stairs, making sure she was out of arm's reach. He took one step at a time, favoring his left leg.

"You got no fuckin' tits," he added, when they was halfway up the staircase.

"And you have no fuckin' manners, Bailey." This is where, if she were in her own martial arts movie, she thought, she would give him a front kick that would propel him down the stairs, impaling him on a sharp iron object that happened to be at the bottom.

At the top of the stairs, Abby waited for him and then walked to the front door. He was behind her. She walked outside, holding the door for him. He limped out behind her. She walked down to the sidewalk. He followed. She turned to him, making sure she wasn't too close.

"Bailey, I can't let you come back here. If you do, I'll call the cops."

"Fuck you."

"Let me explain why. You drink too much, and with the condition of your leg I'm afraid you'll fall on the stairs and injure yourself. It's for your own good."

"Fuck you, bitch." They were really cookin' now.

"I knew you'd feel that way." She dropped her voice, so no one by the open windows could hear her. "Fuck you, too, Bailey."

"Fuck you," he repeated. Finally, having run out of things to say, he started limping across the square toward the railroad-track crossing. Abby watched him. *With luck, he'll get run over by the next freight train,* she thought. He turned and looked at her. She stood there for a few moments, and then went back inside.

The phone rang as Abby was finishing her dinner. Dulcie had already gone home, and Abby was left to lock up. She could just reach the phone from where she was sitting, which was good, because she was too exhausted to stand, and her feet felt like watermelons.

"'Tween." Too late for unnecessary syllables.

"I got a message that Abby called—"

"Speaking."

"Abby, this is Sean Kenna." She could hear a radio in the background. The hiccup of a country-western voice.

"How can I help you?" Abby waited for Sean Kenna to get on with it.

"I'm the plumber. Mike Testarossa's assistant. You've been calling."

"Oh, right. Well, it's a little late now. We're all well done and steamed alive, like fresh lobster. A few hours ago you could have heard us screaming."

"Yeah, well, I'm sorry about that, but we were shorthanded. I can come over right now and look at your unit. I've worked on it before."

Abby looked at her watch. Too late. But tomorrow was Saturday, and if she didn't let him come over, Dulcie would be stuck chasing after him.

"Okay. Soon?"

"Yup." The phone went dead. The staff, finished with the chores, came by to pick up their tips.

" 'Night, Abby."

" 'Night, guys." Henry had changed into his civvies, and had already taken a cigarette out of his pocket. He would light it precisely before he walked out the back door, so he could deposit a belch of smoke in the little back foyer. He was leaving with the newest waitress, a sweet, pretty girl who was still learning how to manage an entire station without bringing the dessert out before the main course. She had changed into a tight, short dress, and Henry was talking to her, leaning in close. She was giggling. If they weren't already sleeping together, then tonight was the night.

"Go away, you guys," Abby said sourly, "you're steaming up the windows. They're bad enough as it is." Henry grinned. Abby looked at the new waitress. "You know, Henry's a lowlife."

The poor girl smiled. "I know, that's what I like about him."

A lost cause. Still bumping into each other, they left.

When the back door opened a few minutes later, Abby thought one of the staff had forgotten something. She glanced up. A man she didn't know walked in.

"You Abby?" he asked her, waiting. She stared at him. She wasn't expecting to see a sexy-looking man, not at the end of a long shift. Tall, muscular, dark wavy hair, not long, but just long enough to look as if he hadn't paid much attention to it in the last few weeks, wide shoulders, worn jeans. Needed a shave. His dark eyes looked tired. He didn't smile.

"I'm Sean," he tried again. "You Abby?" Abby thought of Dick and Jane.

She nodded. She felt self-conscious, as if they were on a blind date and she had forgotten to have a shower and brush her teeth. She started to stand, but he gestured with his hand out, as if pushing her down.

"Don't get up. I know where everything is." He went over to the thermostat and turned it, listening.

Finally, Abby managed to get out a sentence. "Just let me know if you need anything."

He turned to her. "I need to go up to the roof to see the unit."

"I'll take you up."

He shook his head. "I know my way."

"Oh. Well, let me know if you need anything," she repeated.

He looked at her briefly, as if considering her offer. "I'll get my tools."

When he came back in, Abby ignored him. She heard him go up the narrow back staircase. She went into the kitchen to see how the cleanup was going. George and Sandy were long gone. Dan the Man was still wading through the pans. He would be there for at least two more hours, sweeping and swabbing down the floors, taking out the heavy black rubber mats, leaving the place ready for George the next day. He had turned the radio dial to a religious talk show. When he saw Abby, he smiled. He only had a few teeth left in his mouth, though he was just in his late thirties. Abby took the back stairs down to the corridor behind the bar.

Here everything was in order, ready for the day cleaning man. The chairs were on the tables, shelves restocked, bar inventoried and cleaned. The musty air hit her. She went along the corridor to the metal door that opened onto Route 46. Propping it open with a milk crate, she stepped outside. A breeze brushed her face, and she took a deep, slow breath. The night was dark and cooling down. She shut her eyes. A car came up the hill, the headlights blinding. She backed into the doorway.

"Abby?"

She jumped. She had forgotten there was anyone else in the building other than Dan. The plumber was standing in the hallway, his lean frame backlit by the light bulb hanging from the ceiling behind him.

"Oh, hi."

"You need new filters." He rubbed his eyes with his hand. "It's not a big deal. I'll drop 'em by tomorrow."

"Great."

He turned as if to go.

On impulse, she said: "Do you want a beer, or something? I was just going to have a beer." The invitation popped out, maybe because he seemed tired and the bar looked like a bar. A place of hospitality. Maybe because it was dark and lonely in the corridor and she didn't want him to leave just yet. He looked at her, considering.

"Sure, why not. I'm done for the night." She wondered if he was married, and had someone waiting up for him. She didn't see herself in the role of the other woman, so maybe a beer with her was okay, like grabbing a quick nightcap with the boys. Then Abby wondered what she was doing, having a drink after closing with a plumber she didn't know. Next it would be the milkman. She opened the cooler.

"Heineken?"

"Sounds good." He held up his hands. "I've gotta wash the oil off my hands." While he was in the bathroom, she lined up the scotch bottles, making sure their labels were all facing the right way. Sean came out of the men's room, and pulled up a barstool. He took a long draw from the cold bottle.

"Ahhh." He exhaled audibly and smiled. "Thanks."

They drank in companionable silence. At least, it seemed companionable to Abby, but it might have been that the man's thoughts were so far away he had nothing to say. She stole a few looks at him. He was something. Maybe mid-thirties. His Adam's apple moved as he drank. The top button of his shirt was unbuttoned. The skin of his chest looked tanned. She imagined herself slowly undoing the other buttons.

He glanced at her. "Mike Testarossa's daughter seems to have run away from home. We were shorthanded today."

Mentally, she pulled her hands away from his shirt buttons. "Oh, I'm sorry. That's terrible."

"Yeah. It's hard for him."

She tried to change gears and imagine what it must be like to realize that your child hated living with you. Enough to jump out into the world, alone. "Is she very young?"

"Not really. I mean, she's an adult, she's twenty-three, but she's pretty immature. Stubborn."

Abby was puzzled. "Why didn't she just move out, tell him she was going?"

He shrugged. "I don't know. Maybe she wanted to rub his nose in it."

She felt a flicker of concern for the girl. "Wouldn't he let her live on her own?"

He smiled at her, as if guessing her thoughts. "He has a house up on Malden Street. She has her own apartment attached to it. Separate entrance. Her own car."

"Was she in school?"

"A job. Hudson."

"How does her father know she ran away? That something didn't happen to her?"

Sean twirled his beer bottle. "She packed a bag. Left him a note." He emptied his bottle. "I should go. I've got an early start tomorrow."

Abby nodded, and he stood up. She felt a stab of disappointment. She couldn't remember the last time she'd met a man whose shirt she had imagined taking off, even though he had showed no interest in her. And now he was leaving. She couldn't stop him.

"Thanks." He smiled again, and started up the stairs. He stopped, and turned around. "So, Abby, do you have a boyfriend, or a husband?"

She blushed. Oh, shit, he read her mind. Feeling like a traitor, she shook her head. "Nope. My husband died two years ago." And then, in case he hadn't caught it the first time: "I'm a widow." Whenever she said that word, she saw herself in a long black dress, no legs, her face covered by a black veil. Keening softly, her mouth invisible. Only her eyes showing, red-rimmed and old.

"Do you ever go out to eat? I mean, to other restaurants?"

"I—"

"I mean, would you go out sometime with me? To dinner?"

She pretended to hesitate. "I could do that."

"Okay." He looked as if he was going to say something, but changed his mind. He nodded, turned, and she watched him walk up the flight of stairs. His hips were narrow, the muscles of his rear rounded and solid. She swallowed. She poured what was left of her beer down the sink. She didn't want to go out to dinner with him, she didn't want to talk. She just wanted to climb on top of him and fuck his brains out. Oh, god, listen to this. She would make up some excuse and cancel, if he ever called her. But as she turned off the lights, she thought, *Why the hell should I? I may be a widow, Jonah, but I'm not a dead one, not yet anyway.*

# CHAPTER SIX

Walking past the liquor store on Monday on her way to the café, Abby saw Judy, the shop owner, gesture to her. Abby pointed to herself, then looked behind her, the way people do when they think that they have stepped between communicating bodies. *Yes, you,* Judy mouthed, and came to the door.

"Sweetie," she always called Abby something tender, "Sweetie, a customer of mine left you a note and a set of keys."

"Really?" she asked, intrigued.

"Yup. Mr. Leighton."

"Oh, right." Cyrus. Abby had forgotten about him. She followed Judy into the store, and waited while the woman retrieved an envelope from behind the counter.

"He seemed very concerned about leaving his keys with you. He kept telling his wife you would have parties at their house. She kept saying he was being silly."

"Maybe I should have a toga party. I could order a case of tequila from you, put it on his account, and invite the local Harley chapter."

"Oh, you're joking. I know you. You'd never do that." She laughed, but glanced at Abby to make sure.

Abby opened Cyrus's note as soon as she was outside. She was unable to leave any message unopened. She read all her mail immediately, even the junk. There was a chance it might be important, even wonderful or life altering, like a letter from a dearly loved friend, an announcement from the sweepstakes people, or a job offer in Paris. You could never be sure until you opened it.

However, Cyrus's note held nothing wonderful, just instructions on how to use his computer, and warnings about what she would owe him if she invited people over to his house while he and Paula were away. He also left her his phone number in California. His house keys were on a key ring with a neon yellow plastic tag, shaped like a number one, printed with the address and phone number of a local hardware store. Number One, of course, Abby thought.

Outside felt warm, definitely early summer. Which fit in with Abby's theory about spring in upstate New York, the week or two when there are buds on trees, but the hillsides are still brown. That it's not a real season but a momentary condition nature finds itself in, a bridge between two heavyweights. When she was ten, her parents had taken her on a weeklong vacation to England, and she thought of spring as something like the changing of the guard at Buckingham Palace. You wait and wait, and just when you are ready to give up, suddenly there is fanfare, some marching around, saluting, turn right, step forward, turn left, more marching, and it's over. If someone isn't holding you up over the crowd, you miss it.

Abby walked diagonally across Main Street to Victor's Café, a coffee shop/ice cream parlor/diner in an old storefront. It was next door to the old Texaco Station, Dick and George's garage, gone now and divided into a few little boutiques, one selling antiques, the other a travel agency. Victor's Café was originally opened and run by a young, handsome couple, avid hikers, who named it The Blue Ridge Café. They worked hard, gradually losing their wholesome outdoorsy looks, becoming pale and tense. Before either was found with a pick embedded in his or her throat, they sold the café to George's cousin Victor, who used to work at the InnBetween. Victor took down the posters of craggy mountain ranges, and added a little more backbone to the menu. He was a small, intense man, who solved the labor problem by staffing the place with slow-moving, sometimes surly teenagers, driving them with paternal affection and a bullwhip. He left the coffee strong, satisfying the regular customers, who accepted the change of leadership without a backward glance.

Abby took her soup and roll outside to a picnic table. She had been looking for a little company, but was the only customer. She ate her soup, enjoying the sunshine. When she finished, she sat with her eyes closed, feeling the white light on her eyelids. She let her mind wander, and found herself thinking of the plumber, Sean Kenna. The thoughts sneaked in unguarded. She imagined kissing him. They were taking it very slowly, though she couldn't make out where they were. Was it a car? No, that didn't feel right. The street? Too public. Maybe a hotel, no, no, not spontaneous. She was struggling with the location, while simultaneously running her hands through the man's hair as she pressed her body against his. Her breathing was growing shallower. Suddenly, a woman's high-pitched voice cut in.

"Abby? May I join you?" Abby opened her eyes. Shit. Malaria.

"Okay," she said, ungraciously. Malaria was carrying a plate of food, a vegetable mixture with chunks of tofu on it. Abby remembered that she was some sort of alternative therapist, specializing in couples, which was funny, because she usually came into the restaurant by herself.

"How's it going?" Abby asked her, just as Malaria forked in a large mouthful of tofu. Bad timing. The older woman held up a finger as if to hold her at bay, and chewed rapidly. She obviously wanted to answer the question. Abby looked away, wishing she could recapture her sunny fantasy.

Her companion swallowed noisily. "I'm okay. Okay. Actually," she tilted her head, considering her answer, "I'm better than okay. I'm fine. Quite fine."

She was an attractive woman. She was dressed in a grown-up hippie style, wearing what were most likely the same colors and patterns she had worn twenty years before, but now came from expensive catalogues, sewn from natural, hand-dyed itchy-looking fabrics. On both wrists was an assortment of heavy, silver bracelets. She had large, slightly protruding eyes, the lids darkened with kohl. Her hair was long and wavy, gray at the roots and head, reddish brown by the time it reached her shoulders. Abby looked at the ends, imagining them up by her scalp, framing her face. No, they'd look dry, like kindling, and stick out around her face. Then she imagined her with her hair cut short, the color all gone, the gray hair dominating. She would look better, more elegant, but older. Maybe she was right, leave the hair long, as a reminder of youth, and the disappearing color as an honest expression of middle age, part young, part old. Very honest. For herself, Abby thought, she'd cut it off and dye the shit out of it.

Abby was staring at her head, her mouth slack, thinking her shallow thoughts, when Malaria interrupted her with a question.

"Do you want some?"

"What?"

"You're watching me eat my food. Have some."

"No, no thanks. I had soup." Silence, conversation all dried up. Feeling a little bad about the makeover fantasy, Abby asked: "You're name's Mal—Ahrah, right?"

Malaria shook her head, as if Abby were a bad girl. "I'm offended. I know your name and you don't know mine. Oh, I'm just kidding, don't look so bad. It's Aliara. Alee-ah-rah."

Abby nodded. "Do you live here full-time?"

"Actually, I moved up about six months ago."

"You're a therapist, right?"

"Couples. Do you and your mate need roadside assistance?" She laughed, charmed by her own wit, and then continued. "In fact, I'm the one needing assistance. I'm looking for a place to rent. A one-bedroom apartment, or an adorable little house. Know of anything?"

"No, I don't. But I will keep my ears open," Abby lied.

"I heard that there's an apartment on Malden Street available. The tenant ran off with a rich boyfriend and left the landlord high and dry. Do you know who that might be?"

Malden Street. That sounded like the plumber's address. The plumber with the runaway daughter. The last thing he needed was this woman breathing down his neck. "Sorry, no."

"I don't want to miss my chance."

"You'll find something." Abby stood, picking up her bowl. "Well, I gotta be going. Bye bye."

"I'll see you soon," Malaria said warmly.

*Not if I see you first*, Abby thought.

In the afternoon she did laundry and cleaned her trailer. As she swept the small space, she imagined a self-cleaning trailer. Why not? First step would be to secure all loose belongings in drawers or cupboards, like on a ship before a storm. Next, you flip a switch—vents would open, the engine would start up, and all the dirt would be sucked out. Bingo. Think what this could do for the lives of working people, Abby thought. Great for national morale. And it would permit women to spend more quality time with their children. Because let's face it, who does most of the housecleaning in this country, Abby asked herself, as she pushed the broom under her dresser. You would just have to make sure to get the pets and toddlers outside, before throwing the switch. An image appeared in her head of Rick with his hair standing on end, stuck to a vent, his eyes wide in fear. Abby stopped moving, appalled at herself. "Sorry, Ricky," she murmured.

The next morning, the sun shining on the hood of her car, Abby drove down the hill toward West Bantam with Cyrus Leighton's letter on the seat next to her. Of the five Bantams, West Bantam was the farthest. Bantam was the main town, and Bantam Center was not much more than a crossroads, though it did have the Town Hall. Appropriately, Old Bantam, with its rolling pastures dotted with horse farms, was where old money lived, or used to live before it sold to new money.

She knew the general area and only had to look at the letter after leaving the main road. Cyrus's directions were precise to the point of patronizing, so she found her way easily. At Purvis she took a left and the house was the second mailbox on the left. She pulled into the driveway, the gravel crunching under her tires. The house was a distance from the road, new, built in the old farmhouse "vernacular," meaning it was generally in the style of, without the headaches. All straight lines, no sag, and the trees around it were young, no wolf maples to give it tenure and resonance. In forty years this house might start to look good, though the roof might be leaking. She walked past the usual manicured perennial beds. At the door, she found her Number One key chain, and fitted the key into the lock.

Inside, she heard the busy roar of a vacuum cleaner. She followed the sound through a small mudroom and into an open-plan kitchen that gave onto a long, airy living room. A bank of windows looked out on the back lawn, where she could see a pool, a tennis court, and the back edge of the parking lot. A short, stocky woman was pushing the vacuum around. She moved it rhythmically, focusing hard, and she hadn't heard Abby come in. Abby stood still for a moment, and when the woman didn't look up she shouted: "Hello!"

The woman gave an involuntary yelp. Then she snapped: "God Almighty!" as if Abby had deliberately crept up on her. She turned off the machine.

"Sorry if I scared you—"

"You didn't scare me—"

"I didn't mean to make you jump. I'm Abby Silvernale, I'm here to—"

"Take off your shoes, leave them by the door."

"I'm a friend of—"

The woman waved at her, as if she were a gnat. "I know. Paula said you'd be here. I'm Mrs. Merchant. The Leightons call me Betty. This is my day." You'd never guess from her expression.

Abby smiled ingratiatingly. She practically wagged her tail. "Don't worry about me, I'll be in and out."

"His study's in there. Don't mess with anything."

Abby wondered how she was meant to work if she didn't mess with anything. Movement caught her eye, and she glanced out the French doors. Betty's gaze followed hers.

The water of the pool was choppy, as if someone had just jumped in. Sure enough, a head bobbed up, and then gave a sideways shake. It was a boy gesture. Abby had an older cousin who used to do that. She watched the figure in the pool swim to the edge and pull himself gracefully onto the side, without using the ladder or steps.

"Who's that?" Abby asked, gesturing to the dripping figure. It was definitely a boy. She could tell by the oversized trunks he was wearing. They came down to his knees and clung to his legs, bunching up and wrinkling. He pulled them away from his body. No wonder, it must feel like swimming in an evening gown. Betty was watching him, too.

"That's my son, Joey. He's got no school today so I brought him with me."

Her eyes were on him as he dried himself off and started walking toward the house. His chest was narrow and Abby could see his ribs.

"I better stop him, before he drips water all over the house again. No matter how many times I tell him, he still comes in the house."

She hurried out the French doors, crossing the lawn to meet the boy. He stopped walking as she approached him. She started saying something to him, and placed her hand on his arm above the elbow. He glanced over at the house, shrugged his shoulders, and Abby saw him pull his arm away from Betty. He turned and headed to the parking lot. His mother stood watching him, then turned back to the house. She reentered, carefully wiping her feet on the mat.

"He looks tall. What grade is he in?" Abby asked, trying not to feel as if she were spying on a family's privacy.

"He's sixteen. Growing like a weed. I've got to buy him new sneakers, so I'm leaving early. But normally, you know, I like the place to myself, I've got a big house to clean here. And," she added, "at the end of the day, I've got my own place to look after." She gestured with her head in the direction of the parking lot, as if she were really talking about her son.

"Oh, sure. I'll probably be done by next week, anyway. Well, I'll get my stuff." Abby had nothing but a turkey sandwich in the car, but she wanted to get out of the housekeeper's way. With relief, she let herself out the front door. In the parking lot, the boy was looking through the driver's window of her Bronco. He started when he heard Abby and stepped back from the car, as if she'd caught him doing something wrong. Up close he was a good-looking boy, though he was going through that awkward stage, all legs, nose, and Adam's apple.

"She's pretty cute, isn't she?" Abby patted her boxy little vehicle.

Joey glanced at her, and back at the car. "Yeah. Late seventies, right?"

Abby smiled. "Seventy-five. Only forty-seven thousand miles. You know about Broncos?"

He shrugged. "Some. I really like old trucks. One day I want to get an old Dodge. My friend's dad has one. He races it."

"Is that the green one, a fifty-six or fifty-seven, lives on Railroad Avenue?"

The boy smiled broadly. It warmed his eyes, and made him look younger. "Yeah. Fifty-eight. He lets me drive it sometimes. It's pretty cool."

"Joey, right? Your mom told me about you. I'm Abby." She stuck her hand out, and after hesitating a moment, he shook it. On impulse, she added: "Hey, I have a yard with some old trucks in it. It's kind of a private bone yard. Do you want to come check it out sometime?"

His eyes widened. "That would be amazing." The boy glanced up at the house. Abby's eyes followed his. Betty was carrying a purse and closing the front door. She started down the path, watching them.

"What's your number?" he asked, suddenly in a hurry.

"Five one five one. Three eight two, five one five one. Easy to remember. Call me when you have some free time and I'll show you around."

Abby climbed into her car and pretended to look for something in the glove compartment. Betty unlocked her car, and when she and her son were safely inside it, she backed out and drove down the driveway, kicking up gravel as she went.

• • •

Cyrus's office was a large, comfortable room on the ground floor. The walls were covered with black and white photographs of showbiz people, some of whom she recognized. A younger, much thinner Cyrus appeared in many of the pictures, grinning, shaking hands, often with a cigar wedged between the first two fingers of his left hand. All of the photos were autographed. Near the door she noticed a shot of him standing with Al Roker. It was at least a couple of years old, because the weatherman was still really big. She knew the reporter had bought a country house in the area, and the background of the picture seemed to be the living room of Cyrus's house. However, when she looked more closely, she realized it probably wasn't because the furniture was different. Maybe it was Al Roker's new pad. Old Cyrus sure got around.

Cyrus's desk was blond wood, a Scandinavian design, and it was bare, not a pencil on it. Betty had probably vacuumed everything up. On a smaller desk under the window sat a computer, its monitor small and dark. She followed Cyrus's directions, and on a bookshelf she found a statuette. Underneath it was a key. As she lifted the statuette, she realized it was an award—a woman with some kind of a sphere around her. Abby took a bow, then holding the figure above her head, gave it a victorious shake.

The key opened the cabinet beneath the statuette. In the cabinet were neat piles of lined yellow legal pads. Abby leafed through them. They all were covered with small spidery handwriting. Christ. What had she gotten herself into, she thought. She pulled out the whole stack, and carried it over to the desk. Each pad was numbered, and they were in order. That was a blessing, but so much for thirty pages. There were five pads. About the size of *Bleak House*, had Dickens chosen to use legal pads. Abby carefully moved the computer to the big desk. She followed Cyrus's instructions on getting into his writing program, and with a sigh she started work.

To her surprise, it went faster than she expected. It might have been because the handwriting was clearer when seen from the right side up. Sometimes it seemed a little rushed, sloppier than usual, but she assumed that was toward the end of the day when the author was getting tired. Or when he needed a vodka or four. But the real surprise was in the story itself, which she found she actually enjoyed. Cyrus was so fond of telling her how good he was that she had stopped believing him.

She worked through the morning, stopping to stretch her back and look in the fridge where Paula had told her she would find juices and sodas. At lunchtime she sat by the pool and ate her sandwich. By mid-afternoon she had only finished one notepad. It was discouraging, because she thought she was doing so well, so she tried to remember that longer hours meant more money. She found some chocolate chip cookies and ate them in front of the computer, and then, thinking of Mrs. Merchant, she carefully dusted the crumbs into her hand before putting them in her pocket. By four o'clock she couldn't sit any more. She made a notation of her hours, and escaped.

The next morning, it was pouring. The cows in the next-door pasture huddled under trees, all facing the same direction. Was that just a coincidence? The rain rattled on the metal roof and sides of the trailer, and the dogs sat on chairs staring stonily out the windows at the cows. It was cozy and she didn't want to go out, but by 10:00 A.M. she dragged herself to the car. Parts of the road were thick mud, but the Bronco, with four-wheel drive, was made for country roads. She drove over to Cyrus Leighton's. By lunchtime she was well into the second notepad.

She thought Cyrus wrote screenplays, but this appeared to be a novel of sorts, about Hollywood. The character she liked best was a UCLA student. The story cut back and forth among the various characters, and by early afternoon she had returned to the student, who was in a bit of a jam. He needed to find a way to get from his house to school three days a week, and he didn't own a car. He was thinking about his dilemma, gazing out his window. And this is where Abby did a double take. She stopped typing, and reread the paragraph.

The student is at the window, absently watching his neighbor who is standing next to his car, dressed for work. His neighbor works nights and drives a new, dark blue VW Beetle. The young man watches his neighbor as he tries his car door then peers into the driver's window. Surprisingly, the neighbor walks to the rear of the car and crouches down. He seems to be reaching under the rear fender, feeling with his hand, looking for something. The student realizes his neighbor is probably retrieving his spare key from a magnetic box in his fender. He must've locked the key inside the car. Sure enough, after his neighbor has opened his car, he returns the key to the hiding place. Good thing he has a spare, thinks the student. And that is when he has a revelation. A brainwave. Instinctively, he backs away from the window so his neighbor won't see him watching. A spare key. He needs a car during the day. His neighbor works nights and sleeps days and he now knows how to get into his neighbor's car. He can make a copy of the key, and, voilá, unless the neighbor changes his schedule, he has wheels. Just take the VW while the man is sleeping. And all he has to do is make sure he replaces the gas.

Abby sat for a minute in her chair, amazed. She read it again. She wondered if this could be a coincidence. The thing is, she didn't believe in coincidences in a small town—there just weren't enough people or possibilities for events to duplicate themselves by chance. For example, in Bantam, if she saw Mrs. Jones on Main Street, and two hours later saw her husband on Findlay Street, she wouldn't think anything of it. Life in a small town. However, in Manhattan, if she saw a man on West End Avenue, and three hours later saw his brother on St. Mark's Place, she'd be struck by the coincidence, the sheer randomness of it. No, if events or people seem connected in a small town, they usually are. So, why was Cyrus choosing this particular month to write about a person who secretly borrowed a car? And what was the connection to Dulcie's minivan?

She dialed Dulcie at the restaurant. Dulcie answered on the second ring.

"Hi, it's me, Abby."

"You looking for work?"

"No, I want to ask you a question."

"Only if you work tonight."

"Maybe. Tell me, did you ever mention the car borrowing to Cyrus Leighton?"

"God, no. I don't talk to him. You're the only one who talks to him."

"Okay. Did you mention it to anyone?"

"No, I didn't. I still feel kind of strange about it. Why?"

"Just something I read. Probably a coincidence," she lied.

"Not so fast. I'll see you at four, okay?"

"Fine. See you at four."

Abby put the receiver down, then went to her purse and rooted around until she found Cyrus's letter. She picked up the phone again and dialed his number in L.A. Better to do it from his phone. He was far richer than she would ever be.

It turned out she was calling the Bel Air Hotel. Not bad. Let them watch him spit his food around, at least he was paying them well for the privilege. The receptionist told her he was out, but coolly agreed to take a message.

Abby only had a few more hours before she had to be at work and the dogs needed food and attention. When she reached her hilltop, the sun had come out, creating a brilliant emerald and soft blue display. Against such a beautiful setting, she thought, the trailer seemed like an ugly, misshapen gingerbread cottage. Or like a loaf of mustard-infused bread. She took the dogs for a walk across two large pastures: she sidestepped the cowpats, while the dogs carefully sniffed each one. They cut through the farthest field and trudged down to the abandoned railroad track, a straight, raised path occasionally used for jogging or riding, but otherwise deserted. The rails had long since been pulled up, but the grass still grew sparingly through the gravel surface and the trees had grown around it creating a tunnel of greenery. There was an eerie quiet to the track, and because she was afraid of it, Abby forced herself to walk there, calling for the dogs when they lagged behind. When she turned around and headed back up through a field, the dogs seemed energized by the open space and the sunlight, and ran ahead.

That evening the InnBetween was busy. People came early, in loud clusters, eyes darting over the room, smelling the food, looking for the best table. They were all thirsty and hungry. Downstairs, Abby was busy mixing drinks and running orders up to the kitchen for customers who were eating at the bar. The kitchen was in a controlled frenzy, orders being called out by the waiters, the pick-up bell ringing constantly. The cooks were an overheated miracle to watch. Sandy, scuttling between the grill and the fridge, slicing and turning, George at the stove top, sautéing, flipping, pouring, stirring, the air a dangerous mixture of steam, smoke, and flames. It was a pleasure to escape down the back stairs to the air-conditioned bar.

She was making half a dozen frozen margaritas, the blender grinding harshly, customers two deep (great business for a small, basement bar), when the intercom buzzed. She grabbed it.

"Call for you on line two," Dulcie told her quickly, and hung up. Abby pushed the flashing button, and a raspy New York voice started talking.

"So, girlie, did you burn my house down?" Cyrus Leighton.

"Only part of it." She had to shout to hear herself over the din of the bar and the speakers. "Don't worry, you can't see the damage from the driveway. How's the land of the lotus eaters?"

"Full of assholes. They hate me. Why are you shouting?"

"Because we are crazy busy here, and I can't hear a thing."

"If you haven't burnt the house down, what have you done?"

"I have a question about a source of yours."

"Oh, no."

Oh, no was right. He might just not tell her for the fun of it. She shouldn't have used the word "source."

"Jimmy, the student in your book, he uses his neighbor's car. I need to know where you got the idea to write about that."

His voice came back at her an octave higher. "I made it up, nobody gave me the idea, I made the goddamn thing up!"

"Cyrus, come on now, I need to know. I don't have time to mess around. I've got people waiting for six margaritas, a pitcher of martinis, and a double shot of Glenlivet. Please."

"Fuck 'em. When I get back, you can give me a blowjob. Then I'll tell you."

"That's disgusting." Abby paused for a moment, and then said slowly: "I'm thinking of having a little shindig at your house. I know these wild transgenders who collect showbiz memorabilia . . ."

He barked, a mixture of a laugh and a cry.

"I'm melting, I'm melting! Okay, Dorothy, you bitch. It was the kid who comes and mows my lawn." His voice got fainter as he turned away. "Paula, what's his name? The kid who mows the fucking lawn? Where the hell is she? It's Dick. Something like that."

"Okay, great. What day does he come?"

"I don't know. Thursday, I think."

"You're a star. Well, I've got to run."

"Wait, I—"

She put the receiver down. In the two days she had worked at his house, she hadn't seen anyone mow the lawn, so Thursday was probably right. At least she didn't have to go back when Betty was there. Just then the intercom rang again, and Dulcie told her that it was for her, again. Cyrus, no doubt. He just wouldn't quit.

"Cyrus, I'm thinking of setting up a Battle of the Bands on your tennis court—"

"Abby, Sean here."

"Who?"

"Sean Kenna, the air-conditioning guy."

Abby blushed. Thank god he couldn't see her.

"Oh, hi."

"Are you busy?"

"A little, yeah."

"Are you working Friday night?"

She hesitated. "Actually, no," she lied. "I'm not."

"Can I pick you up at seven?"

"Seven? That's perfect, fine."

"You sure?"

*Do it.* "Yes, sure."

"Okay. Good."

"Bye." She started to hang up.

"Wait—" he called out. "I don't know where you live—"

"Oh. Sorry. You know the Silvernale farm? On River Street? I mean, I don't live there—"

After she hung up, as she poured the Scotch, it came to her that this was her first date in more than seven years with someone other than Jonah. The thought left her a little short of breath.

"I hope that's for my customer. He could use it." Henry tapped the glass she had just filled to within half an inch of the rim.

"Fuck," she said.

Henry took the glass from her and put it on his tray. "Gimme. It's good. He'll tip well, for once."

On Thursday morning she was back at Cyrus Leighton's desk. There were no more interesting tidbits in his manuscript, though she did find a description of a bank manager who reminded her of Mrs. Whitley at the bank. Or at least "the whistling sound her thighs make as they rub together when she glides through the foyer, a credit slip or personal bank-ruptcy form permanently in her left hand." She kept one eye out for the lawn-mowing boy, Dick, and a little after noon she heard the deafening roar of a riding mower burst into life right outside the window. She hadn't heard a truck pull up, but she went outside, and found a team of three males starting to work. A boy, who looked about twelve, was carrying a weedwacker. He started it up just as she stepped outside, and began moving along the side of the house. Another slightly larger boy was already pushing a hand mower around the garden, and the largest of the three was riding a small tractor around the lawn that ran down to a line of trees by the road. All three had white blond hair and scowled as they worked. The three billy goats gruff.

She went up to the boy with the weedwacker, and yelled hello at him. He looked up, startled.

"Yeah?" he yelled back, his face crumpled up with concentration.

"Hi. I'm looking for Dick," she hollered. She hoped he would turn off his machine, but he didn't. "Which one of you is Dick?" She smiled as she shouted over the scream of the engine, hoping to break the ice.

He smiled back, not, as it turned out, in friendliness, but at her ignorance. He yelled: "There's no Dick here." He pointed to the riding mower. "My big brother, he's Richie. But he ain't no Dick." Couldn't let it go, the little shit. Abby wondered if Cyrus had been well aware of the correct nickname and just wanted her to look bad. The boy shook his head at her ignorance and returned his attention to his machine, bits of greenery flying around him.

Abby walked away from him, toward his brother, who by now was on the far side of the lawn, the mower roaring under him. Richie seemed to be moving very fast; she felt vulnerable walking out in the open. He looked her way, and she waved, her arm a flag. He kept going. He seemed to be ignoring her when all of a sudden he swung around and came at her full speed. She had to fight the urge to turn and run back to the safety of the house, but she wondered if that's what he wanted, so she stood her ground. Within two feet of her legs, he came to a stop. He turned the key, and the engine died. He looked at her questioningly.

"That was fun. Richie, right?"

He nodded, waiting. He was in his mid-twenties, with lean, sharp features. Good-looking, at least for now. In fifteen years he would have the face he was meant to have, hard, all youthful softness burned away from the inside.

"Hi. I'm Abby, I'm doing some work for Cyrus and I wonder if you could tell me something."

Richie shrugged, noncommittal. She plodded on. "I came across a great little story in Cyrus's manuscript, asked him where it came from, and he told me to ask you."

Richie's white blond hair had fallen in his eyes, and she couldn't read his expression. "I don't talk much to Cyrus. What little story?"

"Well, the story of someone secretly borrowing a neighbor's car when the owner isn't using it. You know, on a regular basis, to get to work."

He slumped in the black vinyl seat, his wrists resting on the steering wheel as if it were the pommel of his saddle, and looked at her. His young face was already weathered from so much time outdoors. He would've made a good cowboy, except for the tractor.

"Oh, yeah. I made that up." Right. He spoke slowly, and she felt he wanted her to believe he was simpleminded.

"You made it up? Why?"

He shrugged. "I dunno. I got a good imagination, I guess. Cyrus got a kick out of it, so I told him it happened to a friend of mine."

Before she could say anything, he turned the key, and the engine roared back to life.

He shouted over the racket. "Hey, I gotta go. My brothers and me, we got two more houses to do before lunch."

He shifted into gear, and lurched off. Abby stood there, watching him go. He was lying, she was pretty sure of it. She walked back to the house, wondering what to do next. She glanced down at her legs, and saw they were covered in grass cuttings.

She stayed as long as she could at Cyrus's, working well after the lawn boys had finished. She watched them as they were packing up to leave, and she could tell they were talking about her. Li'l Weedwacker was telling his brothers something, smirking and rolling his eyes. Then all three of them looked over at the house and laughed. Probably the Dick story. Not really that funny. She shrugged and turned away from the window. When she was done, she wrote up her hours, and headed into town.

On Main Street, she met Dulcie, who had run out of latex gloves so she'd gone to Victor's to borrow a box. No, she couldn't stop, she was expecting a visit from the Board of Health. No one used the gloves, but if the inspector didn't see them in the kitchen, he'd fine her. She also had to get one of the staff to clean out the grease trap, or she would have to do it herself. Abby took the opportunity to tell her she wouldn't be working on Friday. After fussing over a replacement, Dulcie wanted to know why. A date? When Abby wouldn't tell her who she was going out with, Dulcie shook her head as if she were dealing with a naïve child.

"Oh, please, I'll find out. One of the customers will tell me, or Henry will know." She smiled slyly at Abby as she walked away, her box of gloves under her arm. *The doctor will see you now*, Abby thought, watching her.

Abby went into the café and ordered a bowl of lentil soup to go.

# CHAPTER SEVEN

By the time five o'clock on Friday came around, Abby had done everything but boil the trailer. The day before, she had driven into Pittsfield to buy new sheets. On Friday morning, she washed them and put them on the bed. She then scrubbed the shower, sink and toilet, and the kitchen. She mopped all washable flooring, and vacuumed the carpet in the bedroom. She went through the refrigerator, emptying it until it looked barren. She folded and refolded the clothes in her closet. She cleaned the windows, twice pinching her fingers in the latches. She then decided the new sheets looked too new, so she stripped them off and put on her old ones. Clean towels in the bathroom, naturally. Finally, all that was left was herself. She had to wash, do all the bathroom things, and dress. He was coming to pick her up at seven.

Any fluttering of panic she shut down unmercifully. She was going to go through with this. She had no idea what this man was like, but he seemed like a nice guy, he was attractive, and she was going to take him to bed. It was time. If she waited any longer, she would forget what the whole business was about. She would regain virgin status.

At six-thirty, she got under the covers in her underwear and stared at the low ceiling. She tried to slow down her heartbeat. She imagined herself floating, looking down from above into her tin shelter, onto her bed. She was afraid. Afraid to go out with this stranger. Just don't answer the door, she said to herself. But she pictured him driving up and seeing her Bronco out front. He would know she was hiding inside. He might call the police or break down the door and find her cowering in her new black lingerie. As she got dressed, the dogs lay on her bed, watching her. She had decided on a low-cut red top and black jeans. Come-hither clothes, but adaptable to different environments. And pants were a good idea, because she could run in them if the situation got unpleasant. She neatly remade the bed.

The dogs began to bark before Abby heard Sean's truck whining up the road. By the time he knocked at the door, she was as ready as she would ever be. She wiped her sweating palms on her thighs, took a deep breath, and opened the front door. The dogs were a useful icebreaker, jumping on him, sniffing his shoes, finally moving off to his truck, smelling the tires. By the time Rick lifted his leg onto his front left steel-belted radial, she was ready to offer him a drink. He accepted, looking at her carefully. She avoided his gaze. They sat rather stiffly in her tiny but sparkling living room talking about the dogs, while Sean rubbed their ears.

Finally they left, driving down the hill in his pickup. They took Route 46 toward Hudson and stopped at the Blue Moon Tavern, where the only vehicles in the parking lot were Harleys and pickups. Abby had been hoping they might go to Massachusetts, a place full of strangers. But this was definitely local.

Inside the tavern, the room was long and narrow. On the left side, a heavy mahogany-stained bar ran halfway down the length of it; about six small tables lined the right side. It was early, so the place wasn't jammed, but it was already noisy. Half of the tables were occupied, though the bar was busier, with some people sitting, some standing, laughing and talking across each other. At the end of the bar, a woman was feeding coins into a jukebox, while a man stood behind her, his arms around her waist. The music playing was country-western, twanging loudly about the usual heartbreak and abandonment. Beyond the jukebox the room opened out into a dining area. Sean guided Abby along the bar to one of the tables at the back of the room.

A plump young waitress in a short skirt and a low-cut top came out of the kitchen. She stopped at the service station for silverware and menus. She glanced at Abby, then smiled broadly at her date. "Hey, Sean! How are ya, babe?"

She leaned over him from behind, ostensibly to put a menu down in front of him, and rested a large breast on his shoulder. He didn't seem to notice. He and Abby ordered a couple of beers on tap and the girl finally left, taking her breasts with her, after whispering something in Sean's ear and making him laugh. He looked at Abby apologetically.

"They know you pretty well here," she said, trying to sound merely observant.

"I come in a couple of times a month. They're friendly people."

*Yeah, I'd say.* "So, tell me how you got into the plumbing business." She put her elbows on the table, and looked politely at him across the table.

"Sounds like a job interview," Sean remarked.

She shrugged. "Sorry. You don't have to answer."

After a pause, he started talking. "I was working on a construction site in Brooklyn. When we finished, the owner asked us to put an addition on his country place. It turned out to be in West Bantam. I spent two weeks up here that summer, and liked it."

The waitress came back with the beers. "You guys eating?"

Sean looked at Abby. "They have great ribs."

*No one forced you to go out with this guy,* Abby said sternly to herself. She tried to take the iron out of her smile. "Ribs sound great. I'd like that."

"How about that platter, the big one with coleslaw and fries?" Sean asked the waitress.

"You planning on stopping your heart tonight?" She smiled suggestively. He laughed, and shook his head at her, either to deny what she was saying, or in mild reproach.

After she left, conversation took a few uncomfortable moments to find its way back to the rather dull subject of plumbing. Sean continued: "After I moved up here, as the weather got colder, it was harder to find construction work. So I took a temporary job with Testarossa. One of his workers was sick. Then the poor guy got even sicker. Finally had to quit. So Mike offered me a permanent job."

"Wow." Abby tried to lighten the moment by looking at him in mock suspicion. "What did he get sick from, arsenic poisoning?"

He laughed kindly and played along. "Hey, it's cutthroat out there, in the plumbing world. You take your chances." After a pause he asked: "So, tell me about you, where are you from?"

"Oh, here and there." Abby shrugged. "My father was in the military, so we jumped around a lot. He retired when I was in tenth grade, and we moved to Goose Creek. He had spent summers here when he was a kid, visiting an old aunt, and he always wanted to come back. So I spent my junior and senior year here in Bantam. Did you know that Goose Creek is in the Bantam district?"

Sean shook his head. "I didn't, but I'm glad I do now. So, been here ever since?"

Abby took a long drink of her beer. The knot in her stomach was starting to loosen. "Not a chance. After high school all I wanted was to get out of here, go to New York. Seek fame and fortune. So I did. I mean, seek them." Abby laughed.

"Then what?"

"And ten years later, I came back, married. My husband was from here, and his father was dying." She felt herself flush, as she did whenever Jonah came up.

"Are your parents still alive?"

"In Arizona. My father had never actually spent a winter upstate until we moved here. January and February finally got to them."

"Did you and your husband date in high school?"

"We overlapped one year in high school, but we didn't know each other." She figured she should get this over with. "He died, two years ago."

Sean just nodded. "So you said."

"He committed suicide," she added.

She didn't elaborate on the drinking, and the pills and the mess of that last day, when she'd driven off in a rage, wishing he would jump off a cliff or walk into a semi. She didn't tell him about the terrible guilt and sadness that ate at her for the first year, and could still put her into a trance of remembering, and how even now she could not stand being in the farmhouse. And how she knew that if she had only stayed home, she could have talked him out of it. When you start imagining how you might have done things differently, the choices you made seem so poor, so mean, so avoidable.

Instead they went on to talk about local people, and movies they had seen. Their food came and Abby bit into one of the ribs. He was right, it was really good. They ordered two more beers. Abby started to enjoy herself. The place filled up and the noise level rose accordingly. Abby needn't have worried about being recognized. This was Sean's turf. Once in a while someone would call out to him, or pound him on the back as they passed by. Near the jukebox, a few people were dancing.

Eventually, the ribs were gone and they couldn't drink any more beer. There was an awkward moment when they both acknowledged it was time to move on.

They were working their way through the crowd toward the door, when a voice raised itself above the noise. "Hey, Sean, ya dog, how's it goin'?"

He was standing at the bar, holding a bottle of beer, his blond hair combed neatly off his forehead, exposing a band of deathly white skin normally hidden under his hat. It took Abby a second to place him. Richie, the senior lawnmowing brother.

Sean raised a hand. "Hey, Richie. How're you doing, man?"

A girl standing next to Richie called out: "Sean, honey, why you leavin' so soon?"

"Hey, Sarah. Got an early call tomorrow." Sean kept walking, gently steering Abby to the door. They emerged from the packed bar into the fresh night air. It was drizzling lightly, a damp mist. Leaving the warm, dark, smoky bar was a little like leaving the womb. Necessary, but a shock. And maybe it's true, Abby thought, you spend the rest of your life wishing you could crawl back in.

"I know him," she said, "he mows lawns for people."

Sean raised an eyebrow. "Actually, he farms. Has three hundred acres he works with his dad and brothers. But you're right, he does yard maintenance in the summer. Pays the bills."

She felt suitably chastised. The gravel crunched underfoot as they walked to the pickup.

"How do you know him?" she asked.

"Through his girlfriend, Sarah. That was her in there. She's one of Connie Testarossa's best friends. And his older brother and I work together at Testarossa's."

"He has an older brother? I thought he was the oldest."

Sean laughed. "No way. He's practically the baby. Has three older brothers. Six boys all told. No girls."

Abby was silenced, thinking about their mother. Giving birth to, and raising, six boys. Like a pioneer family. Or a golden retriever.

Sean reached over to Abby and took her hand. The touch seemed frighteningly personal to Abby, as if he had suddenly fondled her breast, and she had to resist the urge to yank her hand away. When they reached the truck, he kept her hand in his while he unlocked the passenger door. Before he let her climb in the cab, he raised her hand to his lips and kissed it. His lips were warm and dry. To Abby the contact felt deeply, silently erotic, there in the darkened parking lot. Overwhelmed, she laughed, embarrassed. He held the door for her as she climbed into the pickup. They didn't touch again, but the heat between them stayed with her, and seemed to change the air in the cab.

By the time they drove into Bantam, Main Street was deserted and dark. Eleven-thirty, and even the lights of the Kipling Movie Theater were out. A solitary person was walking down the sidewalk. It looked like a boy, by the slouch and the wide pants dragging on the concrete.

Sean was obviously looking at him, too. "Kids here don't seem to have anything to do, anywhere to hang out." As they drove by, the boy glanced up, and she recognized him.

"Wait, Sean, pull over."

He put on the brakes, and brought the truck to a standstill. Abby rolled down the window. By now the figure was quite a ways behind them. Sean went into reverse, and they whined backward down Main Street until they were level with the boy.

"Joey!" He looked over at her, and kept walking. "Joey, it's me, Abby."

And when he still didn't respond, she yelled: "Seventy-five Bronco!" He stopped moving, and turned to her.

"Joey, you okay?" she called out.

He nodded, slowly.

"Can we give you a ride home?"

He stared at her, and shook his head. She could see his face was wet. It looked like tears. Or maybe it was the rain, which was still coming down very lightly. Abby opened her door, and started to get out of the cab of the truck, but Joey shook his head and put his hand up, like a traffic cop, keeping her away.

"I'm cool. I don't need anything," he said. His voice carried well on the night air. As if to prove a point, he smiled stiffly at her. It was more of a grimace than a smile, but she had to accept it at face value. He turned away, and started walking, his long frayed jeans scraping on the sidewalk. He hunched his shoulders, as if he could feel her eyes on him.

She sat in silence for a moment. Sean looked over at her, waiting for her verdict. She shrugged. "Let's go."

They drove up to her house in silence. She wondered what a sixteen-year-old was doing walking around alone, looking so unhappy. But she comforted herself with the thought that he could do that, and he was safe. That was the beauty of a town like Bantam.

The dogs went berserk when the truck drove up, their barks harmonizing and echoing over the hills. Sean got out and they both stood awkwardly.

"I had a good time," he said, looking at her.

"Me, too," she answered.

"Okay, well, I should go." But he didn't move.

"Be careful of the dogs when you pull out," she said, walking toward him, instead of away.

He gave a lopsided smile, as if he could read her mind. It was her move, his hands were tied. So to speak. She liked the feeling, though she was dimly aware of some shortness of breath, as if by walking across the gravel she were stepping off a rooftop, solid ground falling away behind her. Before she could think about it too much, she closed the distance between them and, putting her hands on his shoulders, she kissed him. Big move. He seemed to know it was, and he pulled her into him. She felt the electrical charge move quickly from his warm mouth and tongue and travel down through her body, between her legs, wrapping around her thighs. She had to lock her knees to stop them from buckling.

It seemed as if her trailer had shrunk. They crashed into furniture that seemed closer together than usual and set at odd angles. Abby knocked over a lamp. Once they got to her room, Sean reached out a foot and kicked the door shut just in time to close out the dogs. In the confined bedroom, it suddenly felt as if they were strangers, both running away from the same danger, who had barricaded themselves together in a storage room at a train station. Abby stood by her bed. Sean looked around, touched the dresser, and glanced at the calendar picture of the farmhouse.

Quickly, Abby pulled off her red top.

He looked at her. "You're beautiful," he said. He spoke with reverence, all awkwardness gone. He moved close and stood in front of her. She put one knee on the bed and unbuttoned his shirt, just as she'd imagined, and he waited for a beat but when she fumbled he helped her by undoing his jeans and pushing them down over his hips. His fully erect penis sprung out.

"Thank God," said Abby, without thinking.

Sean laughed. "You surprised?"

Abby blushed in the dark. "No, it's just been such a long time, I didn't think I'd recognize it—"

He pushed her onto the bed. His body was lean and muscular, which suited her fine after so long with nothing but soft and feminine.

Those next few hours, Sean was tireless and focused his intense energy on her. He wasn't always gentle, but then neither was Abby. Occasionally they would hear the snuffling of a wet nose under the bedroom door, and they would be distracted, but only for a moment.

Eventually, they slept. At dawn, Abby got up stiffly, put on a tee shirt, and lay down again. Sean's breathing was steady, and she watched his chest rise and fall. It occurred to her that, while they sleep, some people look like children, while others look like corpses. She wondered at such a morbid thought and was relieved to be able to see something childlike and trusting in Sean's sleeping face. She tried to pretend that she was used to him, that she loved him. For a second she pretended that he was Jonah. As if sensing her thoughts, he turned on his side and opened his eyes. He saw her watching him.

"You okay?" he asked.

Abby nodded. "I'm good. You?"

"More than good."

She moved in close to him, the tee shirt giving the contact a new innocence. Sean held her for a moment, and then rolled away and sat up.

"What's wrong?" she asked, and then kicked herself.

He stood, picking up his clothes from the floor at the foot of the bed. "Have a six A.M. call. Gotta go home, shower, get my stuff."

Abby nodded quickly, pulling the sheet up. "Oh, right."

Abby didn't offer him tea or coffee. With only jeans, a shirt, and car keys to collect, a person can be ready pretty quickly. Before he left, he sat on the side of the bed.

"Can I call you?" he asked, brushing the side of her cheek with his finger.

Abby smiled at him.

"Sure," she said, not meaning it.

When she heard his truck start up, she went to the living room window and watched him drive away. After the sound of the engine had faded, she turned back from the window. She felt a general, undefined sadness. She looked at the lamp lying on the floor. Proof, along with her sore body, that she had spent the night with a man. She picked up the lamp and set it back on the table. In her bedroom, the sheets and mattress pad had come off entirely, exposing the mattress. She took a deep breath. She stripped the bed and put the sheets in the laundry. She found the other set, the new one, and remade the bed. The calendar from Hudson River Bank had fallen off the wall. She hung it back up, straightening it carefully, before getting in between the cold, fresh sheets.

When her breathing began to slow, she remembered Joey. She should have made sure he got home all right. She should have insisted. But this was Bantam, for God's sake. He was fine.

# CHAPTER EIGHT

Abby didn't fall asleep until after six, and then she slept as if she had been hit on the head with a mallet. A drool-on-your pillow sleep. At 8:00 A.M. the phone rang, dragging her awake. She couldn't make out the low voice at the other end of the line.

"Who is this?" she asked groggily.

"Joey. It's Joey. I'm in trouble."

Abby was starting to focus and she could hear the fear in his voice. "Okay, Joey. Where are you?"

"I'm at the police station."

"In Bantam?" Abby forced herself to think clearly. He was probably picked up for vagrancy last night. Why couldn't the cops have just driven him home? The Bantam police seemed to make it their life's work to harass teenagers. All they had to do was drive him home, for God's sake.

"Give me twenty minutes." Abby hung up and moved as quickly as she could to the shower.

Seventeen minutes later, she was at the traffic circle in front of the Inn-Between. She ran up the steps of the Lacey Memorial building, which housed the police station, the mayor's office, the building inspector's office, and the town clerk. She turned left, and left again, and knocked on the heavy wooden door marked POLICE. She only had to wait a moment before the door was opened by the chief of police himself, whose surname, oddly enough, was Sheriff. Chief Sheriff was in his late forties, medium height, trim, with a full head of dark, wavy hair, and thick dark eyebrows that accentuated the waxy pallor of his skin. He had a patient and gentle way about him, was a family man and Little League coach. People in Bantam liked and trusted him, even though his brother was mayor. Stranger things had happened. Chief Sheriff stood in the doorway, blocking her entrance.

"Hello, Abigail Silvernale." He always called her by her full name, an ungainly pile of syllables. It made him sound as if he had been studying her file. "You're up bright and early. What can I do for you today?"

"Chief, I got a call a little while ago from Joey Merchant." Chief Sheriff stared at her for a moment, then stepped back, indicating that she should come into his domain. She followed him down a narrow corridor, and into an office. It was a small room, with gray metal filing cabinets, and a gray metal desk. He shut the door behind her, and gestured to a chair. He sat down behind his desk, making a slow noisy sigh, like a deflating beach toy. When he was empty, he took in a deep breath, and shook his head.

He looked at her questioningly. "Why'd he call you?"

She shrugged. "I don't know. I gave him my number a few days ago. My trucks, you know. Where's his mom?"

The chief sighed again, looking suddenly older by about fifteen years. "She's dead. Shot in the chest."

Abby gasped, shock and disbelief knocking the wind out of her. "I only just met her," she said, as if that invalidated what he said. As if people can only die violent deaths once you've known them for a while. "How's the boy? Is he okay?" A sudden picture of Joey shuffling down Main Street flashed through her head, his face wet with rain or tears.

The chief must've seen something in her face. "What is it?" he demanded.

Abby shook her head. "I saw him last night, in town."

"What time?" He picked up a pen and made a note on a piece of paper.

"I'm not sure. I'd say it was eleven-thirty, quarter to twelve."

Chief Sheriff grunted, still writing.

"Anyone with you can verify that?"

Abby hated having the town know her business, but her sex life seemed trifling compared to murder. "Yeah. Sean Kenna. He was just driving me home." She glanced at the chief. She thought she detected a slight lift of a dark eyebrow as he scribbled down that tidbit. "So who do you think shot her?"

The chief looked up from his book, closed it, and slid it back into his pocket.

"I hate to say it, but young Joey is our best candidate."

"You're kidding, he's just a boy." She realized as soon as she said it how old-fashioned she sounded.

The chief looked at her with sad skepticism. "I was the first one to interrogate Sam Bates." He was referring to a sixteen-year-old who ten years before had massacred three members of his own family, one of them a small child. In West Bantam.

"Come on, I'll take you in to him. But I'm going to be present."

They found Joey sitting on the bench in the holding cell, his head in his hands. He looked up at the sound of footsteps.

"Hi, Joey. Abigail Silvernale's come to visit you." The chief pulled up a chair for her, and she sat down, looking at Joey through the bars. He seemed ragged and sunken, like a sick kitten. They sat in silence.

Finally the boy whispered: "Did they tell you my mom's dead?"

"Yes. I'm really sorry. She was a good lady. I could tell she loved you very much." Abby doubted if the boy could even hear her trite words.

"What do I do?" He looked at her. His expression was desolate, abandoned.

Abby swallowed, pushing down an urge to run. "Do you have any family members I could get ahold of? Did your mother have brothers or sisters?"

Joey shrugged. Abby couldn't tell if the answer was no, he didn't know, or he wouldn't say.

"Joey, do you know a lawyer?"

He shook his head. His body seemed to slump lower at the mention of the law.

"Okay." She felt herself being squeezed by the oppressive air of the small space. "I'm leaving now. I'm going to find you a lawyer. See if we can work something out. Don't talk to anyone until we get someone in here, okay?" She glanced at the chief, who nodded. She stood up.

"Wait, don't go." Joey glanced up at her.

"Okay. Okay." Reluctantly, she sat back down.

"I've got a dad. I don't see him much."

Abby nodded encouragement. "That's great. We should call him. Does he live far?"

"Malden. But I don't want to call him."

"That's okay, I'm sure the chief would be happy to." Abby looked at the officer, who nodded again.

Joey shook his head. "I want you to go see him. Tell him, you know, in person."

Oh, shit. She didn't want to get sucked into this. "Listen, Joey, I'm—"

"Please. Just tell him what happened, but tell him I'd never hurt her. I mean, she could really get to me, you know, but I'd never hurt her. Kill her."

He looked so desperate. She couldn't say no. "What's his name?"

"Roy Goodrich. He lives on Calvin Road, next to the post office. It's like a dirt road. His house is up at the top."

Abby waited a moment, and when she realized they had said everything there was to say, she nodded good-bye, and left.

# CHAPTER NINE

As Abby walked down the steps of the Lacey, she thought with dismay about her promises to the boy. First, she needed to find a lawyer. Abby stood in Central Square, and looked around, thinking. Lawyer, lawyer. There was Hadley, two doors down. He was pretty good, but dealt mainly in estate law, closings, and divorces. Most country lawyers do a bit of everything, she was sure, but she wanted one with some background in criminal law. Anyway, more than once she had seen Hadley leaving his office at lunchtime, carrying golf clubs.

Abby glanced across the street, and saw Franklin D. Van Renesse's sign. Of course. She'd forgotten Franklin was a criminal lawyer. Franklin had even been in the news for the last few months as the defense attorney for two really nasty characters. They were both accused of their respective crimes in Hudson, a town known as a mecca for drugs and antiques about half an hour south of Bantam. One of the accused men was a tall cross-dresser who ran a "modeling" agency. He had routinely abused the young boys who signed up as talent, promising them careers and telling them this was the best way to get them ready for showbiz. Some folks might even agree with him. Anyway, Franklin D. Van Renesse had represented him and lost the case. Good for society but bad for Franklin D. The other case was a man who had stabbed his wife repeatedly while she was on the phone with the police, crying and telling them what was happening. She died holding the receiver. Another lost case for Mr. Van Renesse, defense attorney. But, come on, she couldn't hold those losses against him.

She turned into the little front yard of his building. Most of the buildings on Main Street were three-story brick with copper cornices and old-fashioned storefronts. This house, however, was the last wooden house on the street, and the only one with a front yard, which in spring and summer was a mass of flowers and colors. The house was tiny, a dollhouse, and the sign, hanging from a sort of gallows at the edge of the flowers, read: FRANKLIN DELANO VAN RENESSE, ATTORNEY-AT-LAW.

After negotiating the sloping, springy stairs to the second floor, she found Franklin's receptionist at a small desk on the landing. She looked up from her pile of papers, and smiled. She looked familiar, but Abby couldn't place her.

"Is Franklin around? It's kind of urgent."

"Why, Abby, good morning."

Abby suddenly remembered how she knew her. The restaurant, of course. She came in most Friday nights with two girlfriends, drank margaritas, no salt, got loud and down and dirty with Henry. She seemed very different here today, serious and professional.

"He's on his way to court. But you can probably grab a few minutes." She used the eraser end of her pencil to point at his office door, which was closed. Abby knocked softly. No answer. She knocked again.

"Come in, if you're going to do it at all," yelled a deep, impatient voice.

She turned the handle, and pushed. It was a good room, big bay window looking out onto the garden and the street, wide oak partners' desk, built-in bookshelves filled with rows of bound legal books. A few black and white photographs on the walls. Franklin had his back to the door, and was pulling a book out of the bookshelf. He turned around, and smiled when he saw her.

"Well, well. Hello, Abby Silvernale. This is a treat." He came around the desk, and shook her hand. "Good to see you again. Have a seat."

There is a substantial black community in Bantam that can trace its roots back to the Underground Railroad. Many of the families have the same surnames as their white counterparts, and even though their children go to the same schools, they seem to live in a separate though parallel world. Franklin was one of the few visible members of that community. Abby first met him when Jonah died, when she needed someone to help her sort out the mess. She walked in off the street. He did a good job, and, aware of her financial situation, only charged her $285. Since then, they had even had lunch together a few times. She considered him an early-stage friend.

They both sat down, he behind the desk, she opposite him. A good-looking man, high cheekbones, skin a medium brown, with a few darker freckles across the wide nose. Tired eyes behind wire-rimmed glasses; closely cropped hair. Probably in his forties, he stood about six feet tall. His expression was usually quite serious, that is, until he laughed, when he didn't seem quite so lawyerly. She knew very little of his personal life, but she did know she liked him, and found him a kind, considerate man who knew the law. And that seemed to be what Joey needed.

"I have a client for you, Franklin. A teenage boy." Franklin nodded. "It looks like he might be accused of killing his mother." Franklin raised an eyebrow. "I don't know him well. In fact, I only met him once. I gave him my number because he likes old trucks." Franklin nodded again. He knew of her rusted collection. Abby continued. "He called me this morning, they have him at the Lacey. He has a father, might be a deadbeat, I don't know. Joey wants me to go see him and give him the happy news."

"What's his name?" Franklin started writing on a pad.

"The boy's Joey Merchant. He's sixteen. His mother was shot."

Across the desk, Franklin looked at his watch. He stood up and grabbed his briefcase, opening it to put the pad inside. Abby stood also.

"I'm due in court in an hour and a half. I'll stop by and see him first." As he passed her, he patted her on the shoulder. She followed him out of the office. On the landing, he said something to his receptionist. He walked down the flight of stairs, and Abby followed. Outside, she watched him turn left and stride toward the Lacey. She walked more slowly. Time to meet the dad.

The day was warming up. Abby headed out Route 103 and as she crested the hill above Bantam, she could see south and east for miles. Clear and perfect. The hills rolled and curled, a painting of fields and woods. Abby crossed the Taconic State Parkway, and slowed down through the quaint little village of Spencerville, known as Expensiville by some of the locals. Past town, the road cut through woods as it headed due east toward Massachusetts. At Malden it dead-ended, and she took a right, driving south on Route 22. A few miles down she passed the post office. She slowed down, and turned left on Calvin Road. The road wound up the heavily wooded hillside. There were few driveways off the narrow, dirt road but none after the first mile. She had to stop for a large buck, standing gracefully in the middle of the road. He stared at her, flicking his tail. Abby opened her window.

"Move," she said in a loud, firm voice. He waited, so she would know her order had no effect on him, then stepped delicately into the trees.

Abby kept going and just when the road seemed about to end there was an extension, a narrower, steeper version that ran another hundred yards. She had to go considerably slower, to avoid the ruts and rocks. Finally, around the last bend, she came to a small cabin in a clearing. A blue Dodge Ram, an NRA sticker on the rear window, was parked to the right of the house. She parked her Bronco next to it, and sat, looking around. The house was solid, sided with aged, rough lumber, a porch running the length of it. A huge pile of firewood was stacked neatly to the right of the porch. She expected to see a deer carcass hanging from a tree, even though hunting season was a long way off. This was definitely the home of a country boy. Sure enough, if she craned her neck, she could see a gun rack in the back of the pickup. She sat a little longer in the Bronco. Dog time. Finally, when no yellow-eyed drooling rottweiler came tearing around from behind the house, she climbed out and walked up to the porch. She knocked on the front door. No answer. She considered turning tail, but it had taken too long to get there. She banged on the door with the flat of her hand. Finally, the door opened part way. A tall, middle-aged man stood there, in dungarees and a tee shirt, thin, crew cut, wearing a two-day growth of beard and an unwelcoming expression.

"Roy? Roy Goodrich?"

He looked at her, his mouth tight with suspicion. His eyes were his most remarkable feature: bright blue, slightly protruding. He stared at her, unblinking. Finally he spoke. His voice was slow and caught on air pockets, as if he hadn't used it for a while.

"You a Witness?"

"A witness to what? I didn't see anything," she said, thinking about murder and shotguns.

"What d'ya want?" He wasn't getting any nicer.

"My name is Abby Silvernale. I'm a friend of your son's."

Roy nodded. "What son?"

"How many do you have? Joey Merchant. He is your son, isn't he? Maybe I've got the wrong house." She made as if to turn around and leave.

He opened the door another inch. "What did he do?"

She stopped moving and looked at him. "I don't know that he did anything, but for some reason he wanted me to come talk to you."

He jerked his chin up, as if telling her to continue.

"Betty Merchant was murdered last night. Shot to death. Joey is in jail, the cops think he did it."

Roy kept staring at her. One hand went to his chest in a strangely effeminate gesture. Otherwise, he didn't move.

"I'm sorry." Abby said uncomfortably.

He continued to stare at her. He must have blinked by now, but she had missed it. He stepped onto the porch, and carefully shut the door behind him, as if there was something inside he didn't want her to see. He was wearing a red, full-length apron, the front of it stained dark. She backed up, making sure there was a good ten feet between them, and carefully put her key ring in her fist, with the keys sticking out between her knuckles. A makeshift weapon: one of those self-defense tips she had picked up years before, probably from a cereal box.

Roy looked at her blankly. His gaze went down to her hands. Abby blushed. She released the keys, trying to do it casually.

"So," he said, "what happened?"

"Well, I don't know much more. Joey called me this morning. I live just outside of Bantam so I got down pretty quickly. He doesn't know any lawyers, so I found him a man called Franklin Van Renesse—"

"He's that black man, has an office on Main Street?"

So here it was, the country boy showing off his colors. "Look, Roy, Mr. Van Renesse is an extremely good lawyer—"

"Yeah, I like him, he's fair. Defended Jim Walker's sister when she burned down her neighbor's barn."

Abby missed a beat. Roy smiled slyly.

Abby refused to be baited. "Anyway, your kid is sitting in a holding cell. He wants me to give you a message."

"He does?"

"Yeah. He wants you to know that he didn't hurt Betty. That's it. He didn't do it."

"Yeah, well I wouldn't blame him if he did. She pushes, doesn't let up."

"Joey says he doesn't see you much."

Roy shrugged. "I'm a mechanic at Fred's Lawn and Tractor." He said it as if it explained everything.

"So?" Abby asked.

Reluctantly, he continued. "His mother says I'm a bad influence on the boy."

"Her job to look after him."

Goaded into defending himself, he retorted, his voice louder: "She wants him to go to college, get a good job, but the boy's a motorhead, loves to tinker with machines, wants to grow up to be a race car driver. Hey, I tell him, you should learn engineering, work for a big corporation. That's where you make the real money. But Betty, she don't care, she don't like him hanging around me. She thinks I'll contaminate him."

Abby could hear the resentment in his voice.

"She very controlling of him?"

Roy gave a snort of laughter. "More like, afraid of him turning out like his dad. But he's a good kid, no matter what he did."

What happened to innocent until proven guilty? Especially your own flesh and blood?

Roy moved back to his front door. "Sorry to cut this short, but I've got work to do."

Nosiness overcame her reluctance to pry. "What are you doing, if you don't mind my asking?"

He stared at her, and his eyeballs seemed to glisten in the sunlight.

"I do some taxidermy on the side. I'm stuffing a coon right about now."

"Oh." She nodded, as if plenty of people she knew were busy stuffing coons and she, for one, understood the time constraints.

He stood on the porch watching her turn the Bronco around. She paused, weighing the situation. Then, when the front of her car was pointed toward the driveway, she leaned out the passenger window.

"I hope you'll go see him. He could use someone on his side." She waited a second, and when he didn't say anything she took her foot off the brake and accelerated down the hill.

As she reached the end of the dirt road, she wondered about Roy. How far could resentment like that take him? She glanced at her watch. It was past lunchtime, she was hungry, and she had to be at the InnBetween by four o'clock. She pulled out onto the surfaced road, and drove back to Bantam.

# CHAPTER TEN

In town, she bought a sandwich at Victor's, and sat inside at the counter. She ate quickly, nervously, taking big bites. As she ate, she thought of Joey in his cell. She hoped Franklin could help him. Maybe she should've found some high-powered weekender lawyer who would intimidate the shit out of the local powers-that-be, someone who could get Joey out in a heartbeat. Yeah, maybe she'd screwed this up. Abby took a long drink of her iced tea. No, she should give Franklin a chance. She looked out the window, thinking of the ripples of pain and disruption caused by the shooting. Joey was alone now, and at the mercy of the adults collecting around him. She hoped they wished him well.

She wasn't ready to go home. Maybe it was empathy for Joey, or her night with Sean, but she was feeling more vulnerable than she liked. She hated herself for that needy moment when he was getting ready to leave. It made her blush with shame. The problem with letting someone get their big toe into your life is that you become dependent, you need to know where they're going, why they're going. And if they're ever coming back. Not what she was looking for. She was obviously still not emotionally stable enough for a purely sexual relationship. It was time to take stock, get organized, and focus on other things. Much better to think about Joey, who could actually use her help. For some reason her thoughts moved to Richie, the lawnmower boy she had seen the night before at the Blue Moon Tavern. Six brothers. They could start a pizza parlor. There was definitely something she didn't like about Richie, the middle brother. She thought about his evasive answers at Cyrus's, which led her back to the Car Borrower. She was still intrigued, even though it was pretty much a dead issue; by now Dulcie had changed the locks and reclaimed her vehicle. But she wasn't quite ready to give up on it. So. What did she know so far? That Richie Callahan had told Cyrus Leighton a story about a similar set of events. Maybe one of his brothers was the Car Borrower. Why would they need to steal a car? No, she had seen her—it was a girl. Who had Richie been with last night? His girlfriend. Maybe his girlfriend was the one who told him the car story. Abby tried to remember what Sean had told her about Connie. Oh, right. Sarah, Connie's best friend. Small town. Everyone related or going to be. The plumber's daughter's best friend. And the plumber's daughter was gone. What if *she* were the Car Borrower? She left town, and the minivan hadn't moved since. Of course, Dulcie had changed the locks, so it was hard to know if one had anything to do with the other. But just out of curiosity, she went over what she knew about the girl.

First, her name. Connie. Connie Testarossa. What had Sean said? She had an apartment in her father's house up on Malden Street. She worked at a hospital somewhere, maybe Hudson or over in Pittsfield, Massachusetts. But didn't he say she had a car? The information she had on Connie was pretty skimpy and she could obviously use a little more. Maybe Sarah was the person to talk to.

The Necessary Bagel Café, around the corner from Main Street, had been in existence a few years longer than Victor's Café, and was owned by sisters, both born and raised in Bantam. They served lots of coffee and donuts and bagels covered in homemade toppings. Abby didn't go in often, but she liked the owners. And the Bagel Babes, as they were sometimes referred to, knew everyone in town.

It was early afternoon by the time she walked in. The place was almost empty, with only two of the tiny tables occupied by one person each, both of whom were reading while they ate. There was no one behind the counter. Abby waited for a minute and then saw Corey, the older sister, in the back kitchen. Her given name was Coriander, and her sister was Rosemary. Their parents had an herb farm. Corey had an apron on and was walking past the door, holding a large bowl. Abby called out to her.

Corey turned her head when she heard Abby. Even with a green bandanna wrapped around her head, she managed to look elegant. About twenty-five, she was tall, with red hair worn in a short blunt cut. Her features were chiseled and even. Her sleeves were rolled up.

"Can I come and talk to you?" Abby gestured, not wanting to disturb the librarylike atmosphere of the place. Corey nodded, and Abby walked through the service area to the kitchen.

"Everyone okay out there?" Corey pointed with her chin to the table area. Her voice was surprisingly high and sweet, nearly squeaky, belying her racehorse look. "No one's chokin' to death?"

"They both looked okay to me. Quiet and well behaved. What're you making? A spread?"

"Yeah, curried veggie cream cheese." She went back to her cutting table and started slicing an onion with precision and speed.

"Corey, do you know a girl called Sarah?" Abby asked.

Corey paused, and looked up.

"Sarah who?"

"I don't know. She goes out with one of the Callahans. She's best friends with Connie Testarossa."

"Oh, sure. Let me think. She was in Rosie's class at school. What a bitch. Sarah—? Hmm. I don't remember her last name. I'll have to ask Rosie. She'll know."

Rosie, it turned out, was in Boston for the day at a food show. Abby told

Corey she would come back the next day, thanked her, and started to leave. She was at the glass door of the café when Corey came out of the back room, holding her knife in the air.

"Do you need her last name, or do you just want to find her?"

Abby shrugged. "I'd settle for finding her."

"That's easy. She works at the pharmacy. Out on One-oh-three. Can't miss her. The only bitch there." She smiled pleasantly at her customers, and went back into the kitchen.

Abby drove along Main Street, crossed the train tracks, grateful that the yellow and black barrier was up, and out on to Route 46. At the traffic light she turned left on 103. A short way up, in the old Finast supermarket building, was the pharmacy. She pulled into a parking space, turned off the ignition, and went inside.

As far as she could see, the place was empty of customers, just row upon gleaming row of stuff: hair stuff, skin stuff, pain stuff, greeting cards, and junk food. The only salespeople in sight were a middle-aged woman at one of the checkout counters, and a dark-haired man in a white coat behind the prescription counter at the far end of the store. Abby walked up to the woman behind the cash register.

"Where can I find Sarah?" Abby hoped there was only one Sarah working today.

"Hum. I would guess out back, doing inventory. It *is* Saturday." Of course. Saturday. Abby thanked her, and walked toward the back of the store. She stopped, and studied a row of refrigerator magnets, with customer-like interest. One of the magnets looked like a tiny boom box, with push buttons. One button had PLAY written on it. She pushed it. The three-inch magnet started playing an earsplitting percussive version of the Macarena. There seemed to be no way to turn it off. The tune reverberated throughout the large, empty store, and she saw the saleswoman stop what she was doing and look at her. She picked up the magnet, trying to cover it with her hand to muffle the sound while she walked toward the back of the store. Abruptly, the racket ended. She was out of sight, behind the hair dryers and the douche bags. In front of her was a swing door, with a sign on it: *Personnel only*. She glanced around, then pushed her way through it.

She was in a large, poorly-lit storeroom. She couldn't tell how big it was. Shelves stocked with cases of products lined the perimeter of the room, with more rows of steel shelving creating walls and aisles down the center. She let the door swing closed behind her, and stood still. There was silence. She took a few quiet steps forward. Suddenly, she heard a crash. Then a low murmur. It sounded as if it was coming from the far end of the long room. She walked carefully down one of the aisles. Further into the room, the lighting became even dimmer and much less uniform, the tall shelves casting dark shadows. She was starting to feel afraid, the way she always did when she was doing something she'd been told not to do. Even by a Personnel Only sign. Abby had to remind herself that yes, she was in a storeroom that was off-limits to customers; no, she was not robbing a bank.

Abby came silently around the corner of one row of shelving, and for a minute she saw nothing. Then she noticed movement at the far end of the aisle, about thirty feet away. It took her a minute to figure out what was going on. Someone seemed to be sick. No, having a seizure. She started to move toward the person, ready to help. And then the sick or dying individual groaned, and something about the groan, and the way the body metamorphosed for a second into two bodies, then back into one, made everything clear. She still couldn't make out the details, but she had never seen other people have sex, except in the movies (and once her college roommate, freshman year), so she stood still. Maybe it was the intensity of the moment, but she found herself experiencing a sort of flashback to the night before. Her brain shut down, and a sort of sensory lightning bolt shot through her, complete with smell, sound, and touch. Abby's eyes closed with the power of it and she felt overwhelmed with longing. She stood in the dark, musty storeroom, one hand on a shelf so she wouldn't lose her balance.

Thankfully, she was brought back to the present by the low grunts and groans of the couple she was spying on, who sounded as if they were rhythmically squeezing a chewy toy. Abby shook off the weakness. What the hell was wrong with her? She focused on the grinding bodies in front of her.

Who were they? She assumed one was Sarah, but who was the man? Probably her Callahan boyfriend. Some inventory.

Just then the pair moved and began to thrash against the metal shelving. It looked like the whole thing would come down. If Abby wasn't careful, she would be crushed to death. She crept back to the swing door, taking care not to walk into a crate. She needed to talk to Sarah and she didn't have all afternoon. Before she left the storeroom, she took the little boom-box magnet that was making dents in her hand, attached it to a metal post, and pressed PLAY. She pushed out through the door into the store. The door swung behind her. Abby could hear the muffled notes of the Macarena beating behind her. She imagined them reverberating shrilly through the large storeroom.

Abby left the store and went to her car. She pulled out of her parking space in front of the store and pulled around the building, so that she faced the side of the building. She wanted to be able to see both the front and the back doors. She sat in the driver's seat and slid down in her seat, trying to make herself less visible. She waited. Within minutes, she saw a man leaving the rear of the building. He walked quickly to a tan Subaru wagon. Medium height, hair hidden by a baseball cap. He was too far away for Abby to get a good look at him. He started the car and, instead of driving by her, drove around the back of the store so she didn't see his face. Nonetheless, something about him was familiar.

Abby went back into the store. Sarah was at the cash register, talking to the older woman. She looked very businesslike, a clipboard held against her chest, as if the information on it was of grave importance. As she approached, however, Abby noticed that the back of Sarah's skirt was tucked up in her black lacy underpants. Couldn't she feel the breeze?

Abby walked up to the cash register and stood next to the two women. They kept talking. Finally, she interrupted them.

"Excuse me," she said. They both looked at her with irritation. Sarah was a pretty girl, with eyebrows plucked to a single line of hairs, like dominoes that have been knocked over onto each other. The hair on her head was surprisingly neat after what she'd been up to. It was teased into a blond wall over her forehead and around her face, but flat at the crown of the head and in the back. Like some women newscasters, all fancy and tall from the front, but if they turn sideways, they look as if they've been run over by a steamroller.

"You're Sarah?"

She looked at Abby, raising what was left of her eyebrows. "Yes?"

"Could we talk for a minute? Privately? I'm a friend of Cyrus Leighton, the writer."

"I don't know any Cyrus Whatever. I'm in the middle of doing inventory." She started to turn away. So rude. Abby placed a second little boombox magnet on the counter. She pressed PLAY, and the Macarena drilled and pulsed into the quiet of the store. Sarah glanced shiftily at her boss. Abby smiled at her.

"Isn't this more fun than doing inventory? Though I guess it depends on what kind of inventory you do. Some inventory can give real satisfaction." Abby had to stop herself from jiggling her eyebrows suggestively, like Groucho Marx.

Sarah glanced at the older woman, who was listening to Abby with a frown. "Maybe I'll take my cigarette break, now. Okay with you, Marlene?"

Abby followed Sarah out the front door of the store. Once outside, Sarah walked to the right, so she was no longer visible from the front door. She stopped. She pulled a pack of cigarettes from her pocket, and lit up angrily, turning to Abby.

"Who the fuck are you?"

"I just want to ask you a few questions, and, frankly, I didn't have the time to wait for you both to get off."

Sarah looked at her with as much disdain as she could muster. "So ask."

"Somebody told Rich Callahan a little tale about a student who borrows someone's car using their spare key. I think you told Rich, and I want to know who told you."

The girl seemed surprised, even relieved. "Why? Why do you want to know about that?"

Abby shrugged. "Because I think one of you did it to a friend of mine, and I want to know who. And why. I have no interest in going to the cops. I just want to know."

Sarah smiled contemptuously. "Why should I tell you?"

"Because if you don't, I'm going to call your regional bosses, people who don't know you, and don't give a shit about you, and tell them I saw you banging some guy in their stockroom, at two in the afternoon, no less. They won't be pleased."

Sarah didn't look pleased, either. Her resentment of Abby was tangible, a gluey quality in the air around them. It made Abby feel a little queasy. She didn't like people to hate her.

Sarah seemed to cave. Maybe it didn't matter to her that much anyway.

"Yeah, yeah. I told Rich, and he told the guy he works for."

"So who did it? You?"

"I wish. I think it's a cool idea. Nah, it's Connie."

Well. So there it was. No big deal, just a cool idea, a lark. Abby pictured the girl walking quickly toward the dark car, letting herself in, claiming it, the scent of lemon lingering after she was done.

"Why did she do it?"

"She needed a car, obviously." The *stoopid* was implied. Sarah was beginning to have fun.

"I thought she had a car."

"She did, but she needed *another* car." She was grinning. We were now playing Twenty Questions. Abby didn't mind as long as the girl answered them.

"Why?"

"Because she didn't want her father knowing she was going out late at night."

"How would he have known?"

Sarah had to think about this for a moment. "I guess he would've known when she took her car out. He made her park it in an indoor garage. Attached to his house."

"Where was she going? To work?"

Sarah laughed. "Hell no. She works days at Columbia Medical Center. No, she was going to meet her sweetie."

"Who's her sweetie?"

The girl took a long drag on her cigarette, her cheeks sucking in with the effort. She stared down her nose, watching the tobacco burn. It looked as if she was crossing her eyes at Abby.

"What's that got to do with your friend's car?"

Abby smiled. "I'm just nosy."

Sarah smiled harder. "Well I don't know who her sweetie is. She keeps it a big secret."

"She must've told you something about him. You are her best friend," Abby pressed.

"She keeps this one very close to her chest." She laughed at her own play on words.

"Why? Is he married?"

Sarah was tired of Abby's questions. "How the fuck should I know? Maybe he's married. Maybe he's just shy. Maybe he's a fuckin' leprechaun." She threw down her cigarette, and ground it into the gravel, hard. "I gotta get back to work."

She turned, and walked back to the door of the drugstore. Abby watched her. Her skirt was still wedged up in her panties, her left cheek jiggling seductively as she moved.

"Sarah!" Abby called out, but Sarah just held her right hand over her head, middle finger extended. Oh, well. Sooner or later someone would tell her.

Before going home, she bought Joey a donut from the Necessary Bagel, and a Calvin and Hobbes anthology from Margie's secondhand bookstore. When she got to the police station, he was curled up, fast asleep. She left her offerings with the chief, who said that Van Renesse and the boy had spent a good deal of time together and seemed to have come to some kind of arrangement. That was the best Abby could hope for at the moment, so she drove home.

Abby had two messages from Sean on her answering machine. In the first one he told her he had a good time (that's her, Good-Time Abby) and in the second, he asked her to call him when she got in. She hesitated, then she erased them both. She took a long shower, and dressed for work. She had no time for him. That moment of longing in the storeroom was something she didn't need right now.

# CHAPTER ELEVEN

Abby was twenty minutes late by the time she walked into the restaurant. Her shoulder-length hair was tied up in a knot, and she wore all black—a ribbed black turtleneck, and a black skirt. She had found the skirt at the Salvation Army in Pittsfield, for a buck. She pulled a black InnBetween tee shirt over the turtleneck.

Abby was stationed upstairs with Mindy, and Henry was at the bar. It was the weekend, and the crowds started early. Everyone was feeling good, happy the week was over. The weekenders were happy to be out of the city. The place smelled good, the temperature was just right, and Dan the Man was at his dishwasher. Dulcie was wearing a green and gold low-waisted Earth-mother dress, the kind that makes you look fat no matter what your body type. She was seating people, smiling, adding up checks, clearing forgotten tables, eyes constantly roving around the room.

In the center of the dining room, two tables had been pushed together. Jamison Brown, the artist whose success was a thorn in Cyrus's side, was presiding over the gathering. On his right sat two men who were often with him. Abby knew that one was an art critic and a "Jamison Brown" specialist; the other was Jamison's dealer. They looked alike, both of Jamison's generation, both beautifully spoken, both Williams educated, and Abby didn't try to tell them apart. Across the table from Jamison sat his wife, Dolores, a woman with a braying laugh, who favored work clothes. On her right sat their future son-in-law, Keith Ryder, a handsome man in his early forties, dark hair brushed off from a high, sensitive forehead, a mouth that promised warmth and intimacy. On Keith's other side, leaning into him, sat Dolores and Jamison's daughter, Josie. Josie was slender, well dressed, and beautiful. She had thick, dark brows and dark eyes, offset by streaked blonde hair. On the table in front of her was a small food scale.

Abby and Mindy, during a lull in the long evening, stood against the wall by the cash register. Surreptitiously, they watched the Brown group talk animatedly about a show they had seen on Houston Street, while Dolores and Keith drew on the butcher paper.

"One of these days, Jamison's going to sketch something, and they're going to forget to take it with them," said Abby, remembering how often they had watched as his entourage made sure to leave no crayon mark of his behind.

"Wouldn't that be awesome?" breathed Mindy. "Would it belong to Dulcie?"

"Hell no," replied Abby. "Finders keepers."

"Isn't his daughter beautiful?" said Mindy, watching Josie look up at Keith adoringly.

"She's crazy. Look, she's weighing her food. She's giving it all to Keith."

Mindy, the kind soul, said: "She's sweet."

Abby shook her head. "She's nuts."

Mindy jabbed her in the ribs. "Aw, she's looking after him."

The night marched on, lots of lamb and blue mash, martinis and crab cakes. Up and down to the bar, in and out of the kitchen. The cooks started sending out warning messages: OUT OF LAMB was the first one, followed by OUT OF SHRIMP. Abby hadn't even realized there was a shrimp special.

For most of the evening, the adrenaline kept her from noticing how tired her legs were, but by quarter to ten she was beginning to feel it. The main dining room was still going, with at least six tables of people eating, and a couple more drinking coffee. Jamison raised his hand and caught Abby's eye.

"Abby, we're ready for dessert," he announced. "What d'you have?"

Abby knew that she could double her tip by selling dessert. She began describing the kiwi strawberry tart.

"Ooh, that's what I want," sighed Josie.

Abby moved on to the crème brulée.

Again, Josie piped up. "Oh, god, no, I want that."

Dolores looked warmly at Keith. "What are you going to have, darling?"

Abby kept going. "We have a warm chocolate mousse cake—"

Keith interrupted her. "Is it really rich and deadly?" He turned to his future mother-in-law and spoke softly to her: "I need rich and deadly. Come on, Dolores, join me."

Abby saw Josie dart him a look.

"Yes it is," answered Abby. "It's delicious. One for you?"

"Come on, what about it, Dolores?"

"No, no, I'll be a truck."

Abby managed to sell a bread pudding to Jamison, no surprise, he always ordered bread pudding. Josie changed her mind three times and ended up with the tart, Keith went for the chocolate cake, and Dolores settled for pear sorbet. The art critic and the dealer both ordered espresso.

Fifteen minutes later, while the Brown group was finishing their last course, the front door opened and a squat, gray-haired man blew in. It was too late to order food, and if she hadn't been so tired she would have gone over and told him so. He brought a bullish energy into the room with him, and when he stopped moving, the energy seemed to swirl and regroup around him, like a magician's cape. Abby noticed Jamison glance up at him, the way people do in restaurants when someone new comes in. He raised a hand to him. The squat man walked over to his table, and they shook hands. Abby was expecting him to pull up a chair and join the table, but instead he looked around, and when he saw her, he started her way. Maybe early fifties, short, bulldog-like, with a square jaw. His eyes, however, took her by surprise. They were a dark, soft velvety-brown. Turned down at the edges, they gave him a melancholy expression.

However, there was nothing soft about his body language. He stopped about eighteen inches from her. Way too close. She expected him to grab her arm in his teeth and shake it back and forth. When he spoke, his voice was abrasive.

"Abby, I'm lookin' for someone called Abby," he snapped.

She stepped back a foot. "I'm Abby," she said with a frown. "Who're you?"

"Mike Testarossa."

Aha. The Plumber.

"Aha," she said out loud.

"What does that mean?" He closed the small gap she had made between them. Abby tried to step back, but by now she was up against the railing of the staircase.

"Look, Mr. Testarossa. You seem upset. I—"

"I am upset. I am very upset. I hear from a concerned person that you have been nosing around into my daughter's personal business. Is this true? That you have been pokin' around? Is this true?" He was getting louder with each "true."

"Hey, Mr. Testarossa, move away. I can't breathe." He paused, seemed to realize that this was not proper restaurant behavior, and stepped back. He took a deep breath. He took a handkerchief from his pocket and wiped his face.

"Jeez, it's hot in here." For a moment, he looked so miserable she couldn't help but feel sorry for him.

"Mr. Testarossa, let's go and sit at a quiet table. I'll bring you something cold to drink. Maybe we can talk for a minute, okay?"

He nodded his head, temporarily defeated, and let her walk him to the table in the alcove near the top of the stairs. She went into the kitchen, and brought him a tall glass of water with ice. She figured, in his state of mind, he shouldn't be drinking anything with caffeine.

She slid into the seat opposite him, and made a tent with her fingers, her elbows resting on the table. She wanted to look professional, and calm. She needed to keep the edge she had just acquired, or this guy was going to trample her. She was starting to understand why his daughter might have taken off.

He took a gulp of water. His hands were meaty and red. He put both fists on the table, the gesture seeming to overpower her woven fingers. She spread her smaller hands flat on the table, to give them the illusion of size. It occurred to her that they were playing a silent game of rock, scissors, paper. Paper covers rock, so she was ahead.

"Okay," she began. "Let me tell you where my interest in your daughter comes from. I have to go back a few days."

He nodded slowly. Abby proceeded to tell him about Dulcie. Actually, she didn't mention her name, but she did tell Mr. T. about the car, and the borrowing. He never interrupted, just nodded. She told him about Cyrus Leighton, and the description of the incident in his manuscript. She told him about waiting for the lawnmower brothers. He smiled grimly when she told him about surly Richie.

It wasn't until she mentioned Sean Kenna that he started to look noticeably unpleasant again. Abby told him that when Richie Callahan's name came up, Sean told her that Richie's girlfriend, Sarah, was an old friend of the boss's daughter. Mentioned it just in passing.

"Yeah," snarled Mr. T., "and did Sean mention just in passing that he was engaged to my daughter for a year? That she broke it off, because she said he was screwing around? Ah, what the hell. That's ancient history. Sean's a good guy, works hard."

He picked up a red crayon from the cup in the center of the table, and absently drew a tiny circle on the clean white paper in front of him. He drew over and over it. Abby couldn't help thinking that because of that tiny circle they were going to have to change the whole sheet of paper. Eventually he looked up at her.

"So, you think it was Connie taking your friend's car? Why would she do that?"

"That's what I asked her friend Sarah. She claims Connie did it so you wouldn't find out she was going out late to meet a man."

Surprisingly, Mr. T. nodded proudly in agreement. "That would be like her. When she wants something, she goes for it, no matter what." He started to draw a second circle next to the first. Same color. Around and around.

Finally he looked up. "So tell me, what's in it for you?"

Abby was puzzled. "You mean, money?"

He tilted his head, and shrugged. "I mean, why are you chasing this down? My daughter's left town, she's not taking the friend's car anymore. Most likely she's whoopin' it up in Texas or California. She hates the weather here."

"Have you heard from her?"

He sighed. "Not yet. She packed up and left a note. Since then, nothing. But you, what's your interest here?"

Abby took a moment, trying to organize her thoughts.

"To tell you the truth, I've wondered the same thing. And the best I can come up with is this." She looked at him, trying to make him understand. "I sat in the bushes, and watched your daughter take my friend's car. Steal it. I couldn't see much, and I certainly didn't recognize her. In fact, I could barely tell if it was a man or a woman. But when she first got in the car, she looked happy. Excited. Makes sense now, I guess. Anyway, I was kind of intrigued."

Connie's father was watching her. Abby couldn't tell what he was thinking. She kept talking. "I wanted to find out something about her. What kind of person would do this—I guess it's more to do with her than my friend's car. Anyway, I'm glad everything has ended well." She stood up, smiling politely, eager to end the conversation.

But she was forgetting that she was dealing with a bulldog. He looked at her suspiciously. "Are you trying to tell me, that's it?"

"Well, she left town, she's trying to get settled in a new location, I would say it's nothing to do with me, wouldn't you?"

He looked at her. "Not really. But I swear, somethin's up. Sit back down. Please."

Reluctantly, Abby obeyed. "Mr. Testarossa, Mike, she has her reasons for not calling you. She'll come around." She wasn't going to play along with the paranoid fantasy of a parent who was paying the price for trying to tether his child.

"It's just that she's not afraid of me," he kept on going, completely ignoring Abby's attempt to end their tête-a-tête. "Yeah, yeah. I know what you're thinking, this guy's pushy, bossy, gotta be real tough on the poor kid. Look at her, having to steal someone else's vehicle to see a boyfriend. Boo-hoo, yeah, he must be a real pain. But d'you want to know the truth? The truth is, I'm a real pushover with her. She does whatever she wants. Ask Sean, ask anyone. I give in to her all the time.

"One time, when she was about fourteen, she was invited to go with a friend to the Cape for the weekend. They'd be unsupervised, and I had a bad feeling about the older sister who was taking them, so I said no. No way. Well, Connie she begged and pleaded, but I hung in there. I didn't think she'd be safe, I'd heard the sister wasn't a good driver. So finally she seemed to accept my decision. She stopped talking about it. I told her I would take her to the mall instead. Saturday morning, I get a call from the Massachusetts State Troopers. She'd been picked up on the Mass Pike, hitchhiking. She'd gotten as far as Worcester." He snorted. "I ended up driving her to the Cape myself, and spending the weekend in a hotel. You think I'm tough? Forget it. She's the tough one. By far."

Abby was not convinced. "Then why wouldn't she use her own car? Why go through the trouble of stealing Dulcie's?"

Mr. T. smiled craftily. "Dulcie, huh?"

"She owns this restaurant. Big deal," Abby snapped.

"Oh, I know who she is. Remember, I service her air conditioner."

"Yeah, well maybe you shouldn't bill her for a couple of months."

"Maybe I won't. So, what kind of a car does Dulcie have?"

"A minivan. Why would Connie bother with a minivan?"

"I don't know why." He looked suddenly lost. "Maybe she did it for fun. Kicks."

"She does things like that for kicks?"

"She's a moody kid. One day she's down in the dumps, the next day she wants to go skydiving."

Abby wondered. "So, she could've gotten a double charge out of taking someone else's car, and maybe seeing a guy she knew you wouldn't approve of."

He started nodding slowly, gaining momentum as he went. "So she didn't want me to know anything about it. That would make sense."

Henry came over to the table. "Sorry to interrupt, but I'm outta here. Will you finish this table?"

Abby looked around the dining room. Since they had been talking, the rest of the room had emptied out. Some of the staff were already putting chairs up on tables, and Mindy was collecting salt and pepper shakers. The music was louder.

"Sure. Thanks, Henry." Abby looked back at Mr. T. and stood up. "Look, Mike, I've had a long night. I'm tired. I've got to go home and walk my dogs."

He grabbed her wrist. "Sure, I understand, just one more quick thing, okay?"

He kept a hold on her wrist and she didn't have the energy to fight him, though she twisted her hand out of his grip.

"What?"

"I want to hire you."

This was too much. Abby had to laugh. "I can't look for daughters who go AWOL."

He shook his head impatiently. "I don't want you to look for Connie. She'll show up when she's ready. No. I just want to find out who she was seeing."

Abby looked at him suspiciously. "Why?"

He raised his hands, as if to show he wasn't armed. "Don't worry. I'm not a violent man. I just want to know, that's all. I just want to know why she would steal your friend's car, why it was so important to keep this man a secret. Please. I'll give you five hundred dollars, plus expenses, to find out."

Abby didn't really want to do it, but she could use the money. And plumbers are rich, everyone knows that.

"Please, just find out what was going on." He held his hand to her. "Come on, let's shake on it."

Abby thought for a moment. "Where does Connie work?"

"Columbia Medical Center, down on Route Forty-six."

"Okay. You'd have to call her boss—I need to talk to them about Connie."

He nodded, and once more held out a strong, stubby-fingered hand. And for no reason that she could understand, Abby held out hers, and they sealed the deal.

That night, Abby dreamed of Jonah. He looked just the way he did when she first met him, thin and young, blond hair too long and falling around his face. He was walking on Main Street as she was driving by. He was smiling to himself about something private, and she knew he would tell her what it was if she could only ask him. She tried to slow down but she couldn't find the brake pedal. She opened the door, trying to get up the courage to jump out. But she couldn't do it, and when she turned around to look, he was gone.

# CHAPTER TWELVE

Abby woke up Monday morning feeling anxious. Too many things left undone. The day was overcast and cooler than it had been lately. She lay in bed, thinking of Sean Kenna. She felt sad, as if her night with him had happened long ago to a more carefree person. The memory of it left her depressed, leaden. She got up slowly. Her joints were stiff. The dogs sat on the floor, watching her; they needed a long walk. She pulled on sweatpants, a T-shirt from her dirty laundry pile, a pair of sneakers, and went outside. Five laps walking quickly around the field were all she felt like, though her blood was actually moving through her body by the time she got in the shower. Clean clothes, coffee, a bowl of cereal, and she convinced herself all was well.

As she was getting ready to leave, the phone rang. It was Franklin, asking her to stop by his office. She asked him how things looked, but he said he would tell her when he saw her. He hung up quickly. Most likely, she was one more item checked off his list. She grabbed a sweater, and said good-bye to the dogs.

In Bantam, she climbed Franklin's staircase. No one was at the secretary's desk, so she went to his office and knocked. When she didn't hear an answer, she opened the door and looked in.

Franklin was sitting at his desk. At first glance she thought he was writing. Then she realized she was hearing a buzzing noise, and saw the pen he was writing with was not a pen, but had a cord coming out of the back end of it.

Abby waited for a minute, then spoke loudly. "Good morning, Franklin."

He looked up, saw her, flicked a switch on the penlike instrument, and the buzzing stopped. He smiled broadly, the way people sometimes do when they are in the middle of something that makes them feel good.

"Hello, Abby. Come on in and sit down, please. Let me just put this away." He unplugged and put the instrument away in a desk drawer. Abby sat down. Franklin dusted off his hands, linked his fingers together, and looked at her. "So, how can I help you?"

He was all business. Waiting. No mention of his phone call an hour and a half before. She thought he was making a little joke but he looked so damned serious. He raised his eyebrows, as if in encouragement. Abby let a little silence accumulate before she spoke.

"Franklin, what's up?"

He stared at her, questioningly.

"Franklin, I'm here about the boy, Joey Merchant." He stared at her, smiling. Then the smile began to break up, like a small craft against rocks.

"Wait." He looked over his desk, searching for something. He picked up a file, opened it, and leafed through it. When he found what he was looking for, he lay the file flat on the table, and started to tap his finger on the page he was reading. He seemed to be muttering something to himself. Then he stopped.

"Abby, I apologize. My mind was wandering. I have quite a few cases open right now, and I simply forgot where I was." Abby nodded at him, hoping he was right. It looked like more than that. But Franklin went on. "You came to talk about Joey Merchant. I saw Joey yesterday, and thank you for steering me his way."

"How was he? How did he seem to you?" Abby dragged her worries away from Franklin, and made herself picture the boy curled up in the cell.

Franklin thought about this. "He is a young man in a very difficult and frightening position. He feels very alone in the world. And the case against him is circumstantial, but quite strong."

"Jesus. What happened?"

Franklin glanced down at his file then looked up at Abby. "According to Joey, he walked home after school, and did his homework. His mother was still at work, not due to arrive until approximately six P.M. Joey finished his homework then watched television for a while. His mother returned a little later than usual, and lost her temper with Joey because he had left his schoolbooks on the dining room table."

Abby could picture Betty finding that a punishable offense. Franklin seemed to be thinking about that as well. He was looking at the wall behind her.

"Go on," Abby encouraged him, wanting to hear the rest of the story.

"Right. So: they had an argument, voices were raised, a normal parent–kid fight. Joey swears it was nothing more than that, but he does say they fought a lot. He stormed out of the house, swearing he would never come home. He said he told his mother he was going to move in with his dad. That seems to upset him more than anything—that those were his last words to her."

"Jeez. So he left then? What time was it?"

Franklin checked his notes.

"About eight P.M. He went to a friend's house. Name of Matt Wilson. According to the cops, it checks out. He was at the friend's house from a little after eight, to ten-fifteen. Until his mother called."

"Did any of the friend's family speak to Betty?"

"Matt's father. According to the police, he said she sounded upset. She'd been looking for Joey, and she asked, would he send Joey straight home. The father said, sure. And he gave Joey the message. He said when he did, Joey did that teenage thing, he rolled his eyes. Which seemed pretty normal to him. Soon after that, Joey left."

"Did he go straight home?"

Franklin paused for a moment. "Joey says he walked around for quite a while. He doesn't remember too well. But he didn't stop anywhere. He just didn't want to go home."

"So what happened?" Abby was trying to put this Greek tragedy together with the sleepy little town she knew, the pudgy-faced housekeeper, and her sulky child.

"So, he got home. And when he got there, he found the front door unlocked, which was unusual for his mother. He remembers noticing that when he first opened the door.

"He says he found her on the living room floor, covered with blood. There was a shotgun next to her. Her own. He assumed she shot herself, and he tried to see if she was still alive. He doesn't remember touching the weapon, but his prints were on it, and on her. They just got the results back this morning."

Franklin and Abby sat in silence. She thought of Joey finding his mother like that and, unbidden, an image of Jonah came into her head. She put it aside, and tried to think what the next step could be. She glanced at Franklin. He was staring at her. He looked weird.

"Are you feeling okay, Franklin?"

He shook his head, as if to clear something away. "Oh, sure, Abby. Sure. I've just got a lot on my mind. So, what are we going to do to help this young man?"

Abby felt overwhelmed. She hadn't realized she was supposed to help him. Other than what she had read, she didn't know much about the law, and even less about a murder investigation. Or any kind of investigation, for that matter. And what if he had blown his mother away? Didn't teenagers do that kind of thing all the time? Maybe Joey was getting even for too much nagging, or for cheap sneakers. Abby looked at Franklin.

"What do you think? Do you think he did it?"

Franklin shrugged and raised his hands, palms upward.

"It makes no difference to me as his lawyer. I have to give him the best defense I'm capable of. But as an impartial observer, I would guess he's no psychopath. I deal with criminals all the time, and some of them are pretty bad people. He seems to me to be an unhappy kid. Doesn't mean he isn't an unhappy kid who shot his mother. Does that answer your question?"

Abby thought about it. She supposed it did. She couldn't see walking away from the boy. Just because the only evidence there was pointed to him.

"What happens next?"

Franklin looked down at the papers in front of him.

"The arraignment is this afternoon. We'll see what kind of bail the judge sets—I have to convince him the boy's not a flight risk, but truth is, he won't get out if no one wants him."

"I met his dad."

"What kind of a guy is he?"

Abby made a face. "Weird. He skins animals for fun."

"What's his name?"

"Roy Goodrich."

Franklin made a note on a yellow pad.

Abby stood up, suddenly eager to leave. "Keep me posted. I like the boy, and I want to help if I can."

Franklin nodded at her. Abby let herself out of his office. Mary was back at her desk. She suddenly remembered the electric pen and stopped in front of her.

"Mary, does Franklin do some kind of electric calligraphy?"

She chuckled. "Scrimshaw. He does scrimshaw."

Of course. The special engraving tool.

"What does he do it on? Wood?"

"Sometimes. Or on bone. In the old days it used to be done on ivory."

"Does he normally do it when he's at the office?"

Mary looked up at her. "I guess." She shrugged her shoulders, and looked back down at the papers in front of her.

As she let herself out the downstairs door, Abby wondered if she had done Joey a disservice by bringing in a lawyer who had lost his last two cases, couldn't remember a phone call he had just made, and used his work hours to carve little shapes on bone.

• • •

That afternoon Abby fell asleep on the couch, with the dogs curled up next to her. She dreamed she was trying to run down a quiet country road when she realized her legs were encased in hard plastic tubes. She tried to remove the plastic tubes by scratching and pulling at them. Eventually she succeeded in tearing them off, but to her horror, found that under the tubes her legs had become shriveled twigs, decayed and useless. She lay in the dusty road, unable to move, helpless. She tried to call for help, but no sound came out.

Abby struggled up to consciousness, moaning and sweating. After some time her heartbeat slowed down. The dogs, whose solid bodies were pressed against her legs, slept on untroubled. She looked at her watch and saw that it was a few minutes to four. Painfully, she got up from the couch and shuffled like an old woman into the bathroom. She turned on the faucets in the shower and, after taking off her clothes, stepped in. She stood there, hoping the hot water would strip away the sense of loss that choked her.

# CHAPTER THIRTEEN

Abby made an appointment to meet Sally DeCintio, Connie's boss. She drove into Bantam. As she was making the last turn into town, a big pickup coming the other way flashed its lights at her. She slowed down when she recognized the truck. It pulled up right next to her, and Sean looked down into her window.

She looked at his arm, resting on the open window and something about his skin, the way it looked smooth and cool, made her want to stroke it. He smiled, as if he could read her mind.

"I've been trying to get in touch with you, seems like days. How's it going?"

She nodded. "Okay. Running around. You know."

He looked up at the roof of his cab, as if there was something written there.

"So, Abby. Are you giving me the brush-off?"

It didn't seem like a rhetorical or flirtatious question. He seemed to be waiting for an answer.

"I'm really busy. I've meant to call you, but I've been so busy." She was awed by the platitudes that were coming out of her mouth. She was like the fairy-tale princess whose words turned to frogs as she spoke them. Sean watched her, as if he, too, was impressed by the shallowness of her excuse.

"Well, you know where to find me." He sounded as if he had lost interest.

He put the pickup into gear and gave it some gas. It moved off into the traffic circle. Abby watched it go in her rearview mirror.

She headed south on Route 46. The Columbia Medical Center was about two miles north of Hudson. Built during a sixties boom, for the next three decades it was allowed to slowly wear out, like a cheap toaster. Its paint began to peel, the roof sprung a few leaks, and the equipment devolved from state-of-the-art to not-always-reliable. Nurses complained, and doctors tried to relocate. By the early nineties, talk had begun about shutting it down.

However, in the summer of '94 a group of aggressive weekenders and locals got together for a barbecue (and legend has it, many Bloody Marys) and formed what was known as the Coalition for the Aggressive Preservation of Institutions to Save our Health, or C.A.P.I.S.H. Amazingly, rather than being laughed at, they were joined by newly settled families, artists, and, over time, local professionals and businesses. Maybe it was the implied threat of the acronym, with its Mott Street ring, its Italian muscle, or just the fact that plenty of its members were well-connected, moneyed professionals, but people felt that C.A.P.I.S.H. had clout. Dinner parties and gala events were hosted, money was raised, and the local politicos started to believe they had always *loved* the Medical Center. Finally, it was given a new wing, a refurbishing, and the nurses received a well-deserved raise. Safe for at least another couple of decades.

Abby took a right off 46 and up the resurfaced access road. The Center appeared before her, squat and institutional, a classic sixties nightmare softened by time and trees. She had only been to the hospital once before, with Jonah. She went to a movie with a friend and, while she was out, he took a shovelful of pills. She came home at eleven-thirty and found him on the kitchen floor. It never occurred to her to call an ambulance. She dragged him to the car. He was as hard to move as a dead body, but somehow she levered him into the front seat. She had to hold him straight while she did up his seat belt. His head kept rolling around. On the entire drive down to the hospital, she shouted at him, trying to wake him up. She occasionally reached over and grabbed a clump of his hair and shook his head. She turned on the radio, raising the volume as high as it would go. The only voice she could find on the airwaves that was abrasive enough was a hellfire preacher ranting about sin and damnation. The man probably saved Jonah's life. It was just when he yelled something about "grabbing your heart and squeezing the hate out" that Jonah carefully leaned as far forward as his seat belt would allow and barfed out his guts all over the inside of the windscreen. She remembered seeing a semi-dissolved white pill slide down the glass. There she was, doing eighty at near midnight on a country road, and she could barely see out because of the vomit. Automatically, she turned on the wipers. Strangely, they didn't do any good. And then it came to her: no, the storm is on the inside. *The storm is on the inside.* Struck by such brilliant cleverness and deep irony, she started to laugh. Jonah was groaning, the preacher was howling, and she was laughing. And then crying. Luckily that stretch of road is pretty straight, because she could only guess where she was going.

They stumbled into the reception area, Jonah's arm draped around her shoulders, his chin sunk down on his chest, both of them covered in puke and wet with tears. The nurse behind the desk looked at the two of them, shook her head, and said: "Well, someone's been partying." *Stupid observation,* Abby thought at the time. *I mean, does this look like fun?* But later, as she sat in the waiting room, she remembered it, and wondered if that nurse hadn't hit on the truth. Maybe that's what Jonah was trying to do. Party himself to death.

But today she was clean and dry-eyed. She left the Bronco in the visitors' area and walked across the parking lot to the main entrance. The inside seemed dark compared to the bright sunshine outside and she stood still, waiting for her vision to adjust to the change. Abby had spoken to Testarossa before making the appointment, and he'd made a point of telling her to talk to Sally DeCintio (pronounced *Chin-tee-oh*) in Development.

She found her way to the Development office, which was on the ground floor in the opposite direction from the Emergency Room. The hall was quiet, with nothing but the hum of voices and technology, like copiers, and computers. Peaceful. Abby always expected hospitals to be filled with the groans of human suffering, the hallways lined with gurneys, starched nurses squeaking by on rubber-soled shoes. Instead, the only nurses she passed were standing in one small cluster. Suddenly, they all laughed at something. Like a small explosion, the laughter broke up the cluster. The nurses moved off briskly in different directions, shaking their heads and smiling as they walked.

Sally DeCintio was waiting for her. She was older than Abby had expected: judging by her voice, Abby thought she would be closer in age to Connie, but she was about fifty. She was slim, dressed in a dark blue tailored jacket over a white silk blouse, and a mid-calf skirt.

But there conservative ended. She was like a Barbie Businesswoman doll whose head had been pulled off and replaced with that of a Barbie Drag Queen/Streetwalker doll. She had a shock of dyed red hair, permed into a mass of ringlets that fell to her shoulders, a lacquered curl decorating the middle of her forehead. Her eyes were ringed in charcoal gray eyeliner, her eyelashes so heavy with mascara Abby wondered if she could close her eyes. Her real eyebrows had been removed, and false ones drawn above the bone ridge where the originals had once grown. Her lips were sculpted with a dark pencil into a Cupid's bow. It was as if she had taken one look in the mirror, shaken her head and said: oh, no, this is all wrong. Or maybe she was in a low-budget, witness-relocation program. No money for reconstructive surgery so it all had to be done with paint. Abby tried to imagine what she looked like before bed, her face washed, but failed.

When she was able to drag her eyes away from Ms. DeCintio, she looked around. They were standing in a large interior room, the light source strips of fluorescents on the ceiling. Two young women were working at computers. It was a drab but functional space, made homier with travel posters and a few potted plants. Sally led her through a dark wood door with her name and the words *Director of Development* below it, into an attractive private office that looked out onto a back garden. When they were inside, Sally closed the door. There was a large picture window and sitting on a bench in the garden, profile to her, Abby noticed a woman in a bathrobe. She was very still.

Sally was briskly friendly, and offered her coffee or tea. Abby politely accepted tea with a little milk. Her hostess disappeared for a minute, and Abby watched the woman on the bench, who looked as if she were made out of stone.

"Car crash. Head injury. We're hoping she'll come around," Sally said when she came back in. She stood next to Abby's chair, her eyes also on the woman, then she shook her head, tut-tutted, and put a cup and saucer in front of Abby. There were two sugar cubes on the saucer. Sally circled the desk, and sat down with a sigh. She straightened a pile of papers by holding them upright and knocking the edges against the desk, then put them back down carefully. Her fingernails were surprisingly short, with only a subdued pale pink lacquer on them. She looked at Abby, eyebrow ridges raised expectantly, painted eyebrows momentarily disappearing into her forehead crease.

"So. How can I help you?"

Abby stirred her tea. "I'm not sure. I'd like you to tell me what you know about Connie."

Sally DeCintio opened a file she had lying on her desk. "After Mike called, I pulled her file to refresh my memory. So. Let's see." She scanned a few pages of the thin file. "She's been working for us for about a year. A nice girl, friendly, outgoing, well liked. No complaints from anyone." She looked up at her. Abby smiled encouragingly.

Ms. DeCintio frowned, wreaking havoc with her eyebrows. "You know, this file is confidential. I wouldn't normally do this, but I understand why Mike is concerned. I would be, too. But there's nothing in here."

"Who hired her? Did you?"

Sally glanced once more at her file, then looked away, as if remembering. "Yes. We put an ad in the *Register Star*. Clerical work, etcetera. Not highly skilled work, but we had trouble finding someone who seemed right. Then she came in and I hired her within the week."

"You knew her father?"

Sally nodded. "Mike and I went to Bantam High together. He was a few years older, but we were both in a production of *Damn Yankees* my sophomore year. I had the lead, you know, Lola—" for a second her eyes drifted away, remembering, before she yanked her fringed gaze back to Abby, all business, "and he and some of his jock buddies were recruited to play the baseball players. We became friends. I saw less of him after graduation. I got married, had kids. My husband and I divorced seven years ago, and Mike's wife died three years after that. We ran into each other at the Bowling Lanes about a year ago, and got reacquainted. It was about that time he mentioned that Connie was at loose ends, looking for work. I said she should apply for the job." She looked at Abby and then went on, "But Mike's not why I hired her. She was the best qualified. The one with the best people skills."

That struck Abby as odd. "Why would she need people skills for clerical work?" Abby gestured toward the door, where on the other side sat the two young women, typing.

Sally smiled. "For the etcetera part. We use our office staff to help with hospital functions." She saw Abby was still puzzled, so she went on. "We're a nonprofit organization, and we depend a great deal on charitable donations, both private and corporate. That means, frankly, that we throw a lot of parties, everything from art shows and antiques auctions to clambakes and hoedowns. You name it, we host it. So our staff has to help out with mailings, planning, and even take a turn passing the hors d'oeuvres. Connie is perfect for that."

Abby watched Sally carefully. "Is she having a relationship with anyone at the hospital?"

Abby thought the woman's gaze became guarded, thoughtful. The grid of mascara around her eyes seemed to tighten. Then she shrugged. "I have no idea. No one that I know of, anyway. I can certainly ask around for you. Though it would be very awkward for the hospital if something unsavory were going on." She emphasized the word *unsavory*.

"I hadn't been thinking of anything *unsavory*," Abby replied. "I mean, she's young and single, she's entitled to a boyfriend."

Sally's eyebrows shot up. "*She's* entitled." Abby was left to decipher what she meant, and stared at her blankly. Then she got it. Connie might be entitled, but the person she was seeing might not be, if for example, he were married.

Abby nodded, slowly. "I see what you mean. I have no interest in doing any damage to the hospital. I'd just like to know if anyone went away with her. Did any other member of the staff leave at about the same time she did?"

Sally thought for a moment. "I really don't know. We have a pretty big staff."

"Can you find out?"

Sally nodded, her curls bouncing. "I'll do a little detective work for you. That's the best I can offer right now."

Abby sensed that she was out of time. She looked at her watch. She had been there for about twenty minutes.

"Did she give you any warning that she was leaving?"

Sally shook her head. "Not that she was leaving. She left a message on my voice mail, saying she wouldn't be coming in on Monday, she had something important to do. I expect her back any day, though I can't promise her job will be waiting for her." She stood up.

"One last thing. Can I see her desk?"

"Sure. It's right here." She led her into the outer room, and pointed to a metal desk against the wall.

Sally returned to her office, leaving Abby to look at Connie's work area. It seemed sadly empty for someone who had been there for a year. Pencils, paper clips. Abby quickly looked through the rest of the drawers, but found nothing that seemed relevant. Finally, she went back into Sally's office to get her things. She glanced out the window, looking for the woman on the bench, but she was gone; someone must have taken her in. Sally was at her desk, reading a letter.

"Well, I'll be going," Abby volunteered. "I'll tell Mike you were a great help."

Sally looked up at her and smiled. "Don't worry. I'll tell him myself. I have an appointment with the Board in less than an hour."

Abby let herself out. Walking down the hallway, she wondered what she had learned about Connie's life. By the time she reached the reception desk, she remembered what Sally had just said. She would be seeing Mike herself. Did that mean at the board meeting? Was he a board member? She turned around, and hurried back to Sally's office. The director was standing, putting papers into a briefcase. She looked at Abby with faint irritation.

"Still here?"

"One favor and I'll be out of your hair," Abby said unwittingly, then with a glance at the red curls, stumbled on, "I just wondered if you could give me a list of the board members. Oh, and the volunteers who work for the hospital."

Sally went back into her office and lifted a piece of hospital stationary off a stack on a side table, and presented it to Abby with a flourish.

"Tah dah. Board members. As far as the volunteers go, I can't help you. They come and go. Just as I have to do right now." She turned to leave, stopped, then turned slowly back, looking at Abby curiously. "Didn't you come in here a couple years ago with a young man, a suicide attempt?"

Abby had the eerie sensation that Sally had found out about Jonah by looking in her eyes. "My husband, yup." She folded the piece of stationary in half, then half again, ironing the seam with her thumb and forefinger.

"I remember you. I was working out front then. Lucky you got him here so quickly," Sally said.

"Yeah," Abby agreed. "It was lucky."

"Beautiful young man," Sally concluded. With that, she picked up her briefcase, herded Abby out of her office and left, her heels clicking. Abby put the folded paper in her purse and retraced her steps to the double front doors. The sun was still shining brilliantly, and she squinted as she crossed the parking lot, thinking of windshield wipers.

She stopped for coffee at Victor's. She sat outside on one of the picnic tables with a large double caffe latte, a small notepad open in front of her. She made a list, trying to see what she had left undone, and what loose ends, if any, she had succeeded in tying up. None. On the Connie front, she hadn't learned much. She had discovered that the girl's boss did not know or would not say if she had a lover. Abby suddenly remembered the piece of stationery Sally had given her. She fished it out of her purse, and looked at the list of names.

At the top was a wealthy New Yorker, Maurice Mullendore, a regular customer at the restaurant. He was on every arts committee in Columbia County. A tall, white-haired man, late fifties with a slight stoop. He spoke in a mutter, so you had to lean close to hear what he was saying, even though you might regret the effort as he could be arrogant and dismissive. His wife, Ellie Birch, was also on the list. She was quite a bit younger, with a pretty smile and a tendency to wear muumuus and wide floppy hats. The word was, she was his secretary before she got upgraded. Cyrus Leighton's wife, Paula, was there, and so was Mike Testarossa. Further down was the founder of the largest local real estate company, and below him the woman who owned Burnt Hills Stud Farm, who was also the Master of Hounds at the Old Bantam Hunt Club. Most of these people she saw quite often at the restaurant. They liked to meet with friends, throw parties, and all of them had either money or connections. Many of them had both. Abby wondered how Mike found himself in the middle of this group, but she guessed that an organization like a hospital needed a few working stiffs to anchor the group to the community.

Abby was staring blankly up Main Street, when Franklin D. chose that very moment to open the iron gate out of his small front yard, and step out onto the sidewalk. He hesitated for a moment, and then started walking in the opposite direction.

She decided this was a sign, and she grabbed her purse and followed him. He turned the corner just past the Fleet Bank, and she broke into a trot. She wanted to catch him before he drove away. She ran around the corner of the squat, ugly building, and stopped short. At first she couldn't find him. Finally she caught sight of him fitting his key into the door of a dark maroon sedan parked in the bank parking lot. His briefcase was upright between his feet.

"Franklin! Wait up!" He looked up in surprise as she walked toward him.

"Oh, hello, Abby. Beautiful day, isn't it?" He smiled at her. Then he frowned. "I'm having the hardest time unlocking my car." He jiggled his key in the door. "Now the darned thing seems stuck," he added, shaking his head. He dropped his hand, and stood still for a moment with his eyes closed. Then he went back to jiggling the key.

"Maybe it's bent," she suggested. He made a hopeful sound, and tried to take the key out of the lock.

"It's stuck alright." He shook his head, and bent lower, face close to the lock. "I thought nothing went wrong with these Swedish cars. I guess they all trip you up sooner or later."

Abby looked at his car. "Franklin, come on now, one Ford driver to another, I take offense at you pretending to drive a set of foreign wheels."

Abby expected him to make some kind of joke. Instead, he looked up at her and smiled absently, still jiggling his key in the lock. "My dear, last time I drove a Ford I was in high school. Can't go wrong with a Saab. You should return that Bronco to your father-in-law's field."

Abby walked to the back of his car and looked at the name. "Franklin, this is a Ford Taurus, you do know that, don't you?"

Franklin looked up at her, suddenly serious, his expression fearful. He picked up his briefcase, and walked around to the back of the car. He stood there, staring at the name *Taurus* in chrome script. "Hell. This isn't my car. Whose car is this?" He sounded accusing, as if someone had pulled a fast one.

"Is your car this color?" Abby suggested. This vehicle looked nothing like the Saabs she knew, but maybe he had a model she hadn't seen before.

"A little bit. My car is brownish red. Hell's bells. No wonder my key's stuck." He walked back to the driver's side, and took hold of his key. He started to wiggle it gently, and Abby held her breath. Finally it popped out. Franklin held it against his chest and sighed.

"Are you okay?"

He shook his head, and looked around the parking lot. Across the street, parked on Findlay, was a rust-colored Saab 900 with a black top. He saw it about the same time she did, and pointed.

"There it is." It didn't look anything like this car. Strange.

"Franklin, let me buy you a cup of tea." He looked at her, and to her surprise nodded calmly. They walked out of the parking lot and back toward Victor's.

Once they were sitting at the most remote table she could find, he with herbal tea and she with another caffe latte, she turned to him and asked softly: "So, what's going on?"

He took a moment to answer. "I don't know, Abby, but I've been doing some weird things lately."

"Do you have a fever? Maybe you've got the flu."

He shook his head. "It was the garbage, I'm sure."

"The dump?" she asked. Some people are very sensitive to the toxicity of dumps. He looked at her and shook his head. "I don't go to the dump. I'm very busy, so I have garbage pickup."

Abby nodded, hoping this was going somewhere.

"I have a nice wooden bin at the end of my driveway. The top is so heavy even the raccoons can't lift it. I made it myself out of treated lumber. Last Wednesday I took out my garbage, lifted the top up, put the bag inside, but I must've knocked the support out, because it fell on my head."

Abby gasped, imagining the blow. He kept talking. "I must've passed out, I don't know for how long. I live alone, so no one came looking for me. Finally I made it back inside and lay down on the couch. I slept there for the rest of the night. Next morning I got up with nothing worse than a big bump up here." He patted the top of his head. "I thought everything was fine."

Abby was watching him carefully, remembering their last conversation in his office, when he seemed to have forgotten his phone call to her. "But it hasn't been? Fine?"

He shook his head. "I've been doing some weird things. Some of them kind of embarrassing." He lowered his voice. "The other day I went to the bathroom to pee. I found myself urinating in the wastepaper basket in my bedroom." He glanced at her, and any desire she had to laugh dissipated. He looked frightened. "I've been forgetting things, appointments, information, names."

"You must've done something to your head, something more serious than you know. I actually listened to a program about that on NPR, that you can have brain damage with relatively small bumps. If you hit your head in the right place. I mean, the wrong place."

Franklin looked at her and shook his head. "You're making me feel so much better. What you're saying is, I've just given myself a front-yard lobotomy?"

Abby took his hand. "That is clever, for a vegetable. You know what the worst part is, for a lawyer? You can't even sue anyone, unless it's the raccoons."

He laughed. "You think I'm making too much of this?"

"Actually, no. I think you're making too little of this. Do you have a couple of free hours?"

"I was on my way to Albany, to the library."

"Instead I think I should take you to the hospital."

"Not a chance."

"Come on. We can talk about Joey, and you can get someone to actually look at you and put your mind at ease. If there's anything left of it."

"I don't need a babysitter. I can do it alone."

"I know you can, Franklin. But that's one of the bad things about living alone, isn't it? No one to notice if you pass out by the garbage cans. Anyway, you'd do the same for me, wouldn't you?"

Abby couldn't face another trip to the hospital she had just come from, so she set out for the Berkshire hospital, in Pittsfield.

On the way he told her about Joey's standing, and what was going on with the police investigation. "In fact, nothing much is happening. They seem content with the evidence they have, and the district attorney is pleased as punch with the obvious interpretation of that evidence. My problem is that I've been over everything with a fine-tooth comb, and see nothing that points to a third party. If I could find that, then everything against Joey would be seen for what it is, purely circumstantial."

Abby remembered something she wanted to ask him. "What about those people Joey was visiting the night of the murder? Would they take him in?"

Franklin shook his head. "I've already asked them. They aren't comfortable with it. They've got kids, neighbors, you know. Bottom line is, they don't know if he did it or not. And they're afraid they'd be inviting a killer into their home. You can't really blame them."

Abby shook her head. "It's hard to think of Joey as a killer."

The emergency room at the hospital was nearly empty and it wasn't long before a nurse was able to see Franklin. While he was gone, she glanced through the only material she could find, a pamphlet on tooth decay. It was full of pictures of open mouths, the one on the left healthy, the one on the right showing inflamed gums barely holding on to rotting teeth. Who posed for these pictures? Was the one on the left a well-to-do professional with a dental plan, and the one on the right a single woman, no insurance, living in a trailer? She checked her teeth with her tongue. She wondered why the pamphlet was in a hospital. Maybe it was a "there, but for the grace of God" kind of thing. Intended to make people feel grateful for what ailed them, the simple gunshot wound or splintered bone. She put the pamphlet down, feeling agitated.

An hour later, Franklin appeared, talking to a man in a white coat. Abby stood up, and Franklin nodded to the doctor and walked toward her. She tried to guess from his expression what was going on. He wasn't smiling.

"What's up? You gonna make it?"

Franklin smiled faintly. "Are you kidding? They're trying to kill me. I was fine until I let you talk me into coming here."

"So?"

"They want to keep me here overnight for some tests. Can you pick me up in the morning?"

Overnight. Tests. Abby had a quick vision of dark, silent corridors and being woken up from a deep sleep to painful punctures performed by shadowy, unidentifiable figures hidden behind masks.

"Sure. Hey, it's a good thing, you know that." Abby let her voice drop to a whisper. "Think of the poor wastepaper baskets."

He shook his head. "I have a meeting with the judge tomorrow. I hate to do this, but can you be here by seven A.M.?"

Abby feigned cheeriness. "Sure I can," she said. "I like getting up early."

By the time she got home it was late afternoon. She fed the dogs, and took them for a walk. She carried a quilt outside, spread it out in the field behind her trailer, lay down, shut her eyes and listened to the field around her, the birds, the leaves rustling, the insects.

She tried an old exercise Jonah had taught her. She imagined that she was a bag of sand. A nice, big, fat burlap bag full of sand. Then she carefully imagined tiny holes in the bag at her elbows, hands, neck, small of her back, knees, and feet. She imagined the sand running out through the holes. Thin streams of clean, white sand. Like the sand in an hourglass. She forced herself to breathe in and out, slowly. The sand kept running out, forming little piles around her body, covering the ground. Gradually, she began to relax. Her limbs began to feel heavier and heavier, just as they were supposed to. Her breathing slowed. She was sinking into the ground. Deeper, deeper. The sand was endless, trickling out.

She was so relaxed she didn't feel the first drop. But she felt the next. Darn it, rain. Dragged back to wakefulness, she opened her eyes. Delilah the pit bull was standing over her, her muzzle one inch from her face, a third teardrop of drool ready to fall. In her mouth was a filthy, torn tennis ball. She was watching Abby through pink-rimmed eyes, motionless, ears cocked. Abby could see her crooked lower teeth between her velvety black lips. What a face. If Abby didn't love her, Delilah would be straight out of a nightmare. Abby jerked out of the way, just in time to miss the globule. Which reminded her of something, but she couldn't think what it was. Just a little thought, flickering through her consciousness. She slowly groaned herself upright. "You disgusting creature." Delilah dropped the ball at her human's feet, and watched her, her whole body tense and waiting. A shiver passed through her. Abby had no choice. She leaned down and picked up the slime-covered ball, and threw it as far as she could manage from a sitting position. While the dog was retrieving it, Abby slowly got to her feet, shook out the quilt, and started back.

She was walking through the door when the phone rang. She went to it slowly, a voice in her head warning her not to pick up the receiver. But she didn't listen. Sure enough, it was Dulcie. At 5:00 P.M. that could only mean one thing. "Hey. Where are you?"

"What do you mean? I'm here. You just called me."

"I know. But what about the job?" She sounded upset. "You should be leaving here in forty-five minutes."

"Dulcie, what are you talking about?"

"The anniversary party. In Goose Creek. Don't tell me you've forgotten. I told you about it last week."

Maybe this was what she had been trying to remember. Glob of spit—anniversary party? Was there a connection?

Dulcie kept going. "It's a great job. You're the only one who can do it." A lie, Abby knew. "Please. We'll do all the donkey work, we'll load the truck. Just be here."

In fact, Abby didn't mind catering. The InnBetween didn't take big, formal jobs. Usually no more than fifty people: the staff set up the tables, unpacked the food, made sure everything was just right. The work was pretty painless, and the money was good. Simple, elegant menu served buffet style. The hardest part was working in someone else's space.

"This one is easy. Henry's going, too. I need you to set up at the house, keep an eye on things, make sure the table stays looking nice, then transfer the leftovers to *their* dishes—they specifically asked for us to leave the leftovers—then pack up and come home to mamma. You should be back by ten-thirty."

"Okay. But I've got to jump in the shower. I'm covered in dog drool."

Dulcie snorted. "You need a man, my friend. I'll see you soon."

# CHAPTER FOURTEEN

D ulcie was way off, because it was past midnight by the time Henry and Abby drove through the empty streets of Bantam and pulled up in front of the side door of the restaurant. They both sat for a minute, eyes closed, leaning back on the headrests. Then Abby straightened her head and, like synchronized swimmers, they both climbed slowly out of the van and began unloading their stacks of dirty hotel pans. The door had been left open for them, propped with a brick. Inside, Dan the Man was mopping the kitchen floor under bright fluorescent lights. The radio was playing gospel, and the smell was of drains and disinfectant, steam and grease. With a bitter undertone of sweat. That special restaurant blend. Abby couldn't wait to have a shower. She and Henry put the pans and dishes on the counter and Dan shook his head at them, as if they were naughty children caught bringing back the empty pans of pies they had stolen. No one spoke. There was nothing important enough to say, and they were too tired for chitchat. When the van was empty, Abby and Henry started cleaning the pans, spraying and scrubbing them down. They filled the dishwasher, and ran a load. When they were done, Dan waved them away, and they were happy to obey. On their way out, they took out the brick that was propping the door open. On the sidewalk they breathed in the fresh cool night air.

" 'Night, Henry." She raised a hand halfway.

" 'Night." He nodded, lit a cigarette, and walked off, his step sprightlier than hers. He was heading for a tavern in Goose Creek. The girl who worked the bar was a tall SUNY Albany senior and she was getting off work in about an hour. Abby stood there, staring at the black sidewalk, her eyelids half closed. She shook her head to clear it, mentally located her car, and made herself move up the street toward it. Sure enough, it was where she had remembered leaving it, and she felt an unexpected sense of relief. She let the engine warm up before pulling out of the parking space. She drove slowly through the dark streets.

At home, Abby made a cup of chamomile tea and sat on her front step, listening to the dogs snuffle around in the dark. She thought back over the catering. The evening had begun pretty smoothly. It was still daylight when she and Henry arrived at the new saltbox about a mile outside Goose Creek. The host and his wife turned out to be a couple she had waited on many times at the restaurant—in their sixties, celebrating their first wedding anniversary.

Janine, the wife, said to her in a stage whisper: "Abby, this is my third marriage, and the fourth time around for Toady. (Unless Abby had mis-heard, that seemed to be his name.) "So you can see that we don't take any-thing for granted. We feel every step should be celebrated. 'Cause you never know." She ended the sentence with her mouth in an O, and she held it like that, staring meaningfully at Abby, nodding her head. Abby nodded back; she couldn't argue with that. Then, with a sigh, Janine unlocked her lips, and went off to change.

Henry and Abby took the supplies out of the van, and began setting up in the sun-drenched dining room. Janine and Toady had a dramatic view of the distant Catskills, and while both hosts were getting ready, Abby and Henry had the place to themselves. They put the perishable food into the fridge, and decorated the table with freshly cut flowers and fruit. They planned the traffic flow, then set out the glasses and cutlery on the white tablecloth. Henry spent a good deal of time organizing everything in little diagonal patterns. When he was done, he looked at Abby proudly. After putting the beer and white wine on ice, they opened half a dozen bottles of red.

The first couple to arrive was a film critic and her surgeon husband, a reserved man who rarely seemed to speak. Abby knew them from the restaurant. The critic was a complainer, a tall blonde woman who talked enough for both her and her husband. Abby remembered her well because of her daughter. The teenager rarely came in to eat, but the first time she did, her mother held her hand and forked food into her mouth. Abby and the rest of the staff assumed there was something wrong with the child, that she was impaired, challenged, retarded, whatever. However, a week later she came in with her father and she talked, laughed, and fed herself. Sure enough, on the rare occasions when she was with both parents, her mother was an octopus, the girl sitting stone-faced while the woman stroked her hair, talked about her in the third person to the staff, and fed her.

The film critic came over and greeted Abby and Henry as if they were old friends. She accepted a glass of wine. Abby remembered she only liked California wines, sneering at anything European, as if all French and Italian vineyards were finished, played out. Her husband picked out a beer, and they saw him a few minutes later on the front lawn, listening to Toady.

As more people arrived, Henry and Abby had to work harder to keep the alcohol stocked and the hors d'oeuvres circulating. They recognized a good number of the guests. They saw a couple they knew as Mr. and Mrs. Merlot, both dressed in black pants and white shirts: Abby considered giving them a platter of stuffed mushrooms to pass around. She noticed Maurice Mullendore; his wife, Ellie Birch, was holding on to his arm, laughing at something he was saying. The couple was standing with Keith Ryder, his fiancée, Josie Brown, and a stocky man wearing a surprising pair of powder-blue cowboy boots.

Abby and Henry started serving food at seven-thirty. The crowd was already circling them, like sharks around a school of fish, and a long line formed quickly. People were talking and laughing, but Abby wasn't fooled. They were watching the salmon to make sure there was enough, and make certain no one cut in front of them. If anyone tried, they would tighten up the line, covering the defensive move with wisecracking and laughter.

To her surprise, Mack Spear appeared in front of her, holding out his plate. Abby was surprised to see him because Mack was a photographer whose main source of income came from the landscapes he sold as postcards. This didn't seem to be his crowd, as he never had much money, though he knew everyone in the county. He was a tall, jowly man, about one hundred pounds overweight, most of which was hanging over his belt.

"Hey, Mack!"

"Hey, sweetie. Abby, I want a big piece. That one over there."

"What about Tony? You getting food for him?" Tony was Mack's lover, a small, frail man, an expert on Shaker furniture. Abby started serving Mack, gently scooping up the delicate fish.

"He wasn't feeling so hot so he decided to stay in bed today. But I knew you guys were catering, and I'm hungry."

"But he's okay?"

Mack laughed. "He's fine. He just didn't feel like getting up. He does that sometimes—a raging hypochondriac, you know. That's why he loves this bunch," he added, gesturing around the room.

"What's 'this bunch?' " Abby was curious about the connection between all these people.

Mack looked around the room. "Doctors, most of them. Didn't you know that? Tut tut, you should know what your customers do, Abby. Ah, there's Henry. I'm trying to get him to pose naked for me—" Mack winked lasciviously at her and moved down the line, where Henry was dishing out salad and asparagus vinaigrette.

Keith Ryder was close behind Mack in the food line. He was elegantly dressed in a dark-brown leather jacket and a white shirt. "Abby," he said, smiling, "why does it always make me so happy to see you?"

Abby looked at him, holding up her serving spoon. "You're like Pavlov's dog, every time you see me you're hungry, and most times, unless there's a fire in the kitchen, I bring you food."

He looked at her intensely. "Wow. I've made a mental connection between you and food. You're right, of course. I hadn't realized that. Does that mean that I want to eat you?"

Just then, his fiancée, Josie, cut in line behind him. "I'm back."

"What would you like," Abby asked, ignoring his suggestiveness and pointing to the two entrees, "salmon or chicken?"

Keith looked back and forth at both dishes, unwilling to commit to one and give up the other.

Josie, close behind him, whispered seductively: "I'll get one, you get one. We'll share."

A flicker of irritation crossed Keith's handsome face. But it disappeared in an instant. He turned to Josie, smiling. "Darling, you know how to take care of me."

Josie looked at him under lowered eyelids. "I love you, baby."

"So, salmon or chicken?" Abby asked, trying to keep the line moving.

Keith kissed Josie, then leaned toward Abby. "Isn't she beautiful?" His voice was low and intimate, and Abby had the unpleasant sensation that he meant something very different, but she had no interest in discovering what it was. Behind Josie, people shifted from one foot to another impatiently. Without waiting for a decision, Abby put a small piece of salmon on his plate. He didn't need much—after all, he'd be scarfing up Josie's chicken.

Within the next half hour, Abby came to realize that there were a lot of guests. They had been asked to provide a meal for thirty, and George was always generous in his portions, but there wasn't going to be enough to go around. The line was growing faster than she could serve people, and she was giving smaller and smaller portions. Finally, everyone had been given something, though people were starting to come back for seconds. The first chance she got she called the hostess over. Abby turned her back to the guests, who were watching her like hungry cats.

"You've got way more than thirty people here."

Abby watched Janine's face. For a moment, it looked as if she might argue with Abby. Then she changed her mind, and started to get teary.

"I suppose so. But people kept calling me at the last minute. How could I say no?"

"You should have called Dulcie or George," Abby said reproachfully. "He would've made adjustments, stretched it out, added lasagna, chicken. Something. All you had to do was tell us." She thought for a moment. "Do you have any meat? Steaks, maybe?"

"Steaks? I have steaks in the freezer." Janine looked doubtful.

"How many? Do you have a microwave?"

"Maybe a dozen. Yes, yes, we have a microwave."

Abby sent Henry to tell Toady to fire up the grill. She put on water for pasta. Then she and Janine dug everything out of her freezer that was vaguely edible. The steaks were in a beautiful box, hand-packed by a mail order company in the Midwest. She unpacked them and jammed them into the microwave. They came out gray and bloody. George would've been horrified. Henry took them out to Toady with strict instructions not to give them to anyone when they were done, just take them off the grill, put them on a plate, and bring them to the kitchen. Abby made a huge pasta salad, using anything she could find in the refrigerator. She even threw in a few things she couldn't name. As soon as the steaks were done, Henry cut them in thin slices, arranging them on a platter.

By ten-forty, everyone was fed and full. Henry made coffee and Abby cut George's lemon squares into quarters, each portion an inch by an inch. Then they set to work cleaning up. The kitchen sink and the counters were piled high with dirty dishes. They worked efficiently and quickly. Once in a while, a booze-soaked guest would wander in and make lighthearted comments designed to cheer them on.

The man in the powder-blue cowboy boots, who had been talking to Ellie Birch and Maurice at the beginning of the evening, came into the kitchen looking for seltzer. Abby pointed at the fridge. He spent some time moving things around in it, but came out with nothing. She felt obliged to help him and when she thought she saw a bottle nestled in the back, she bent over and put her head inside the refrigerator. Without any warning, he moved in behind her and pressed his crotch against her. Automatically, she jerked away from him, and hit her head on the inside of the refrigerator. The burst of pain translated instantly to rage, and she pulled her head out of the fridge, right arm swinging back at him. She hit him on the side of the head, knocking his glasses off. The leather soles of his new boots had little traction on the dishwater-wet floor, and he went down, legs in the air. Bang. Abby stood there, hot with anger, looking down at him. Henry, who had seen the whole thing, burst out laughing, and kept laughing until he had to gasp for air, leaning weakly on the sink. Keith Ryder, who must've come in on the man's heels, watched, eyebrows raised, from the kitchen door. The man lay motionless for a moment. Abby was afraid she had knocked him out. Then he slowly lifted his head and propped himself up on one elbow and reached for his glasses. Henry laughed harder, bending forward, hands on his knees.

"Henry, would you shut up!" said Abby.

"I can't, I can't, that was beautiful!"

Slowly, the man got to his feet. Abby braced herself, not knowing what to expect from him. He shook his head as if to clear it. Then he slowly held out his hand as if to ward off any more blows.

"I'm sorry. Poor impulse control." He looked at her ruefully, like someone caught stealing a cookie. "Friends?" He held out his hand, as if to shake with her.

"Not a chance." She didn't want to shake his hand. He was the kind of guy who would tickle her palm with his middle finger. Or use her hand to pull her toward him. What she really wanted to do was push him down again.

"My name is Randy Jaglom. And you are?"

Henry's laughter had slowed down to a giggle. She was distracted from her anger by his name. She recognized it. She had just seen it on a letterhead. "On the Board of Trustees of the hospital, aren't you?"

His smile turned stiff. "So?"

She sneered. "Maybe I should write them a letter about you. Let them know about your poor impulses."

Henry started laughing again. Jaglom swallowed hard.

Abby relented. "Just don't ever touch me again, okay?"

"Wouldn't dream of it." He glanced sideways at Henry, smirked, and strutted toward the door. Keith shook his head at him as he walked out the door.

"I apologize for Randy." Keith looked at Abby and lifted his hands in a helpless gesture, then dropped them to his sides.

"Why should you? He's not your responsibility. Or is he?"

Keith shook his dark head of hair. "No, but he brought us here."

Abby shrugged. "No big deal. Hey, he entertained Henry." She gestured to her coworker, who was still smiling. "Henry, would you mind checking for more dirty plates? I don't want to go out there right now. I might run into that guy, and accidentally slide a carving knife into him."

Happily, Henry grabbed a tray and left the kitchen.

She looked at Keith. "He's a friend of yours? Business associate? I wouldn't have guessed you were a doctor—"

Keith shook his head. "Not me. I'm a painter. Randy's a neighbor of Jamison Brown's, that's how I met him. We play tennis sometimes."

Abby nodded. "Of course. Another artist."

Keith nodded. "Exactly. I met Jamison before I met Josie. He was giving a lecture at the Whitney, and I was curious, so I went. He was impressive, let me tell you. If you ever get a chance to hear him speak, don't miss it. When it was over, I went up and talked to him. We ended up going out for coffee. Turns out we have a lot of ideas in common—we're going to have a show together in the fall."

Abby wondered if Keith was more in love with the famous painter than his intense and beautiful daughter. He looked as if he might be quite a bit older than Josie—early forties to her late twenties. Maybe it was a marriage of convenience, marry our daughter, and you get a two-man show with Jamison Brown. Unconnected, but also interesting, was the fact that, once they were alone, Keith no longer came on to her. Maybe he needed an audience, and someone as responsive and adoring as Josie would be particularly satisfying. Abby opened the dishwasher. Steam poured out of it. She started pulling out the clean, hot plates and piling them on the counter.

She thought Keith had left the room, so she was surprised when he spoke. "Well, thanks for dinner. It was good."

Abby glanced at him. "I'll tell George you liked it."

Just then Henry appeared in the doorway with a tray of dirty dishes and glasses. He sidestepped Keith, and put the tray down. "You know, I'm gonna be laughing about that guy for the next six months. Wham. On his ass." He chuckled.

Suddenly, Keith started baying like a bloodhound. When he was finished, he looked at Abby. "Delicious." With a bow, he left.

Henry looked after him in distaste. "Jerk. What was that all about?"

Abby thought about it. "I think that was Pavlov's dog. But I could be wrong."

When Abby and Henry had finished cleaning up and loading the truck, they said good-bye to their hosts. A number of guests were still there. As they climbed into the truck, Randy Jaglom came up to Abby's window. "Hey, you don't hate me, do you? I've been told I behaved like an asshole."

"You couldn't tell? Someone had to inform you?"

Jaglom shook his head impatiently and turned to go.

"Wait," she stopped him. "Tell me something."

"Shoot." He came back to the car window.

"You know Connie Testarossa?"

He looked around guiltily, as if she were trying to pin another infraction on him. "Sort of. I mean, I know who she is. She works at hospital functions, right? Fund-raisers, parties?"

Abby watched him. "What's she like?"

He shrugged. "Friendly."

"Does she have a boyfriend?"

He seemed to lower his voice a notch. "Not that I know of. Not specifically."

Abby frowned. "What do you mean, not specifically?"

"You know, she's friendly."

"Do you mean, she's friendly, or she sleeps around?"

He shrugged again, not wanting to commit himself. "She's available. You know. Ambitious. Looking for love."

Abby didn't know. What did looking for love have to do with ambition? But then, consider the source. Henry suddenly snapped his fingers and pointed at Jaglom.

"I recognize you. You have that company across the river, don't you? The drug company."

The man ignored him. "Well, it was special meeting you all. I look forward to the next time." He walked away.

"Truly an asshole," Abby said, turning on the ignition of the truck.

Henry barked with laughter, and Abby shook her head.

"You think what he did was funny? It was not funny."

He kept laughing. "What was funny was you popping him, and him falling on his ass. It was beautiful, truly."

"No, it's wrong to hit people." But Abby couldn't help smiling as she pulled out of the driveway.

# CHAPTER FIFTEEN

Abby had barely fallen asleep when the ring of the alarm drilled a tunnel into her unconsciousness. She slammed down on the snooze button and swung her feet out of bed and on to the floor. She sat there, blinking blindly, disoriented. It was five forty-five in the morning and she couldn't remember why she had to get up. Then it came to her. Franklin. She had to pick him up and get him to the judge by 9:00 A.M. She stood, and found a pair of jeans that were lying on the floor.

By ten to seven Abby was at the hospital in Pittsfield. She parked, and walked quickly into the reception area. Next to a row of green plastic chairs, she saw Franklin. He was sitting in a wheelchair, and on his lap he was holding a little paper bag. He looked round-shouldered, and pathetic. A refugee, trying to cross the border into the real world.

He saw her, and climbed awkwardly out of the chair. He didn't say anything until they were outside. In the middle of the parking lot he stopped, spread his arms, and spoke in a deep preacher-voice.

"Hallelujah, sister. Just last night I thought I would end my days within those walls. I thought they would sneak in and steal my organs, then use my skin for lampshades. But you saved me. Praise the Lord."

"I would hate a lampshade made of you."

"Do we have time for breakfast?" he asked. "I'm starving."

Abby looked at her watch. "It'll have to be fast."

"Fast, I give you my word."

Over pancakes and coffee, Franklin told her briefly about the tests. Most of the results weren't in, but the doctor thought it would turn out to be damage from the head trauma, and it would need time to heal. Abby could've told him that.

"What's in the paper bag?" She wanted the whole picture.

"Plastic liners for trash baskets. Until I can buy my own."

"Really, what's in the bag?"

"Medication, if you must know. For the pain. And other things. Okay?"

"Okay, I guess."

He shook his head. "God, you are nosy. Being married to you would be hell."

They both laughed, as if that were the silliest concept in the world.

"Finish your coffee, dearest, I don't want you to be late for work," she joked.


When Abby got home there was a message on her machine from Cyrus Leighton. He wanted to know why she wasn't at his house, working on his story. He said he would be home soon, and if she hadn't finished, he would think of some suitable punishment. Abby did feel a pang of guilt, because she'd forgotten about Cyrus. She wondered if he knew about Betty, his housekeeper. She promised herself that the next morning she would spend some time there. She might even water a plant.

By 10:00 A.M. the next morning, she was unlocking Cyrus's and Paula's front door. The place hadn't been vandalized, which was good, as she didn't want him blaming her for breaking into his house. Especially when she had the key. Everything was in order. She watered the plants and started to work.

Abby worked for the rest of the morning, stopping twice, once to walk around and fiddle with the pictures on the walls, and another time to go to the bathroom. At lunchtime she had had enough so she put everything away, and drove into town.

At Victor's Café she ordered Japanese stir-fried noodles, and took her plate outside. This time one of the tables was occupied by a couple with three kids, while the other table had only one person sitting at it. Malaria, the couples' therapist. The last time she had spent any time with Malaria was in the same place, when she had mentally redesigned her hairstyle. The woman must have materialized while Abby was inside the café ordering the noodles, because she hadn't seen her when she first walked in. Before Abby could do an about-face, Malaria looked up and beckoned her over.

"Come on, come on, plenty of space here." The therapist patted the table-top next to her.

Abby sat down, and after a few pleasantries, she began eating her noodles. Malaria told her about an art class she had taken over in Woodstock. It was the most enlightening, the most liberating experience of her life.

"Yeah?" Abby tried to talk between mouthfuls of noodles. "How come? What kind of class?"

Malaria sighed, put her hand to her cheek, and looked up to the level of the top of the three-story buildings across the street.

"It was a painting class."

"Great." Another decent-sized mouthful.

"We did it bare-chested, using our breasts as brushes."

Abby accidentally swallowed a large clump of unchewed noodles. "You're kidding," she croaked through her blocked throat.

Her lunch companion looked at her. "It was mind-blowing."

Abby nodded, swallowing carefully, opening her eyes wide to show enthusiasm.

"You're just saying that, Abby," Malaria protested, even though Abby hadn't in fact managed to say anything. "I bet you think it's weird, don't you?"

Abby shook her head vehemently. "No, no, not weird," she whispered, "great, it sounds great."

"The person who gave the class is giving it again next month. I'm taking it again. Join us."

Abby looked her straight in the eye, the noodles level with her solar plexus. "No. I couldn't do it."

To her dismay, this directness just got Malaria's engine going. She smiled warmly and took her hand. "Don't say no! It is not something you want to miss. I understand your fear. I was there. You begin the class all shut down and tight, and by the end you are using your body as a vehicle for your art, and you reach this level of openness—"

"It's not for me. I'm a very private person."

Malaria looked at her with compassion. "This class can help you with that, honestly."

Abby stood and picked up her plate. "Don't worry about me. But someday maybe you'll show me your artwork." And with that she walked inside. Pretty good closing words, except after putting her dirty plate on the counter, she remembered something she wanted to ask her. She went back outside.

"Remember when you asked me about an apartment in town? You had heard of one up on Malden Street?"

Malaria nodded.

"Do you remember who told you about that apartment? Who told you it was available?" she continued.

The woman thought for a moment then shook her head. "Sorry. No. But if I remember I'll be sure to tell you. When I see you in class." She smiled and winked.

Abby shook her head and walked inside.

Before she left the café, Abby picked up a couple of muffins and a bottle of fresh orange juice, in case Joey was hungry. However, when she got to the police station, she found the door closed. No one answered her knock. She tried the handle. It was locked. She walked over to the village clerk's window, and asked her when the chief would be back.

The white-haired woman answered indifferently. "I don't know his business." When Abby wouldn't go away, she looked up at her and continued. "You'll have to call, or stop back later."

Abby pointed at the door. "So is the boy just locked in there on his own? What if he needs something?"

The clerk smiled. She knew things Abby was not privy to. "The boy has been moved." She looked back down at the papers she was rubber-stamping.

"Moved? Where to?"

"Why do you want to know?"

*Because his mother is dead, and his living room rug is covered with her blood.*

"I'm a friend. I brought him a muffin."

The woman shook her head, and moved some more papers around. "He's going to need a lot more than a muffin. They took him to the County Courthouse. In Hudson."

Wisdom from the county clerk. That's why she had a salaried government job. Abby walked toward the big heavy doors of the Lacey Memorial. She stopped and returned to the clerk's window.

"You like blueberry? That's all they had." She put the bag on the counter.

The woman seemed to take pity on her. "You can go down to Hudson and see him."

Abby shook her head. "No." She pushed the bag toward the woman. "You want them?"

The woman frowned at her. "I can't take food from you."

"Why not? I work in a restaurant, you'd take food from me there—"

But the woman shook her head. "Stop. I don't want your muffins."

That afternoon Abby drove to Vermont. No particular reason, but she needed to get out of town for a few hours. Most of the cars on the road had the easy pace of summer travelers, and driving was pleasant. Abby had forgotten to bring her box of tapes so she turned to the local talk station. It was a science show for kids. Abby didn't care about black holes; in fact, she had never been interested in black holes. She switched to a rock station, but they were playing an uninterrupted hour of Elton John. Too much. She hunted around in her glove compartment, one eye on the road, the car weaving just a little bit, and found one unnamed cassette, dusted with dirt and lint. She wiped it on her lap, and blew onto the exposed tape. Looked fine. She stuck it in the deck, and after a little crackling it turned out to be an album she and Jonah used to listen to, a traveling album, full of songs about roads and gas stations. Perfect. Abby sang along, and the miles flashed by outside her window. She was enjoying herself, until the last song. No big deal, a simple song about missing someone who was gone, missing their company. Abby was blindsided. Suddenly, Jonah was with her. She could have touched him. Her eyes filled with tears, and the tears overflowed and ran down her cheeks, until she could taste the salt on her lips. She was having trouble seeing the road.

She pulled over into an empty lot, where the grass was growing up between the cracks in the bleached cement. She put her head back and shut her eyes. She was sorry Jonah wasn't around anymore, sorry she had gone away that night, sorry she hadn't come home sooner. She sat there, the teartracks on her cheeks slowly drying. What would her life be like if Jonah were still alive? She let her mind travel, imagining possibilities, good and not so good. Eventually her pulse steadied, and she thought about her parents. She should go to Arizona to see them. Which brought her to Mike Testarossa, looking at her across the white butcher paper of the restaurant, the little colored circle marking the spot between them. It occurred to her—maybe he was stuck in time the way she was, in that morning she drove back from New York. Maybe he had the same terrible feeling in the pit of his stomach, the dread, the knowledge that something was wrong but he was too late to do anything about it. But why would anything be wrong? He even admitted that his daughter was the kind of person who might think running away was fun. There was nothing wrong with Connie that a little growing up wouldn't fix.

When Abby was finally ready to head home, she made sure to eject the cassette from the tape deck. She was better off with the science program, black holes and all.

• • •

The answering machine was taking a message as she walked in the door. She recognized Mike Testarossa's sandpaper voice.

"Abby, please call me. It's about my daughter."

Abby grabbed the receiver, but all she heard was dial tone. She found Mike's number and, with a feeling of misgiving, punched it in. Mike answered after the first ring.

"Hello?" He sounded anxious.

"Mike? Abby Silvernale here. Just got your message."

"Oh, yeah. I wondered if you had any news," he said, tentatively.

"No, sorry, nothing yet."

Mike cleared his throat. "What are you doing? Can you come over?"

"Now?"

"I wanted to show you something. This a bad time?"

"No, it's fine." Abby had no plans, just a night at home with her dogs. She had a steak in the freezer she had been looking forward to. "I'll see you in about twenty minutes."

"Do you know where I live?"

"Malden Street, right?"

"As you get to the top of the hill, the third driveway on your left. The mailbox has one of those Chinese things on it, the two shapes that fit in together. Connie painted it on when she was in ninth grade."

Thanks to Connie's yin and yang mailbox, Abby found the house easily. The driveway did one curve to the right, and ended up in front of a two-car garage. A gilded and ferocious American eagle looked down from above the open doors, and Mike's green pickup was parked next to a blue late-model Honda Civic. The house itself was a raised ranch built lengthwise above the garage, with a short el to the left. Abby climbed out of her Bronco, and slammed the door. She could see a flight of wooden stairs inside the garage, on the right wall. It probably led into the main house. The front door proper of the house was out of sight, most likely on the short side of the house, around to the right.

The short el to the left was an addition, about a third the size of the main house. Abby wondered if it was Connie's apartment. It looked bigger than her trailer, so she could see why Malaria might be hot for it. Plenty of room for breast painting in there.

She walked into the garage and moved past the green pickup, trying not to wipe it down with her clean clothes. The walls of the garage were lined in rough-cut lumber. She imagined running her hands down them, the splinters of wood sticking in to the soft pads of her fingers. Holding on to the railing, she walked up the wooden stairs and knocked on the door. Footsteps, then the door swung open. Mike stood in front of her, scowling.

"Why'd you come in this way?" He looked as if he were considering making her leave and come in, properly, through the front door. "Okay, okay. Don't just stand there. I'm right in the middle of cooking. Do you eat meat?"

"Yes, actually, I do." Abby thought of her frozen steak.

"This way." He turned and walked into what was obviously the kitchen. "Come on in, make yourself at home. There's beer in the fridge, glasses over there—" he pointed to a cabinet near the sink.

Mike walked briskly out a back door, letting the screen bang behind him. Abby saw him go to a dark gray grill. Smoke was billowing out of it. She stood in the kitchen, not quite sure how to make herself at home. She opened the refrigerator. A dozen beer bottles were lined up neatly to one side next to whole milk, butter, eggs. She saw a couple of deli counter containers with white food inside, pasta or potato salad, or maybe even rice pudding. She took out a Genny Cream Ale. It was cold, so she decided to do without a glass. She unscrewed the cap and looked around the kitchen. It was a brown kitchen, dark stained-wood cabinets and beige Formica counters. The walls were papered in sepia tones, a pattern of couples in antebellum clothing strolling down tree-canopied avenues, the ladies in hoop skirts and holding parasols. Abby didn't care for wallpaper, it took up too much of her time. She felt compelled to study it, see where the pattern started to repeat itself, and locate all its variations. Actually, for that same reason she thought wall-papering a bathroom a good idea—something to look at when you're obliged to sit.

Abby sipped her beer, eyes on the pattern. The trees curled protectively around the couples, framing and separating one vignette from the next. The couples were all a little different. In one scene the gentleman had a cane, and the lady's hand was curled around his arm. Their heads were leaning in toward each other. In the next scene, the man was bowing to the lady, his top hat in his hand. Her head was tilted to one side, and she was smiling. More like a little sweet smirk, Abby thought. She went up to the wall and touched it. It was smooth. Up close it looked faded, discolored around the stove and sink, yet because of it the kitchen seemed to blossom with the dark, brown cumulus clouds of the trees. Abby wondered if it had been there since Connie was a little girl. If she had grown up with it. If it reminded her of her mother.

Mike came in, and once more the screen door slammed. He was carrying a plate heavy with four huge chops, the flesh between the grill marks glistening. He put it down on the table. He pulled the two plastic containers out of the fridge and put them next to the meat.

"Coleslaw and potato salad. I hope you like pork." Mike took two plates out of a cupboard. He gestured for her to sit.

The meat was delicious and Abby was hungry. They both ate, concentrating on their plates, saving conversation for later. Mike was eating slowly, staring at the wall. Abby wondered if he was seeing the wallpaper couples or if, after all these years, they were invisible.

"So, Mike, are you going to tell me about Connie?"

He finished swallowing, and then nodded. "I wanted to show you the card she left."

"I'd like to see it."

He stood and picked up his plate. He gestured toward Abby's. "You done?"

Abby glanced at the chops left on the serving plate. She couldn't eat any more. "Thanks."

Together they cleaned up the few dishes. Mike left the room and Abby wiped down the table. Then she sat back down at the kitchen table and waited. Her eyes strayed to the wall and the coy ladies with their gallant gents. She started counting the number of ladies from the upper left corner of the wall. Automatically, when she heard Mike returning, she made note of where she was—above the door to the garage—so she could continue later.

Mike sat down at the table and put a postcard in front of her. It was a photograph of a baby in a diaper, one hand on a wooden chair for support. Its fat little feet looked as if they wouldn't be able to carry such a chubby body more than one step. Over the baby's shoulder was a stick with a red bandanna tied to one end, like a hobo's from the thirties. The baby was grinning happily. Abby wondered how long the photographer had to struggle to catch that moment.

She flipped the postcard over. The other side was covered with large, sloping handwriting.

"Dear Mikey,

"Well, your baby is taking the man of her dreams and hitting the road. We plan to get married as soon as everything is sorted out. Truly, all is well, and I am *so so* happy. I'll call when I can. Love ya, Con-con."

Abby looked at Mike, whose eyes were on the card. "Did she write it?"

He nodded, slowly.

"You don't look happy about it."

He raised his eyes to her face. Shook his head. "I don't like it."

"Is there something specific you don't like?"

He shook his head. Finally he spoke. "Maybe I don't like that she's run off with some asshole, and couldn't tell me about it face-to-face."

Abby felt sorry for the man. He was feeling hurt, rejected, and angry. Even jealous.

"From what I've learned about Connie, sounds like she is a bit of a thrill-seeker. Or maybe going through a phase. What d'you think?"

He looked at her suspiciously. Abby barreled on. "It seems to me she enjoys doing things the hard way. The borrowed car, the secret elopement, the postcard with no address. This is all an adventure for her."

He grunted, waiting for her to go on. She tried to think of something else to say.

"I don't think she has any idea how hurtful this kind of thing is."

He took a deep breath. "Maybe you're right. I miss her, is all." He rubbed his face with his hand. Abby picked up the postcard once more. Mike rested his head in his hand, as if exhausted. "Sometimes I feel like her mother is looking down at me, shaking her head. Like I'm doin' a piss-poor job raising her little girl. I tried to get her to go to college, and she went for a semester, then quit. Said it was boring. I even tried to get her to join the service, thought that might give her some focus, some discipline. She laughed at me. So when she got this job at the hospital, I thought, okay. I told her, if she didn't act all wild and crazy, if she came home at a decent time at night, I would take her on vacation to someplace she wanted to go. So she said Paris. She wanted to spend two weeks in Paris, and I said fine. And I kept my fingers crossed. It seemed to be working out real well. She was having fun. Putting in long hours. Sally DeCintio likes her. And then this. I come home and find her gone, suitcase and all."

"Would you know which clothes she took? That might give us an idea of where she was going."

Mike barked with laughter. "No way. She has a lot of stuff, that's all I know. Do you want to see her room? Maybe as another girl, you'll notice something."

Abby thought that was a misguided hope, but she agreed to look. He led her through the house into Connie's addition. There was a small sitting room, with two doors off it. Most likely bedroom and bath. It was like walking into a city apartment, the walls painted fresh pastel colors, and the furniture modern and light, in a downsized Scandinavian style. But the room looked tarnished, dull. Abby realized it was because there was a light coating of dust over everything.

She followed Mike into the bedroom, a generous-sized room with a large window that looked out onto the woods. It was a mess, however, as if someone had torn through the place, or packed in a hurry. The closet doors were open and a number of hangers lay discarded on the floor. The dresser drawers were open. Abby walked over, and peered into the top drawer. The underwear was in a jumble. She picked out a pair of briefs. They were blue cotton bikini pants. She dug through the rest, but every piece she found was similar: sensible and slightly worn. Connie had taken her sexy stuff and left the comfortable pieces behind. Abby looked around the room. A full-length mirror. The bed was a queen-sized, with a black wrought-iron frame. The bedding was pale-blue cotton. Abby touched it. High thread count. There was no desk, just a tall, narrow bookshelf, a few books, a stack of *Elle* magazines on one of the shelves. On a small, stainless steel table under the window was a photograph. Abby went over to it and picked it up. It was a black-and-white nude of a girl lying on her side on a couch. She was leaning slightly forward, so that one rounded cheek of her behind was revealed, but pubic hair and nipples were hidden from view. Though she was obviously slender and girlish, she had an aura of voluptuousness. Abby studied the picture. The impression of overt sexuality came from the eyes, looking steadily and aggressively at the lens, and the Mona Lisa-like smile that hovered on her lips. Dark shoulder-length hair framed a pale face. Abby glanced at Mike. He was standing in the door, watching her. She held up the photograph.

"Connie?"

He nodded slowly.

"Do you know who the photographer is?"

He took a deep breath, as if he had forgotten to breathe, and was now making up for lost time. "No. I noticed it, asked her about it, but she just said a student friend of hers took it. She wouldn't say who. Probably figured I'd want to kill him."

Abby wondered if he was right to assume the photographer was a man. The frame around it was a light wood, with the name *Constance* on it, in a rather curlicued, feminine script. Probably bought at one of those nature stores at the mall, the ones with small waterfalls in the window, where you can buy antistress videos of sunsets.

Abby returned the photograph to the table, and followed Mike back to the kitchen. It was time to go home. She realized she was still holding Connie's postcard and looked down at it, at the large, flamboyant handwriting. An impulsive, larger-than-life kind of girl, no question. Abby turned the postcard over, and looked at the baby in the photograph. The smile was happy and toothless, but if you looked closely you could see that the baby was actually looking over to the left of the photographer. Abby imagined the mother crouching down next to the camera, smiling and encouraging her baby, just out of reach.

When she got home, Abby got a blanket from her bed and sat on her couch, remote in hand, the television bouncing between one channel and the next. She knew what she was looking for, suspense, followed by one of those satisfying moments when the hero finally understands what the hell is going on, and does something about it. The bluish light flickered on her face. She thought of Joey, locked in his cage, while she snuggled up with her dogs. Maybe what happened was, his father Roy showed up, got into a row with Betty, and shot her. Why not? Maybe the reason Betty left him in the first place was because he was violent or abusive. Maybe Joey knew more than he was saying, but he was afraid. Maybe someone threatened him.

Abby thought of her father, with his almost complete American Heritage collection, missing only Volumes V and XVIII. He could order the two thin hardcover books from a dealer, but that would be taking the easy way out; he wanted to find them for himself in a yard or church sale. The last time he came to Bantam they stopped at every roadside pile of castoffs and every junk store. Though both she and her mother complained, her mother found a pair of ceramic candlesticks she liked, and Abby found Rick. He was in a cardboard box, priced to sell at five dollars. Abby picked him up. He wasn't much bigger than her hand. The saleswoman was a girl of about ten with a scar on her forehead and fingernails bitten down to the quick. She told Abby that he would be drowned if he wasn't sold by the end of the day, and though Abby didn't believe her, she couldn't take the chance. After dickering halfheartedly she dug the five dollars out of her pocket. Her father never did find his American Heritage, because Rick was crawling with fleas so they had to take him home for a bath. But it was a good day.

# CHAPTER SIXTEEN

The next morning, Franklin was out and his secretary couldn't tell Abby exactly where he had gone. Was he in Hudson with Joey? Maybe. She trudged down the stairs. Back on Main Street, she turned toward Victor's, thinking she would get a coffee to go, when she saw Malaria walking in her direction. That decided her. She wheeled around and walked quickly the other way. Her car was parked over in the Dollar Store parking, and after rounding the corner she ran to it, climbing in quickly. She backed out, crossed the railroad tracks, and headed south on 46.

When she got to Hudson, she found a decent parking space in Courthouse Square. It is a sedate and peaceful place, built around a grassy park, a wooden bandstand in the center. The buildings around the perimeter are Victorian brownstones, presided over by the imposing columned courthouse. Abby crossed the central green and walked up the few steps to the main entrance. She noticed a discarded candy wrapper on the second to last step. Someone delaying the business of facing whatever waited inside.

The courthouse air was cool, and there was a noticeable smell, maybe ink, or light machine oil. The smell of bureaucracy and retribution, of mills grinding slow but exceeding small. A low-level drone of sound went with the photocopy smell, punctuated occasionally by heels ticking across marble. The last time she was here, to register Jonah's death, she slipped on the marble threshold as she was leaving. She was eager to leave and moving too fast on the shiny surface, but to anyone watching from the outside it might have looked as if the building spat her out, like a bitter-tasting bug.

When she finally found out where they were keeping Joey, a police-woman told her that he was not seeing visitors. She asked the officer to tell Joey who she was, but the woman was adamant and Abby finally gave up. As she was crossing the front lobby, the men's room door opened and Franklin stepped out, carrying his briefcase. Abby felt a surge of comfort at the sight of him.

"Franklin!" she called, wondering if he would treat her like his Saab, unable to tell the difference between her and a Taurus, but to her relief he smiled warmly.

"Abby—" He walked over to her.

"I came to see Joey, but they wouldn't let me in," she said.

He shook his head. "I just left him," he said.

"What's the matter?"

Franklin took her elbow, and steered her toward the front doors. They went outside, and walked down the wide steps she had just come up. The candy wrapper was still there. "He's not eating much. He's lying on his bunk, curled up. Talking in monosyllables."

"Jeez."

"I'm worried about him," he continued.

"Well, I wonder why. His mother's dead, and everyone thinks he killed her. He must be scared shitless. And lonely. Not to mention sad."

Franklin nodded, and they started walking down the path toward the sidewalk.

"Franklin, I need to talk to him about his father. Maybe there's some link there. Will you ask him to see me, just for a little while?"

146

Franklin thought for a moment. "I'm running late now, but I'll be back down tomorrow. Let me see what I can do, okay?"

He patted her on the arm. It seemed dismissive, but she didn't have much choice. Her car was parked in the opposite direction from where they were walking, so she turned back to the main entrance of the courthouse. As she walked by the courthouse steps, the candy wrapper caught her eye once more. She picked it up and tossed it into the large trashcan next to the stairs. At least she could say she had accomplished something.

On the drive back to Bantam, Abby remembered Johnny. When they lived in New York, she and Jonah sometimes talked to a one-eyed, homeless drunk, Johnny, who played an accordion for spare change on the corner of Seventy-second and Broadway. He had been in the Merchant Marines, wore an eye-patch, and his arms were covered in exotic tattoos, pricked into his skin in distant ports.

One day Johnny invited them to a local bar, a dark and sticky place with windows painted black, and an interior that stretched back into darkness. They sat in a booth, and Johnny insisted on paying for their drinks with dirty change he poured from his metal cup on to the scarred tabletop. He flipped his black eye patch from one eye to another, both eyes bright and milky blue, and told them about the detox center in Florida where he spent his winters. Jonah watched him, wordlessly and with utmost concentration. He seemed enthralled, but from that day on he avoided the corner where Johnny played. She didn't know why she suddenly thought of Johnny.

That afternoon she drove down to Cyrus Leighton's house and let herself in, she hoped for the last time. She worked for three hours without taking a break. When she finally finished the last page on the last pad, she was surprised to see it was dark outside. She read through what she had written for any major blunders. When she came to the student who borrowed the car, she thought about Connie. Why hadn't the girl phoned her father since she left home? Was she ashamed of her relationship? Ashamed of leaving without saying good-bye? Or was she just so caught up in her new life she couldn't be bothered? Abby thought about it, trying to picture herself doing the same thing to her parents. Her back felt stiff when she stood up. She tidied up the yellow pads, put them back where they belonged, and saved the work onto a disc. After shutting down the computer she left, locking the front door behind her.

The evening started off well at the InnBetween, with a steady flow of customers. The staff was on top of things and feeling pretty good until Henry dropped a raspberry and kiwi tart facedown on the prep-kitchen floor. He cleaned it up, or so he claimed, but half an hour later George the chef fell down. They found a kiwi slice stuck to his shoe—there was no way for Henry to get around that one. George was in a lot of pain; he seemed to have done something to his tailbone. He didn't want to go home in the middle of a shift, but Dulcie called his wife. With the help of the waiters, George hobbled to the waiting car, calling out last-minute instructions.

Sandy had run the kitchen alone before, but for some reason that was an off-night for him. First, there was the business of the rice and the potatoes. One of Abby's tables wanted to substitute their portions of rice for roast potatoes. Sandy said no. He wouldn't explain why, he just wouldn't do it. In the meantime, orders in the kitchen were backing up. Sandy was having trouble turning out the food fast enough, and people were getting edgy. Maurice Mullendore and Ellie were sitting at a small two-top next to the porch. He complained that his roast chicken was pink. Abby didn't want to point that they were sitting under one of their most flattering lights, a specially-toned bulb designed to make even the grayest skin tones appear pink, so she meekly took the plate back to the kitchen.

When she put it down on the stainless-steel shelf under the warmer, Sandy, who had three sauté pans going, a huge pot of pasta, and was grilling swordfish, snapped: "Don't tell me they don't like the fucking chicken." Sandy rarely swore. He was obviously stressed out.

"No, no." Abby had to speak up to be heard over the crash of pans being washed in the sink, and the clatter of plates. "They love the chicken. They just think it's a little pink. Could you put it on for another minute, just to make Mullendore happy?"

Sandy grabbed the plate and, turning back to the line, jerked it so the meat slid off onto the grill. He slammed the plate down.

By 10:00 P.M. the bar was quiet and Abby was clearing some of the downstairs tables. She looked up when she heard someone coming down the stairs. It was Sean. When he saw her, he nodded. He looked good but he didn't look very friendly.

"Can I get you anything?" she asked.

He shook his head. "No, thanks. Can we talk alone for a moment?"

Abby looked around. The small room wasn't particularly private. She nodded. "I guess so, for a moment. Come around the back."

She gestured to the corridor that ran behind the bar. Sean followed her around, and they found themselves in the narrow, damp space that in one direction led to the staff staircase, and in the other, to the back door.

"What's up?" She leaned one shoulder against the wall, and looked at him.

He seemed to make a decision. He put his hands on her shoulders and turned her so she was against the wall. Then he leaned down and put his lips against hers. She remained motionless, but her eyes closed. He saw this and moved closer so his whole torso was against her. Abby knew she should push him away, but it felt so good. She groaned softly, and opened her lips. His hands went around her, down by her back, pressing her hips into his. Her crotch started pulsing. He pulled her shirt out of her pants, and slid his hand up her chest, under her bra. He took a breast in his hand. Abby groaned again. Her hands went to his buttocks and pulled them toward her.

Suddenly, there was a crash to their left. Startled, they pulled their mouths apart and looked toward the noise. Sandy, the cook, stood there with an empty milk crate at his feet. He must've just dropped it.

"Excuse me," he said in his high voice, tightening his lips disapprovingly, not making eye contact. Sean moved back from her, his hands still up her shirt. Abby stared at Sandy, dull-eyed.

"Sandy, this is Sean. He's the plumber." It was all she could think of saying. Sandy picked up his milk crate, and gingerly sidled by, making sure not to touch either of them. He walked to the walk-in cooler next to the back door, slid the door open, and disappeared inside. They watched him until Sean leaned in again, and kissed her gently on the cheek. He started tucking her shirt into her pants.

"I miss you. I know you miss me. Don't you think maybe we have some unfinished business?" he asked her. She nodded without saying anything. Sandy came out of the cooler, his milk crate full of lettuces and eggplants. He walked by them once more, looking away. He disappeared up the stairs.

Abby followed Sean back into the barroom.

"When are you off?" Sean wiped a strand of hair off her forehead.

"Another hour."

"Can I come by your house tonight?" He watched her intently.

She couldn't remember why she hadn't called him. The reasons had seemed good at the time, but now—Abby nodded.

Sean gave her a discreet kiss on the cheek, and left. Abby went back to her tables. Her shirt was bunched up in her pants, so she had to reach in to smooth out the fabric. She remembered Sarah, and her black lace panties.

When she went upstairs, she found the Mullendores had joined a large central table where the wine was flowing and the conversation was intense, with no one listening to anyone else. She helped the other waiters clear tables and Dan the Man put away clean dishes. While she was refilling the salt and pepper shakers, Abby listened halfheartedly to some of the talk at the big table. They were arguing about how much it would cost, per square foot, to put an addition onto an existing structure. They argued about builders, contractors, electricians, and plumbers. While they shouted across the table at each other, she started to put the chairs, upside down, onto the surrounding tables.

# CHAPTER SEVENTEEN

Friday morning it rained. Abby lay in bed, watching the water from the sky beat against the windows of her little trailer. There was a strong wind blowing, and the trailer seemed to rock with each gust. She lay there, trying to hear her own breathing under the thundering of the rain on the metal roof.

The night before, as soon as she got home she showered and got dressed again, not sure if she should be welcoming Sean in a teddy (she didn't actually have one) or sweatpants. What she was wearing hadn't mattered anyway, as it turned out. Once again, by 6:00 A.M. Sean was picking his clothes off the floor and getting ready to leave. This time, when he sat down on the bed next to her, he said: "I'm like a dog, you have to throw rocks to get rid of me."

"Thanks for the tip. Funny, though, I don't remember throwing any this morning—"

By late morning the rain had slowed to a drizzle. The sun was breaking through in bright patches, lighting the raindrops. Abby looked at the glowering sky and sunny rain, treasuring the oddity of it, its transience. She thought again of Johnny, the drunk from Seventy-second Street. That rainy afternoon in the dark, beer-soaked bar he told them that in East Africa they have a name for that strange and brilliant moment when the sun shines through the glistening rain. They call it a monkey's wedding. Abby had always liked that. Trust a monkey to get it right.

Friday night she was scheduled to tend bar at the InnBetween, so she went in early to check that the shelves were stocked and ready. In the kitchen, George was stirring cauldrons, "Foxy Lady" by Jimi Hendrix playing at top volume on the kitchen tape deck, which, slick and spattered with grease stains, sat precariously on a pile of clean dishrags tied together with string. She helped George set up the salad station and cut orange slices as a garnish for pork chops. When he and Sandy decided it was time to "go to church," she sat at the staff table with Dulcie, who talked nonstop about her son. He had just told her he was tired of the theater and wanted to join the CIA.

"Do you know, for the rest of my life, when people ask me what he is up to, I'm going to have to lie?" she whispered, and Abby noticed she was using her crayon to draw on the linen tablecloth, instead of butcher paper.

"You'll get used to it," she said, taking the crayon out of Dulcie's hand.

It was with relief that she heard George call everyone in for the meeting. He gave them his list of specials, and Dulcie unlocked the front door.

People came early, and steadily. Abby was busy, but she liked it. Sometimes bartending was a satisfying job, she thought to herself. A little science, a little theater, not much food. She could make customers happy by giving them a tiny paper umbrella, or an extra olive. Simple. Yes, it was turning out to be a pleasant night. Good tips, happy customers, and home in a few more hours.

By a little past 10:00 P.M., Becca had taken over the bar and Abby was upstairs eating dinner, when Bailey walked in the front door. Abby looked up to see him limping quickly and efficiently down the stairs. She groaned out loud. She was going to have to face him again. She went over to the intercom, and called Becca.

"Becca, if Bailey gives you any trouble, call me, okay? Also, two shots, and no more, okay? But don't tell him you're cutting him off. Call me, I'll tell him. I don't trust him."

Becca sounded unafraid. "No problem. I can handle this guy."

"Don't be so sure. Is anyone else down there?"

"Oh, yeah. Four tables, and two at the bar."

She was okay for now, so Abby went back to her meal. After she had eaten, she began cleaning up. She forgot about Bailey until the intercom buzzed.

"Hey, Abby," Becca whispered. "He's on his third shot, and just about everyone has gone."

"Becca, I told—"

"I couldn't say no. Get down here."

She didn't sound quite as confident. Smart girl. Abby squared her shoulders and headed down the stairs.

Bailey was sitting on his usual stool at the far end of the bar. But this time his body was draped across the bar, and he was reaching for Becca, who was backed into the opposite corner.

"Bailey!" Abby shouted, as soon as she saw him. He turned quickly, and looked up at her. She stopped where she was on the stairs, trying to maintain height and distance. Bailey frowned, and looked back at Becca.

"You're the one with no tits, right?" he asked Becca. The poor girl looked like she wanted to cry.

"You're disgusting, Bailey," Abby said softly. He whipped his head around like a snapping turtle and looked at her, his eyes small and beady. Maybe the only way to get rid of him was coax him into a large garbage can and move him to someone else's pond. Or bar. And keep your fingers out of the way. "I'm the one with no tits, not her," she continued, "but *you're* the one with no brain."

He kept staring at her, his eyelids unblinking. It was probably the booze at work, but she couldn't shake the feeling that she was looking at a swamp-dwelling predator.

"Yeah, well I came to talk to you."

This was a new approach. He was going to negotiate some kind of a treaty.

"You didn't need to sit at the bar to do that."

"I gotta show you something."

"What, your Japanese etchings? Sure. Look, Bailey, I'm going back to work. I've got customers waiting. Come on, I want you out of here, okay?" Abby waved him toward her, like a traffic cop. "I told you last time not to come back. You're not welcome here."

Bailey laughed, or it was a sort of laugh, a silent grimace, his mouth stretched open, very little mirth or joy in it. When he recovered from it, he looked at her. "You gotta stop being so damn bossy. Like a squeaky, bossy wife. Oh, Bailey," he continued, his voice high-pitched and singsong, "you can't come back, Bailey, I don't want you here, oh, Bailey." His voice dropped back down. "You really want to fuck me, don't you?"

Before she could respond appropriately, he raised a huge, dirt-engrained hand in the air, as if holding her and her lust at bay. "First, I gotta show you something. In the woods."

Now it was her turn to sneer. "Like I'm going to go into the woods with you."

He shook his head, amused at what he seemed to perceive as her playfulness. "I'm telling you, you're gonna want to see this. It ain't pretty, but you're gonna want to see it."

Suddenly, Abby felt as if she were in a plane that had hit turbulence. "What are you talking about?"

He had her attention, and he was enjoying it. He weaved his head, as if he were listening to some heavenly music. "Somebody didn't want me to find what I found, but I was hunting, you know?"

"It's off-season," Abby spoke in a deadpan voice.

"Not for me, it ain't. I consider myself a Native American, you know what I'm sayin'? I was born here, my daddy was born here, I got rights."

"You're breaking the law."

"Hey, No-tits, you're a downer, anybody tell you that? There's a lot of deer in them woods, we ain't going to run out anytime soon."

"So why don't you just go to the police, and report what you want to report, and leave out the deer?"

"Because I shot me a deer, and tracked it, and it was the deer that took me to the body." He smiled slowly, watching her closely, enjoying his revelation.

Abby looked at him, unable to hide her shock. Her voice was dry when she asked: "What body?"

He shook his head slowly, smiling all the while.

"Why are you telling me, Bailey?"

His smile widened, and for a moment he seemed completely sober. "You think you're tough. Let's go look at what I found."

"I'm calling the police," she rasped.

"Don't you go callin' no cops." He tried to stand up, stumbled, and had to hold onto the bar. He belched, a loud wet sound. Abby shook her head in disgust, the smell of bile and alcohol heavy in the low-ceilinged, airless room.

"Bailey, the police won't give a damn about your deer, okay?"

"What d'you know about it? Sonsabitches have it in for me. No, no way I'm talkin' to the cops."

Abby wanted to push him off the stool and stomp on his face. She spoke low and hard, trying to drive her voice through his skull. "Bailey, I'm calling the chief, and you're taking us. No choice, it's your civic fucking duty." He opened his mouth to say something, but she pointed at him. It was all that came to her. He shut his mouth. Amazing. Keeping her finger up, she walked to the phone. He didn't say anything until she picked up the receiver.

"Make 'em swear they won't give me any trouble. Lyin' bastards. They're going to try and make it look like I did it."

Within half an hour, the chief of police was at the restaurant, accompanied by two deputies. Bailey insisted Abby come along. He saw her as his protection against the three lawmen. They all got into one police car, and headed toward Spencerville. One of the young deputies was Robbie Hogen, who had been a busboy at the InnBetween before he went to the police academy. Even at sixteen, when she first met him, he was 6'2" and as big as a linebacker, and now he sat in the backseat of the cruiser, knees up, squeezed uncomfortably between Bailey and the other deputy. Once in a while he would catch her eye, and look away. Both the deputies carried large black flashlights. Before reaching the village, they turned right, up Angell Hill Road. Occasionally Chief Sheriff would ask Bailey for directions, but otherwise they drove in silence. The road narrowed as they drove deeper into the woods.

Finally, Bailey spoke up: "Pull over, Big Boss. We're here."

The chief turned off the engine, and they all climbed out, four doors slamming shut in loud, syncopated succession. The wooded night was as dark and silent as oil, the black shapes of the trees creating an indifferent minefield through which they would be obliged to pass. After the officers had gathered up black bags from the trunk of the car, they set off into the woods, single file, following the fitful beams of the flashlights.

It felt like they hiked through those woods for a long time. They had to move slowly, because of Bailey's limp. Occasionally they would stop, the chief would take a compass reading and talk on his walkie-talkie. Then they would trudge on, trying not to stumble on the branches and rocks under their feet.

Once, Bailey tripped and fell, and the other deputy said, with a chuckle: "How the hell do you get any hunting done, Bailey, those animals must hear you coming a mile off." Bailey stood up, slowly, turned around, stared at him, and then let out a loud, hissing fart. He ended it with a sigh of satisfaction, turned back, and started walking again.

Eventually they reached some place that looked to Abby like every other place they had walked through, but Bailey grunted: "It's there, big Chief Geronimo. Over in them thar trees," and he pointed to his right. And with a groan he let himself slowly down on a fallen tree trunk a few feet away.

The chief told Robbie to follow him, and ordered the other deputy to stay with Abby and Bailey. Abby looked for another fallen tree, but had to settle for a large stone. The surface was cold and hard. Robbie and the chief disappeared among the trees.

Once they were alone, Bailey started shaking his head and muttering to himself. The young deputy, who was leaning against a tree, looked at him nervously. "Shut up," he said. Abby tried to ignore both of them. She waited, the darkness oppressive.

They heard the two men returning before they reappeared, their heavy shoes crunching the leaves and twigs underfoot. Like anxious relatives in a hospital waiting room, the young deputy pushed himself off his tree and Abby stood up. Bailey remained on his log, staring glassily at something only he could see. The chief shook his head, as if trying to throw off a bad dream. He stopped in the clearing, and said nothing for a moment. Then he shook his head.

"It looks like it might be Mike's girl. Can't be sure." He looked down at the ground, as if an explanation might be written amongst the rotting vegetation. "We're going to cordon off this area, and Robbie, take Bailey and Abigail back to the car. Drive her wherever she needs to go. I want Bailey to dry out at the station, I'm going to need to talk to him. I've radioed in for more men, but you're going to have to bring 'em back in with you when you come. The coroner is on his way. Okay, let's get moving here." He turned and walked back into the woods. Robbie turned to Bailey, and the other deputy began unpacking a black bag. Abby hesitated, then followed the chief into the trees. By the time she caught up with him, he was standing, looking down at a shape that seemed to catch whatever moonlight was filtering through the trees. As she got closer, Abby could see it was a human shape, flat out on its back, arms spread wide. The dark hair mixed with the dark ground. The chief's flashlight beam moved slowly up the body. When it stopped at the face, Abby thought the mouth was drawn back in a smile, but as she drew closer she realized that half the face was gone. She gasped, and the chief turned around.

"What the hell are you doing here?" he whispered hoarsely, as if the girl on the ground were sleeping. "Get out, you'll mess up my crime scene. Get the hell out."

Abby turned, and stumbled back to the others. They were all standing there, waiting for her. Bailey smirked. "Told you you'd want to see it," he said. Abby couldn't look at him, and without another word they started back through the trees.

Abby asked the trooper to drop her at her car. As they drove through the dark town, she wondered who would be the one to call the girl's father. Probably the chief. *Thank God it's not my job,* she thought. *I barely know Mike Testarossa.* She couldn't, however, escape from the fact that she felt tied to him. He had hired her and she had failed him. She felt burdened by the heartbreaking news he was about to hear, news that would forever change his life.

As she drove up her hill, she realized grimly that in some way leaving home these days was a setting out, a going forth, an effort. Like pulling on a giant bungee cord. By the end of each expedition she was worn out by the struggle, and when she finally gave in to the pull, returning to where she had started was the only possible ending. The path of least resistance. Home. Her dogs would be waiting patiently, and everything would be as she left it, suspended in time, with only a little more dust on horizontal surfaces, and perhaps some natural settling of the trailer into the earth.

This night, however, as she approached, she could distinguish the outline of a vehicle near the trailer. As she came nearer, she recognized it as Sean's pickup. She pulled in next to him and climbed out of her car. The night air smelled damp and warm, of grass and exhaust. Sean was sitting on her metal chair. He rose as she walked slowly toward him, her feet crunching on the gravel. His face was hard to make out in the dark.

"Sean." She was so tired her arms hung motionless, as if ropes were pulling them to the ground. Sean caught something in her voice. "What's wrong?"

Abby took a breath. "They think they found Connie Testarossa tonight. She's dead."

Sean seemed to lose his footing though he was standing still. "Christ." He put a hand up against the trailer, as if for support. "How do you know?"

"Trust me, she was dead."

"How do you know?" he repeated.

"I was there."

"What happened to her?"

Abby shrugged. "I don't know. She was in the woods. Bailey found her. He took us to the body."

"Shit. Are you okay?"

He sounded concerned, and she felt her chin begin to tremble. A weak little woman, she thought. "It was bad."

He came quickly over to her and put his arms around her. The sudden warmth of his body, shielding her from the light night breeze, released the tension and she started to cry, at first silently and then within seconds, sobbing and gasping. Sean hugged her and patted her on the back, murmuring. She cried until his shirt was wet, and then she pulled away from him, covered her face with her hands, and cried some more. Sean went to his pickup and came back with a rag. It looked like something he might have set aside for checking the oil. Gratefully, Abby blew her nose and wiped her face. Then took a deep breath. Sean watched her.

When she was done with the rag, she gave it back to him. "God, look at me. I didn't even know her. You did. You were engaged to her."

He stuffed the rag in his back pocket, put his arms around her, and pulled her close. She appreciated the comfort of his embrace. She smelled him, a mixture of warm skin and machine oil and wood smoke.

Unexpectedly, he kissed her, at first gently, then more insistently. His grip on her body changed. She tried to move her mouth away from his, but he didn't seem to get the message.

Gently, she pushed on his shoulders. If anything, his grip seemed to tighten. A picture of the dead girl appeared in her mind's eye, struggling for her life. And losing. Sean's arms tightened, feeling suddenly like thick ropes that were squeezing the air out of her. His mouth was suffocating her. She whipped her head to the side, gasping. She pushed harder but he kept his arms locked around her. Panicking, she hit his shoulders and arms. "Let go of me!"

At last, he did. She jumped back, panting. "What the hell are you doing?"

His voice was low, angry. "What the fuck, Abby, I—" He moved slowly toward her.

She was suddenly afraid of him. "I need you to go," she whispered. If he decided to hurt her, there was no one around to hear. She kept her eyes on him, unwilling to turn away. "Sean, don't bully me. I don't like it."

"I wasn't—" He reached for her arm, but she twisted away from him. Angrily, he stared at her then turned and walked quickly to his pickup, pulled open the door and climbed in. He slammed the door behind him.

Unable to resist, she heard herself call out: "When did you last see her?"

"Who? Connie? Why? I—" he paused as he realized what she was asking him. He looked at her, his face hard to see in the dark. "What the fuck are you saying? You think I did something to her?"

She didn't answer.

He turned the key and started the engine. As she stood there, he backed out fast, his tires throwing up gravel and digging ruts in her driveway as he drove away.

Abby hung some wind chimes Dulcie had given her from the front door handle so she would know if anyone tried to get in. Then she went into the bathroom to brush her teeth, but before she could get the toothpaste on the brush, she started to shake. She sat on the toilet, her head in her hands. The dogs kept coming to her, sniffing her. She eventually got up, wondering if they could smell the odor of the dead girl on her clothes. She ran a hot shower and stood in the scalding water, wishing it could burn her clean.

Abby sat on the couch, huddled in her bathrobe, her wet hair soaking into the terrycloth fabric. She couldn't go to bed, but there was nothing else she seemed capable of doing. Finally, the blinking light on her answering machine caught her eye, and she pulled her body out of the couch. There were two messages, the first from Dulcie, who wanted her to call her when she got home. She erased it. The second was from Sally DeCintio. It took Abby a moment to remember that she was Connie's boss at the hospital. Sally was calling to tell her that she had done the research she had promised, and had discovered that no other hospital staff members had gone on vacation at precisely the same time as Connie. "And," she added cheerfully, as if her piece of the puzzle absolved her and her people from any whisper of misconduct, "little Miss Connie is going to hear from me when she gets back."

Later on, she woke up with her stomach feeling tight and acid-filled. Her brain was a washing machine, a confusion of images, colors, and sensations sloshing around together. She turned on the light and sat up. She saw Connie's empty body, lying discarded in the woods; she pictured her earlier, leaning her head against the steering wheel of Dulcie's car. She thought of Sean. Connie and Sean had gone out for a year and Abby wondered what had really gone on between them. Maybe Connie had done something to provoke him, make him jealous. Tonight she had seen a side of Sean that she hadn't met before: was that because she had goaded him? Was Sean a violent man? Or had she imagined the threat?

Out of nowhere, she saw herself cutting orange slices with George in the kitchen, listening to Jimi Hendrix. Had that really happened just a few hours before? It seemed like years.

She didn't fall asleep until a pink dawn lightened her small window. When she did, she dreamed of stumbling through the woods, trying to avoid the rocks that cropped up in the dark path in front of her.

# CHAPTER EIGHTEEN

L ater that morning, tired and slow-moving, Abby went to the court-house and was pointed to the waiting room, where she sat, leafing through a battered copy of *People* magazine. After an hour of waiting she considered giving up. She wondered if this was the best day for her to try to communicate with a depressed, monosyllabic teenager. However, there are times when passive inaction has its own rewards, and she stayed in the waiting room, not quite ready to stand up and walk away. She justified it by telling herself she was doing exactly what that room was designed for, waiting.

A guard she hadn't seen before appeared in the doorway and called her name.

"Follow me," he said, when she stood up.

Joey's cell was small, and he sat on the single cot with his back against the wall, his legs pulled up in front of him. His head was resting on his knees, but he raised it when she was let in. Abby stood for a minute, unsure of what to do, while the heavy door was locked behind her. Then she sat down on the cot next to him. There wasn't anyplace else. She waited for a while before she spoke.

"Joey, it's good to see you."

His skin was a pasty white, verging on gray, and a smattering of pimples covered his chin and forehead.

"Yeah, well." His voice sounded hoarse, from too many tears, or not enough use.

The silence started to build up again.

"How's the food in here?"

He shrugged indifferently. After another pause, she began telling him what she had been up to, beginning with the stakeout of Dulcie's car, moving on to Cyrus, his house, and her job transcribing his book. She told him about Cyrus's storyline, and the car borrower. He looked over at that. Maybe it appealed to the motorhead in him. Or maybe he knew something about it. She decided to leave that until later. She took a deep breath.

"They found the body of a young girl, in the woods. I called the chief this morning, who confirmed it was a girl called Connie Testarossa."

She watched him as she said the name. His mouth opened, and he sucked in a quick breath of air.

"What happened to her?"

"They don't know. No autopsy report yet."

His head sank to his knees, and he seemed to be rocking it from one knee to the other, as if he were trying to work his skull loose from his neck.

"Did you know her?" she asked quietly.

He nodded.

"How did you know her?" she persisted.

He looked up. His eyes were shining, and she could see tears on his cheeks.

"The hospital."

Abby was surprised. "You were at the hospital?"

He shook his head. "No, from the parties."

"What parties?" she asked, confused.

"The hospital parties. What're they called—you know—fund-raisers. She helped organize them, and sometimes I got hired to pass trays, stuff like that, especially if the party was at Mr. and Mrs. Leighton's house."

"Oh, right. Mrs. Leighton's on the board." Small-town living. Everyone connected.

Joey darted a look at her. "Do they know who killed her?"

"No, they don't," she answered, wondering why he looked scared. Maybe for the simple reason that there was a lot of death in his world now.

"Do you know something that might be helpful, maybe something that was on her mind?"

He thought for a minute, but shook his head.

"I didn't know her that well. I mean, we talked, but never about anything, you know, like, personal."

"Did you like her?"

He blushed. And nodded. Abby realized, of course, he probably had a crush on her. Connie was a pretty young woman, and he was a sixteen-year-old boy. Stood to reason.

Abby went on. "I never met her. Just heard about her from different people. I'd like to know what you thought of her."

He shrugged, and blushed again. "She was cool. Funny. She'd make fun of the people at the parties, you know, 'cause some of them were, you know, assholes. It was kind of a game for her. But she was always real nice to them."

"What did she do exactly?"

"You mean, to make fun of people?"

"Yeah."

"I don't know, she would imitate them sometimes, copy the way they talked, or walked. Stuff like that."

"What did she do at the parties? What was her job?"

Joey thought for a minute. "A little bit of everything, I guess. She called herself Twinky, the hostess with the mostest. I mean, only to us, not to the people. She had to let people in the door, take their coats, you know, make sure there was enough food, sometimes introduce people." Joey frowned, remembering. "But I think she was like bait, you know? She was pretty hot, and all these rich old creeps would get all excited, and laugh a lot when she was talking to them, and lean in real close. She'd come back and tell me what they said. One old guy told her to sit on his lap so he could—" he hesitated, "put his burning rod up her." Joey blushed darkly as he said this, scowling unhappily. "It was disgusting, I told her she should tell Mr. Leighton and have the guy thrown out, but she just laughed, and said to forget it, he was drunk. She said she bet his rod," Joey isolated the word to give it quotation marks, "was more like a cold noodle." He added sadly: " I think she kinda dug it when they treated her like that."

Abby thought that was perceptive of him. She could picture it. Connie was having fun, feeling her power. Maybe playing with fire? Or was she just in love, and feeling compassion for other less happy inhabitants of the planet?

"Did your mother know what was going on?"

Joey sighed. "Yeah, she had a pretty good idea. She'd tell her to wear longer skirts and behave herself, said she'd get the wives all riled up, but Connie just laughed."

"Did anyone seem to get riled up, jealous or angry, anything like that?"

Joey considered the question, then shook his head.

"Was there anyone in particular that she seemed to spend time with, anyone she was involved with?"

Joey continued to shake his head. "No one that I can think of," he said, adding, with a flash of insight, "but I doubt she would have told me, you know?"

Abby nodded. He was right. She wouldn't have told him if she was seeing a married man, or an important person at the hospital. But then again, she might drop hints. She might have wanted to show off, let someone know.

"There wasn't anyone that she talked quite a lot to, or even argued with?"

Joey thought about it then snorted. "The only person I saw her argue with was my mother. But a lot of people did that."

"You saw her fight with your mother? Do you know what it was about?"

"Yeah. It was at the Leightons'. My mom was in charge of the kitchen. She said Connie was using the wrong tablecloths. She was using the really good ones, or something like that, and she should only use the cheap ones. Connie was pissed, and said they all looked the same, and called her a jealous bitch. My mother was so damn mad, I thought she was going to hit her."

"Did your mother ever get physical?"

"Nah. She just got all stiff, and stomped out of the room. That's my mother's way of dealing." Joey said this bluntly, as if her anger and poor communication skills were with him, forever, in the very air he breathed.

Joey looked tired, worn out by their conversation. It was time for Abby to leave.

"Joey, thanks for letting me visit. I'd like to come back sometime, maybe bring you some goodies and just hang out. Could I do that?"

"Yeah. Okay." He looked at her sideways. "I'd like that."

Without thinking, she reached out and put an arm around him. He leaned tentatively toward her, and she put the other arm around his broad, bony shoulders. Eventually, she felt him relax against her. *He's just a kid,* she thought, *starved for hugging.* She rocked him gently. And maybe he wasn't the only one.

# CHAPTER NINETEEN

News of Connie's death hit Bantam like an explosion. It made the front page of the local papers, and the *Albany Times Union* and the *Berkshire Eagle* picked it up immediately. A beautiful young girl, local, thought to have eloped with an unknown lover, found dead in the woods. It had all the makings of a real-life soap opera. Suddenly everyone remembered something about her, and grieved for her. According to the papers, there was a sort of gloriously wet indulgence going on, a "flood" of outrage and fear, an "outpouring" of sympathy for the bereaved father. There was even a "deluge" of calls to 911. It was true, for a week no one could talk of anything else.

There were no new developments from the police, though one article mentioned a man being detained for questioning. Abby thought it was most likely Bailey. Probably take him a week to dry out.

In the meantime, Abby neither saw nor heard from Mike. She finally got up the courage to call him, but his phone rang and rang. Eventually his machine picked up and she left a brief message of condolence. Though Mike had hired her to find out who his daughter's boyfriend was, she figured by now it was in the hands of the police. What was she supposed to do?

Abby worked most of the week. One evening Chief Sheriff and his wife, Cindy, came in for dinner and sat in Abby's station. Cindy was a petite blonde, full of energy and smiles. The couple talked intimately through most of their dinner, speaking softly, laughing occasionally, their heads close. Occasionally, when Abby walked by, Cindy would stop her with an apologetic request for "a tiny bit more bread, *please*," or if she could, "a spoonful more of this delicious sauce, but only if you're going that way." Toward the end of their meal, Cindy went downstairs to the bathroom. Abby put down what she was doing and walked quickly over to the chief. She sat down on the edge of Cindy's chair and spoke in a low voice, so no one could hear her at a nearby table.

"Chief, I have one question for you, just one."

He looked at her, the relaxed, contented look dying on his face.

"What is it? I can't promise an answer, you know that, Abigail."

Not a great start, but she leaned forward, keeping her voice low. "About Connie Testarossa." The chief frowned, and she kept talking so he wouldn't have a chance to shut her up. "I was wondering if you could tell me what the autopsy says. I mean, how she, you know, died."

Abby hadn't even finished and the man was shaking his head. "Abigail, I'm having dinner with my wife. I don't want to talk about it now. And anyway, this is police business. Keep well out of it, for your own good. She wasn't in those woods pickin' mushrooms, she was brutally murdered. Can you understand that?" It must've been the wine loosening his tongue. Not that she had expected to hear that Connie had died in those woods by tripping on a root.

"Look, Chief, I swear I don't want you to tell me anything I'm not supposed to know. But can't you give me some general information, the kind of thing you might tell a reporter? Can't you tell me what killed her? How it was done?"

He shook his head. "All I'll tell you is what you'll see in the *Independent* tomorrow. She was hit over the head with something hard, okay? Many times over. Now buzz off, would you? And bring me the check." He was still scowling when his wife sat back down at their table.

For the rest of the evening, Abby pictured Connie's death. She imagined the violence of the act, and the need to kill that brought it about. She imagined the slamming, the breaking and crushing of the girl who, just a short while before, had walked resolutely up High Street, her shoes echoing on the pavement and who had smiled in anticipation, warmed by some secret of her own. As she went through her chores, Abby thought how Connie's brutal murder left her feeling a tangible sense of her own frailty and helplessness. She had thoughtlessly tangled herself up in Connie's life, and now she was part of her death.

Next morning she heard about Joey Merchant. Actually, she overheard. She was at Victor's, drinking coffee, and the two ladies who owned the bookstore were talking at the next table. The odd thing was that she was just thinking about Joey. Nothing specific, just considering if she should let him pick out his own truck from the bone yard at her farm. And suddenly she heard his name. She snapped out of it in time to hear one of the women tell her partner that Joey Merchant had been released into the protective custody of his father. Neither of them knew his name.

"Are you serious?" Abby snapped, turning around in her chair. They both looked at her in surprise, and the speaker nodded cautiously.

"I can't believe they would do that! I can't believe it!" Abby slammed down her cup, and pushed away from the table. Outside, she walked quickly along the sidewalk, in the gate and up the stairs to Franklin's office. His secretary looked up.

"Abby, you can't go barging in there," she cautioned her.

Abby ignored her, and banged on Franklin's office door. She heard a faint "Uh huh?" and pushed open the door. Franklin looked up from his desk. He was buzzing away as he worked on something at his desk. He didn't even look up. She stood there, fuming.

"How could you let him go, Franklin!" she hissed.

Franklin looked up at her, annoyed. "You're upset about something?"

She took a deep breath. "If you would put that fucking thing away for a moment, and think about your client, you might be interested to know that he has been sent home with that psycho, Roy Goodrich."

Franklin put his elbows on the table. "That psycho, as you call him, has my blessing."

Abby felt as if someone had punched her. "You put this together? Oh, God, Franklin, why?"

Franklin seemed puzzled at her response. "It's a good idea, Abby. The boy doesn't have anyone else. Goodrich cares about him, and he seems to like Goodrich. The man put up the bail. I think it's a great solution until all this is resolved."

Abby sat down heavily in one of his chairs. "The guy is a suspect, Franklin. He could've killed Joey's mother."

"Says who? I haven't heard of any evidence or motive to link him to Betty's murder."

"I know, but he shared a child with her, I got the distinct impression he didn't like her, and there could very well be some reason we are not aware of. And have you seen where he lives? He's a redneck, a gun-toting, animal-stuffing weirdo."

Franklin snorted. "Listen to you. Next thing you'll be calling for a lynching. You've been serving food to city folk for too long now, girl."

She shot him a look. "Don't give me that stuff, Franklin. You know what I mean."

Franklin let out a sigh. He put his hands together, as if praying for her to understand.

"Abby, I was worried about the boy. I was afraid, honestly, that he might try to hurt himself. He needed to get out of that cell. Come on now, you saw him."

Franklin looked at her. She shrugged, reluctantly. "I would've taken him."

"Well you didn't ask nor do you have any legal right to, and Roy did and does. Most importantly, Joey seemed happy to be going home with his father." Franklin watched her, shaking his head. "The court had no reason to question his motives, and neither do I. Naturally, if you hear anything different, I'd like to know."

Abby stood up. "Okay, but this isn't over. I'll be working on this."

"Good." Franklin smiled. "I'm glad to hear it." His pleasure annoyed her, and she shut the door harder than necessary on her way out.

# CHAPTER TWENTY

I t was ten-thirty by the time she parked in the drugstore parking lot and entered through the automatic doors. As usual, the place was empty of all but one or two customers drifting along the aisles, slowed down and stunned by all the cheap plastic. She found Connie's friend Sarah in the oral hygiene aisle, where she was filling up racks of toothbrushes.

"Hi, Sarah," she said, as cheerfully as she could.

After staring at her blankly, Sarah scowled. "You."

"I'm glad you remember me. I have another question."

Sarah grabbed a handful of toothbrushes from a box at her feet, and went back to shoving them into their little dispensers. "Forget it, I don't like talking to you."

"Hey, that's not fair. I haven't done anything to you." Abby sounded a little whiney to herself. She lowered her voice, and went on. "Listen, Sarah, I just want to know something about Connie's relationship with Sean."

One of the toothbrushes bounced out and landed near Abby's feet. Abby leaned down and picked it up.

Sarah shook her head in disgust, as if she had just found Abby stealing lipstick. She kept on stuffing the toothbrush racks. "Checkin' up on him, right?"

Abby was quick to deny it. "No, you're wrong, I just want to find out about Connie, what her life was like."

Sarah smirked. "Oh, you're so caring, aren't you. Just want to find out what her life was like. Well, it was just fine. And she and Sean were great together. Do you think they fought a lot? What did you think, maybe he killed her? Wait'll I tell him that, he's gonna love it."

"If they got along so fabulously, how come they broke up?"

"Why don't you ask Sean yourself, huh? Instead of trying to drag it out of his friends."

Abby looked at her and shook her head. "As usual, you've been so helpful."

There was really no point talking to her. Abby walked angrily toward the exit. The automatic door opened and she was just about to step through when Sarah's coworker called out to her from behind the cash register: "Miss, are you buying that?" She was pointing to Abby's right hand. In confusion, Abby looked down. She was still holding the toothbrush.

"Oh, no, I'm sorry, I forgot I was holding it—" she stammered.

From the dental hygiene aisle, Sarah was watching her.

She stopped in the restaurant and used the phone to call Roy Goodrich's number. The phone rang and rang. Finally, someone picked up.

"Hello?" A male voice, low.

"Roy?"

"No."

"Joey?"

"Yeah?"

"Abby here."

"Oh, hi." She could hear his breathing.

"How's it going?"

He didn't answer for a moment. "I'm okay."

"Great. I was wondering if you'd like to come over and see my old trucks. If there's one you like, you can have it." It wasn't what she had planned to say.

This time he hesitated only for a second. "Sure. Where are they?"

"On River Street. Past the bridge."

"Oh, yeah. I know where. That would be cool."

"Is Roy there?"

"No. He's at work."

"Do you want me to come and get you?"

Again, he hesitated. "That would be good."

"Okay. I'll see you in about half an hour."

She hung up, wondering what the protocol was with a suspected murderer, however youthful. She decided to call Roy where he worked, at Fred's Lawn and Tractor, to make sure it was okay to take Joey out. She wanted him to be aware that someone else was taking an interest in the kid.

"Yup?" Roy answered, after she had been put through to him.

"Roy? This is Abby Silvernale. We met when I came up to your house to—"

"Yup. I know who you are."

"I wanted to see if it was okay if I pick Joey up and take him to my house—"

"What'd you want with him?"

"I don't want anything with him. I thought I'd get him out of the house—"

"I don't think it's a good idea, the lawyer says he shouldn't go out much. I gotta get back to work."

The conversation wasn't going quite as smoothly as Abby had envisioned. "I have trucks," she said. "Old trucks."

There was silence at the other end. Obviously, no paternity test was needed to prove fatherhood; she finally had his attention. Not wanting to lose momentum, she kept talking. "I promised Joey I would show him all the old trucks on my father-in-law's farm. Today seemed like a good day."

There was a pause, but she felt now it was more for form's sake. "Okay, but nowhere else."

"Okay. Thanks."

But he had already disconnected.

Joey was sitting on the porch waiting for her when she reached the top of Roy's rutted driveway. Abby turned the car around and he jumped in. It was a clear, bright day, and they made small talk, or at least she did, as they drove along Route 103 back to Bantam. Joey sat still, looking out the window, glancing at her when she said something particularly compelling, answering her with nods, and grunts.

When they reached the farm, she pulled into the courtyard. The discarded farm trucks and vehicles lined the edge of the road and the opposite side of the yard, a rusted metal hedge between the yard around the house and the pasture that climbed the hill behind the barn. Abby got out of the Bronco and walked up the porch steps. She hadn't done that for a long time. She knocked on the doorframe. After a few moments, a stocky woman in her early thirties opened the door, squinting in the light. She smiled when she recognized Abby.

"Well, what d'you know. The landlady."

Abby stood awkwardly, her hands in her pockets. "Hey, Noreen. I'm here with a boy. He's come to adopt a truck."

Noreen looked in the direction of the car. "Yay. Bring more boys, adopt 'em all."

Abby gestured to the porch. "Is it okay if I just sit here while he looks around?"

Noreen flapped her arm dismissively. "Feel free. Your porch. You need me, I'll be out back."

She nodded to Abby, and let the screen door slam shut as she disappeared into the house.

Joey started at one end of the row of vehicles and spent the afternoon going from one relic to the next. Most of them were rusted to a reddish black and there was no way of guessing the original paint color unless he looked inside, or crouched down in the tall grass and peered underneath. Undaunted, Joey made sure to look under each vehicle, and inside every hood he could pry open. He muttered to himself, opened doors, and climbed around. Abby sat on the edge of the porch. She hoped he was up to date on his tetanus shots. After a while she stopped watching him and lay back on the wooden deck, gazing at the tongue-and-groove ceiling. If she tilted her head back, she could see the old iron lighting fixture with its one, single bulb. Upside-down it looked different. She relaxed her neck and shut her eyes. She dozed off.

The afternoon wore on. Joey didn't give up, and eventually he stood at the bottom of the steps and looked up at her. He spoke seriously: "I found it."

He led her to the farthest corner, behind the barn. He explained that it was a Ford pickup, around 1952, original color black or dark green. It was well rusted but, according to Joey, surprisingly watertight, and the interior hadn't suffered too much damage. The engine looked solid. Frozen solid, Abby was sure. She warned him that something had been wrong with it at least three decades earlier, or it wouldn't have been put out to pasture. Joey didn't care. He sat behind the wheel, looking intently at some imaginary landscape where the twisting road disappeared into the horizon.

Abby promised she would let her tenant know that he would be coming for the truck, but first he had to clear everything with Roy. She offered to drive him up the hill to her trailer so he could phone Roy and give him the news. Reluctantly, he agreed to leave the truck. She thought he was going to put his arms across it and kiss it, but he limited himself to a pat on the driver's door.

In the trailer she made tuna melts while Joey phoned his father at work. Roy wasn't near the phone, so he left a message and then sat down at her kitchen table. They drank iced tea while the sandwiches toasted in a frying pan.

"What color are you going to paint it?" she asked, smiling.

"All black, with red and orange flames along the sides," he answered seriously, envisioning it.

Abby did, too. "That's good, you'll be able to find it in the mall parking lot on Thanksgiving weekend."

He smiled politely, barely following her reasoning, or barely interested.

She sat quietly, not wanting to intrude on his quiet euphoria. Finally, however, she let her natural nosiness get the better of her. "How is Roy treating you, Joey?"

He looked at her, a startled expression on his face. Then he glanced away quickly, and she could practically hear the barricades clanging into place. She wondered why he needed that protection, but maybe it was just a natural fear engendered by having a murdered parent, and spending a number of days in jail. Those things can make you paranoid.

"Is there anything I can help you with?"

He shook his head. "No. I'm fine. Roy's a good guy. He wouldn't do anything to hurt me."

Interesting choice of words. Abby nodded. "Well, if you ever need someone to talk to, I'm around."

"Yeah. Okay. But everything's okay. I just have to get through the trial. That's what Roy says. And then I'll be okay."

As if on cue, the phone rang. Abby answered, recognizing Roy's raspy voice on the other end. She handed the phone to Joey, and watched the boy lose his nervousness as he talked about the truck. When he was done, he held out the phone to her.

"He wants to speak to you."

"Yes, Roy," she said, after taking the receiver.

"So this is your truck?" He sounded diffident.

"I've got a yard full of rusted-out wrecks. You'd be doing me and the township a favor if you'd let him take one. He can work on it at your house." She glanced at Joey, who was watching her anxiously, willing her to convince him. "He's a good kid, it'll keep him out of trouble."

"I know that," Roy replied. "I just don't want any legal problems. You know, ownership, liability, that sort of thing."

"I don't have the original papers, but I'll find out from the DMV what I have to do. I'll make sure it's legally his."

There was a silence, then: "Well, that's real generous of you. I know he's happy about it. Tell him I'm coming around to get him, and then, if you don't mind, he can show it to me himself."

Abby sighed with relief, and gave him directions. When she hung up, Joey said stiffly: "Thanks for the truck. It's really cool."

She smiled at him. "Good. You deserve to have something make you happy."

He stood still and his face began to crumple into what she first thought was a smile. Then, to her dismay, he covered his face with his hands and turned away.

Abby put her hand on his shoulder. "Are you okay?"

He hunched over, his face still covered. "Yeah," he lied, the sound muffled by his hands. A racking sob shook him. Then another one. He bent over and cried hard, his whole body heaving, his hands over his eyes. Abby stood there, overcome by his sadness. She rubbed his back gently, the way one would do to a small child. For a while the sobs came stronger and faster. It seemed to her that Joey was keening under the tears, as if the rusted truck were responsible for breaking his heart. They stood like that for a long time. Finally, the strength of the outburst began to subside, and the sobs became fewer and farther apart. She picked up a box of tissues from the kitchen counter, and brought them back to him. He blew his nose, once, twice, gave a last hiccup, then sighed. Eventually he spoke.

"I'm happy about the truck." His face was wet from the tears and blotchy. "I'm happy to be out of that jail, and I feel bad that I'm happy, because my mom's dead. I'm scared they're going to say I did it, and I wonder, did I do it? Did I shoot my mom? Did I blank it out?"

As the words tumbled out of him, he looked at the floor, his eyes bloodshot from crying, the delicate skin around them swollen and red. It wasn't until she heard the distant whine of an engine climbing the hill that he turned to her and announced, wiping his eyes: "I heard someone in the house with my mother." He said it fast, as if he were afraid he might change his mind.

"What?" Abby wondered if she had heard correctly.

"Yeah, but you can't tell anyone. I came home earlier than I said, heard a voice with my mother, and left."

"Why didn't you tell the police?"

He shook his head. "They wouldn't have believed me anyway."

Abby was stunned. "But you can't decide that, it's something they should know. It could help them figure out what really happened."

"Forget it. If you tell the cops, I swear I'll tell them you made it up."

"You know who did it? Was it a man or a woman? Did you recognize the voice?"

Joey looked away. "Nope."

She tried to turn him to face her. "Okay, what were they talking about?"

He shook his head. "I don't know. But they were fighting, I know that. Or at least my mother was. I can always tell when she gets mad. Her voice gets all tight."

They had been so involved in their conversation, it wasn't until she heard a vehicle door slam outside that Abby realized Roy had arrived.

Joey turned to her. "Don't say anything to anybody, okay? I don't know why I told you. You swear, okay?"

Abby nodded, unable to come up with any other response. There was a knock at the door. She looked at Joey, who took a deep breath and squared his shoulders. He walked to the door, and she followed him outside to greet his father.

# CHAPTER TWENTY-ONE

S he was standing outside the trailer, watching Roy's truck turn down the last curve in the road, when her phone started ringing. She walked slowly inside, her mind whirling with what Joey had just told her. Someone in the house with his mother. Well, if she believed he was innocent, then that shouldn't come as a surprise. However, Joey as witness was another thing altogether.

Abby picked up the phone and said hello, her mind on Joey.

"Hello, Missy, it's your boss," rasped Cyrus Leighton, interrupting her thoughts.

She sighed. "Hi, Cyrus."

"Hi, doll, how's my house? Did you trash it yet?"

"Not badly. How's Sunny SoCal? I'm surprised they let you stay this long."

He chuckled. "Don't worry, they hate me. We're coming home tomorrow. You finished the work?"

"Yup, all done," she replied. She suddenly thought of something. "Tell me, Cyrus, where did you meet Al Roker?"

"Baby, you be nice to me, and I'll introduce you to him."

"I don't want to meet him. I want to know where *you* met him. Specifically, where that picture was taken."

"Day after tomorrow, I'll show you. Come by. I may even pay you. Now I gotta go. Lunch."

Abby's first stop was Cyrus and Paula's house. She made sure to wipe her feet carefully, and once inside, she went straight for the Al Roker photograph. She looked at the sideboard, seen near the window behind the weatherman. *It's a shame he and Cyrus were so damn large*, she thought to herself. Between the two of them, they took up most of the frame. She gave up. Taking one last look around to make sure everything was in order and the plants were watered, she left. There was nothing she was going to do about the dust that had settled on the surfaces of the room since Betty had last cleaned. If dirt was what it took to have someone mourn the woman, then so be it. A pretty meager memorial, she thought, as she locked the door and walked to her car.

It was dinnertime at the InnBetween, so she drove into Bantam and parked on Findlay, opposite the dentist's office. There were no parking spaces closer, which meant either the movie at the Kipling was good, or the restaurant was busy. She walked back to the Circle and let herself in the restaurant staff door.

She could tell by standing in the little anteroom that they were full. Waitstaff was slamming in the swing door from the dining room, and during those intervals when the door was open she could see Dan the Dishwasher, sprayer in hand, working in front of a huge pile of dirty plates. Behind him the kitchen roared, punctuated by the loud ding of the bell and George's holler of "Pick up!" heralding plates ready to go, lined up under the warmer. Abby had a vision of a delivery room, all the pain and mess hidden from view and a clean little bundle delivered to the nursery.

Sure enough, in the dining room every seat was taken. Dulcie was standing at a table, laughing at something a customer was saying. She took a credit card and came back to ring it up. When she saw Abby she looked hopeful. "You here to work?"

Abby shook her head. "No, I'm hungry. Can I eat at the bar?"

Dulcie stayed focused on the credit card machine. "Sure, go ahead. You may have a bit of a wait, though. We're backed up."

"Okay. I'll be downstairs if you need me."

Dulcie didn't answer, and Abby walked between the tables toward the dining room staircase. The room was noisy and energetic, full of loud talk, laughter, and argument punctuated by the clatter of glasses, knives and forks on plates, chairs scraping on the wood floor. She padded down the carpeted stairs. Here, though most of the tables were taken, the room was quieter, the sound muffled by the lower ceiling and wood paneling. Henry was bartending, a row of glasses in front of him. He glanced up at her, and went back to pouring out drinks. Luckily the bar itself was empty so she picked an end stool and sat down.

"Abby, stop, don't sit. You need to help me out here."

"Forget it, it's my night off." One of the pleasures of a night off, for any restaurant worker, is to be able to come in, sit through heavy traffic, and watch your coworkers sweat it out. It's the law of the jungle.

Henry ignored her. "I need six house reds, a Bass Ale, and two mojitos. Dulcie needs these upstairs and I've got food orders to bring down."

He wiped his hands on a towel, put his drinks on a tray, and slid the tray onto his right hand. Then he smiled knowingly at her: "Do this for me, and I'll owe you big-time. And I mean, big. Real big."

"Go away."

Henry flared his nostrils at her and moved around the bar, the drink-laden tray leading him gracefully up the stairs.

She wasn't able to be hard on Henry, and he knew it. She went behind the bar, and got to work mixing his drinks for him. When she heard footsteps on the stairs she glanced up. The Mullendores were walking down the stairs. Maurice was in front, and Ellie was following, her hand on his shoulder. After saying hello to Abby, they pulled out two stools. Ellie looked worried.

After she had arranged her jacket on the seat back, she asked: "It's so busy tonight, Maurice is afraid we'll be stuck down here for the rest of the evening." She said this as if she were being forced to spend the night in the New York City sewer system.

"Does Dulcie know you're here?" Abby asked, and when Ellie nodded, frowning, Abby reassured her: "Then she won't forget. Something will open up. Everyone comes all at once." She spoke in short sentences as if to comfort a small child, and she added on reassurances, because Ellie stayed looking concerned, and Abby didn't want her to burst into tears. She leaned on the bar and to distract her, Abby asked: "How is your house going?" She had heard they were doing some major renovations to their sprawling farmhouse.

Ellie sighed. "Well, you know what it's like. Builders, contractors, all that craziness. We're trying to keep part of the house livable, but it's not easy."

Henry came thumping down the stairs, picked up the tray of drinks, and left.

"Can I get you both something to drink?" By the time she had poured Ellie a white wine, and given Maurice a beer, Henry was back, swinging an empty tray. Abby came around the bar and sat down next to Ellie, who was still talking about her house. "The dirt and dust are incredible. I'm afraid we're going to have to wear masks. And the traffic. I mean, I don't know who half the people coming in and out are."

Abby nodded, as if sharing her pain. She thought of her little trailer. She knew when a new mouse moved in by the shifting of the structure on its foundation. She was glad she didn't have a house that was a life force of its own, even though it would be nice to have a little corner to accommodate houseguests once in a while. But then, no houseguest, no problem.

"What work are you doing, exactly?" She took a sip of her Myers and orange juice, and shifted on her stool.

Ellie looked as if she were trying to remember what had started all the fuss in the first place. "Well, they've taken off the back wall of the house, and they're adding a gorgeous structure, partially underground. A workout area below. Above ground all glass, a sort of greenhouse/family room. It's going to be really beautiful, if they ever finish it."

"Won't it be hot in the summer?"

"I asked the architect that, but he said no." She shrugged, as if she had to accept that, because architects are never wrong. "Right now, I wouldn't care if they hammered some plywood over the hole and left us alone. Maurice is away a lot, and I've been afraid to be alone since the break-in."

"You were broken into?"

Ellie laughed apologetically. "Not really, because everything was open. But we were robbed."

"That must've been horrible. Did they take a lot?"

"No, not too much, surprisingly. Just a couple of our bigger pieces."

"Bigger pieces? Of what? Art?" Maybe she was talking about sculpture. They were certainly patrons of the arts. They had a creation on their front lawn that looked like wagon wheels that had rusted together during the harsh winter of Aught-Five.

Ellie was about to answer when Dulcie came down the stairs, scanning the bar. She came over to the Mullendores, put an arm around each of them. Maurice was talking intensely to Henry about football. It's what happens to certain people when you sit them at a bar, even if there's no television. "Maurice, Ellie, thanks for waiting. You're all set," she said.

Ellie jumped up. "Oh, good."

Maurice laid his hands on the bar and pushed himself up. "Finally," he rasped, as if he'd been there for hours. They picked up their drinks, and started up the stairs. Abby called out: "Ellie, what did they take?"

Ellie turned and looked at her blankly. "Who?"

"The thieves. You said they took two pieces."

Ellie turned and kept walking. She talked as she disappeared from sight. "Oh. A hutch and a blanket chest. Pretty ones." Her feet were all that was left, and she was gone. Abby was reminded of the Cheshire cat in *Alice in Wonderland*.

Dulcie was following them up the stairs and she turned to look at Abby, her eyebrows raised, and mouthed: "What was that about?"

Abby mouthed back: "He's with the CIA."

Dulcie turned back to the stairs, and made a dismissive gesture with her right hand, as if pushing both Abby and her silliness away. But at the top of the stairs she looked back down at her, her eyes narrowed.

# CHAPTER TWENTY-TWO

It was past eleven by the time she drove out of Bantam. The wind was picking up as she turned off River Street. The mature maples that sheltered the Silvernale farmhouse seemed strangely agitated: a dark, living wall whose highest branches swayed and rustled against the night sky. There were no lights on at the farm where her husband was born and died, and it looked abandoned, haunted. She wondered if her tenants ever went on vacation. Selfishly, she hoped not. Their distant but steady presence was comforting. When she reached the dirt road that wound up the hill to her trailer, she put the Bronco into low gear. As she drove up the steep, rutted surface she listened sleepily to the whine of the engine, letting it tow her up the incline. In the distance, she heard the welcoming bark of her dogs and they sounded particularly loud, as if the breezy night were carrying the sound down to her, crisper and clearer than usual. The large glass of wine she had had with dinner lulled her into a pleasant state of calm.

She reached the flat parking area near her trailer, and, in the headlights of the car, she saw the dogs, barking and moving forward, as if they were avoiding the vehicle while herding it. Surprised, she braked, and turned off the engine. Before going to Cyrus's house, she was sure she had locked the dog door, which she usually did when she was going out in the evening. At night, they were better off indoors, unable to roam and safe from hungry coyotes. She was surprised to find them out, though it explained why their barks had sounded different from the bottom of the hill.

Abby climbed out, said hello, patted, said hello again. They kept whining and knocking against her, which was unusual. She ignored them and stood still, taking a moment to breathe in the fresh night air and look up at the deep, velvety night sky, speckled with stars. Nothing but a moment, her mind empty of thoughts, while she took in the perfection of the distance over her head, dark, but full of mysterious swathes of light and movement. Then the wind gusted, giving her a sudden chill that cut through her thin summer clothes. She walked quickly to the door of the trailer, the dogs at her side, and stopped while she examined her key chain, feeling for the right key. She had just put her fingers around it, when Delilah did something she didn't normally do. She jumped up, her front paws on the door.

"Deli, what're you doing—" she said automatically. But instead of resisting, the door made a popping sound, and swung open. The handle was broken and hanging from the hole in the door. It occurred to Abby, stupidly, that Delilah had broken it by jumping against it. She flipped the light switch, but nothing happened. She stood, her head a blank, looking in the dark entryway. On the linoleum tile in front of her she saw a black shape, barely visible, motionless. It might have been a bag of garbage, but a stray triangle of moonlight lay on it, causing that one geometric shape to shine dark and wet. The information may have been subliminal, or maybe there was a smell she wasn't consciously aware of. Whatever the reason, in that slow second she knew she was looking at a dead body. Her door was broken, and there was a dead body lying in her house.

Suddenly, those alarms that had refused to go off earlier all began clanging at the same time, and she reeled back in panic. She dropped her purse and ran back to the car, calling the dogs. They didn't want to come, and she screamed louder. The panic and urgency in her voice must have convinced them. Once she was in the car, Delilah jumped onto her lap, knocking the wind out of her. Rick climbed onto the passenger seat. She slammed the door and because her hand was trembling so hard, she had trouble inserting the key into the lock. Finally, she succeeded and the car started up with a roar. She pushed Delilah onto the passenger seat, where she and Rick sat, ears back, panting, their anxiety echoing her fear. She backed the Bronco out, kicking up gravel with her tires. The panic was making a white noise in her head and she turned the wheel and faced the car down the hill. Too fast, she bounced down the road, as if an army of goblins were chasing her.

At the Silvernale farm, Lloyd's hunting dog started baying and Rick and Delilah joined in. Abby ran up the porch steps and banged with the flat of her hand on the front door until Lloyd appeared, blinking and creased with sleep, Doreen behind him.

"I need help—they broke into my house—there's a body—" Abby pointed up the hill, as if it were the culprit.

While Lloyd and Doreen went to get dressed, Abby waited anxiously in the front room of the farmhouse for the police to arrive. At first she paced, and then, when her breathing had slowed down, she took the time to look around. The room looked very different from the way she remembered it. Two years before it had been filled with the Silvernales: the couch a high-backed plaid, with covers over the arms when the fabric had given up; across from it a Morris chair covered in red velour, the seat worn, a faint smell of Grandpa's pipe tobacco released each time anyone rocked back and forth; pictures of Grandma as a young girl standing with her two sisters on a beach, all three wearing black bathing suits; Grandpa as a boy, sitting on the porch with a red fox in his lap; a group photo in the Sunday best, standing proudly in front of a Ford Fairlane; Jonah's dad, a baby in Grandma's arms. And on the surface, a modern and untidy dusting of Abby and Jonah: their movies, books, magazines.

Now, the room looked neat and suburban, with a patterned couch and two matching chairs, a few dried flower arrangements, and the only photograph was a family portrait on the mantelpiece, the edges an oval of soft focus. For the first time since Jonah's death, Abby felt an unexpected nostalgia for the old farmhouse, with all its ghosts and clutter. Jonah would laugh at this room, she thought to herself. But she thought the house accommodated the new look without a fight. Abby sat down on the impersonal plaid couch, leaned back, and shut her eyes.

Within ten minutes, two young officers drove up. They listened politely to Abby's story, and decided the best course of action was for the police car to lead the way, and for her and Lloyd to follow. When the two vehicles reached the top of her driveway, Abby and her tenant sat in the Bronco and watched as the officers got out of their car and, with lit flashlights, walked slowly toward her open front door. After a pause, they disappeared inside.

When they came out, one of the two men said something, and the other laughed. Abby opened her car door and got out, making sure to keep the dogs inside. Lloyd followed her.

"So?" asked Abby, gesturing with her chin to the door. The officer who had been laughing cleared his throat.

"You're not going to believe this," he said, scratching his chin, "but some joker threw a deer carcass through your front door."

The other officer crossed his arms. "Yup. Looks like you made an enemy somewhere."

Abby held out her hand to the first officer. "Can I borrow that?" she asked, gesturing to his flashlight. He hesitated, as if it were against regulations, then handed it over. "Sure."

Abby took it, turned it on, and walked slowly toward the trailer. She stood in the doorway, the broken latch tinkling uselessly when she touched it. She turned the bright beam into the small entrance. Now, she could clearly see where the dark blood had pooled on the linoleum. It was already dull and sticky looking, and the smell was metallic and sweet. Past it, the barrel body created a mound, its white underbelly gleaming in the light. Seeing it lying there, a sight made familiar on country roads, she wondered how she had ever thought it was human.

An hour and a half later she was standing outside her trailer, wearing a warm jacket, watching the locksmith attach a deadbolt to the inside of her front door. He had explained to her that the metal door was bent and would not take a new lock properly, but the bolt would get her through what was left of the night and they could find her a new door in the morning. The dogs were shut in her bedroom, watching everything through the window. They had howled when Lloyd and the cops had removed the bloodied carcass.

Turns out, either before or after the freshly-killed deer had been put in her hall, the power had been turned off at the main switch in the kitchen. Was it done with the intention that, in the dark, she would believe she was looking at a human body? As she stood there watching the locksmith work, she thought over the whole scenario. The police had filed a report, but because nothing seemed to be stolen or destroyed other than her front door, she doubted the incident would get much attention. Abby knew what had really happened. The act wasn't one of vandalism, nor was it a mean prank. It was a threat. She felt violence in the air, like the strong smell of blood that still lingered. Unwillingly, her mind conjured up the image of the body of the girl in the woods, her face blackened and partially missing, the night around her thick and airless. Abby breathed deeply, unwittingly trying for air. Her exhalation sounded like a sigh.

The locksmith glanced at her, then back at the bolt. He straightened up. "Done. You call me in the morning, and we'll sort this out, okay?" He fished a bent card out of his tool chest and handed it to her.

Abby took it and nodded, suppressing an urge to grab his arm and beg him to stay.

He must've read her mind. "You gonna be okay?"

"I'm fine. Really." She tried to keep the need out of her voice.

He looked at her, raising his eyebrows. "You got no idea who did this to you?"

"No."

"You got anyone can come stay with you?"

"No," she repeated, adding, "I'll be fine, really."

He kicked the lid of his tool chest, and it closed with a clang. He shut the clasps, picked it up, and walked heavily to his pickup. She shut the bent door and shot the shiny, new bolt. Outside, the darkness closed in behind the vanishing headlights of the kindly locksmith, who could possibly be, she thought grimly, the last person on earth to see her alive.

When he was gone, she released the dogs, who ran immediately to the entrance of the trailer, their noses to the ground. The smell of the blood had kept them in a state of excitement, and now they were finally being allowed to explore the source. Sadly for them, most of it was gone. Abby had scrubbed up the blood and mopped the floor with a strong antiseptic. "Tough shit, vampires," she said.

Abby didn't sleep much that night. She sat in her kitchen with the lights off, so she could see outside before anyone looking in saw her. She drank tea, and when that got old, she opened a bottle of well-aged port someone had given her a couple of birthdays ago. She wrote sloppy lists of suspects, crossing off motives and replacing them with deeper, darker ones. Just as she was giving up on ever seeing daylight, the night became less dense, and the sky went from black to dark gray, and then to pale. Suddenly exhausted, she left her glass of port on the table and walked shakily to bed. As she was falling asleep, she remembered with a start what she had thought when she first realized she was looking at a corpse. She had thought the body belonged to Jonah.

# CHAPTER TWENTY-THREE

Two days later, she went back to the Leightons'. This time their gray Volvo was parked in the driveway and she braced herself as she walked up the path to the front door. She held the Number 1 house keys in her hand, ready to return them. She knocked on the door, and when no one answered, she knocked again, this time harder.

"Patience, goddamn it," she heard from the other side of the door. It opened. Cyrus stood in front of her, a food-stained robe hanging open to reveal striped pajamas. The buttons on his pajama top were not aligned properly, and she could see a large, sagging breast covered in gray hair. She kept her eyes averted.

"Welcome home, Cyrus."

"Where's my disc?"

"Thank you, yes, I'm well. Your disc is with your notepads. Just where it belongs, Cyrus. May I, Cyrus?" Abby walked past him into the living room. She went into his office. She could hear the shuffle of Cyrus's slippers behind her.

"Don't Cyrus me, missy. If you lost it, I'll—"

Abby opened the cupboard and gestured inside. Sure enough, sitting on the stack of yellow legal pads was a disc in its jewel case.

"Why didn't you say so?" he grumbled.

"I did," she reminded him. "I left you a note."

She gestured to the photograph of Cyrus and Al Roker. "So, where was it taken?"

Cyrus shook his head at her ignorance. "Where the hell does it look like it was taken? In this house, this house you've been fornicating in, having orgies in, where my plants are dying, where my furniture is being stolen—"

"What do you mean, Cyrus?" She raised her voice, interrupting his ravings. Just then, Paula appeared in the doorway. She was also in her dressing gown, holding a cup of coffee. She, however, looked presentable.

"I thought I heard voices," she said sweetly. "Hello, Abby dearest."

Abby smiled at her quickly, unable to give her her full attention. "Good morning, Paula. Have fun in California? Cyrus, you had furniture stolen?"

"You bet your fuckin' ass I did, and those cocksucker Keystone cops in Bantam haven't done a goddamn thing about it—"

"Oh, Cy," Paula interrupted. "Stop being so silly."

"Paula, goddamnit, don't be an idiot."

"Cyrus, please. Just tell me what happened. What was stolen?" Abby didn't want a domestic spat to escalate into a brawl, at least not while she was there.

Suddenly, there was silence. She waited. She could hear and see Cyrus's labored breathing.

"Darling, are you okay?" Paula looked concerned.

He ignored her. "Why do you want to know what was stolen?" He spoke slowly, suspiciously.

"Jesus, because I noticed in that picture of you with Al Roker there was a sideboard behind you, and it's not there anymore. I wondered if you moved it to the city, or sold it. That's all."

"It was stolen," he growled. "Last year, when we were in town."

"Were you broken into?" She tried to ask gently. Understandably, a sore subject.

"No. We got up on Friday night and everything seemed fine. Then on Saturday we were having company and Paula was setting the table. She went to the sideboard to get the good dishes, and the fuckin' sideboard was gone." His voice began to go up again in volume.

"Disappeared," added Paula.

"You didn't notice when you came home?"

"No, we didn't fucking notice. We don't do an inventory every time we walk through the fucking door."

"Was anything else missing?" Abby asked gently, looking from one to the other.

Cyrus answered her. "No, nothing else was missing, but it was pretty fucking weird to realize that someone had come into our house, and carefully taken the most valuable piece of furniture in the damn place, and carried it the fuck out, dishes and all."

"Limoges dishes. Bastards." Paula was the Greek chorus.

"Definitely weird," Abby agreed.

"Weird is an understatement, lady."

"Hey, Cyrus, I was just agreeing with you."

He raised his gravelly voice a notch. "I'm not looking for someone to agree with me. If I wanted someone to agree with me, I'd hire a fuckin' hooker, and I'd make her—"

God, the son of a bitch was easy to dislike. She started to move toward the door. "I gotta run. Here's my invoice, listing all the hours I worked." She handed him the envelope and his keys.

He took them. "First, you tell me what this is all about. The furniture." He looked at her stonily.

"It's really nothing much," she said, reluctantly. "Just an idea of mine."

"So go on." Cyrus pulled out a chair at the dining room table and sat down slowly, a sigh escaping him like air from a balloon. Paula looked on expectantly.

"Well, I was talking with the Mullendores last night, and it turns out, they've had a couple of nice pieces of furniture taken. They weren't broken into, but someone knew the layout, knew what they had, and took advantage of the construction to just walk in. Your robbery kind of reminds me of that. No damage, no TVs or stereos, just some nice antiques."

"Humm." Cyrus strummed his fingers on the table. "So you think the same people did it?"

Abby shrugged. "I think there's a good chance there's a connection. Did Betty work for the Mullendores?"

Cyrus waved the question away as if it were absurd. "Betty was a sour old bitch, but she was no thief."

"Oh, God no," reiterated Paula. "She was so uptight. I mean, look at her with that boy."

"Yeah," agreed Cyrus, "you know that expression 'spare the rod, spoil the child'? That was Betty. Didn't surprise me when the kid blew her away."

"I have an idea." Paula stood up. "Why don't I call the Mullendores? Maybe I can find out something."

Paula stood in the kitchen talking to Ellie Mullendore, while Abby and Cyrus waited, watching her and listening to her side of the conversation. The women seemed to be on good terms, which surprised Abby because she had never seen them together at the restaurant.

"Yak, yak, yak," muttered Cyrus.

"They're friends?" Abby asked.

"They're on some board together." Cyrus shook his head, as if the two women had been caught mooning traffic from an overpass. He would probably have looked more kindly on mooning.

"Of course, the hospital." Abby remembered the stationery given to her by Sally DeCintio.

Paula hung up and turned to her audience, her eyes bright with anticipation. "Guess what?" she said, looking from one to the other.

Cyrus groaned. "No, no, damn it, no guessing. Tell us right now."

Paula shook her head. "Sorry, you have to guess. Come on, Abby, guess what Ellie said." She practically squealed with delight, knowing they'd be stumped.

"It's a long shot," said Abby, "but do they use the Callahan brothers to mow their lawns?"

Paula's face was nearly comical as it changed from elation to dismay. "You cheated. You heard what she said."

Abby felt like a killjoy. "I'm sorry, but it wasn't out of the blue. Everywhere I turn, I run into those guys. And I know a lot of people use them, so it was a pretty safe bet, you know?"

Cyrus stood up. "Hey, Paulie, don't let it get to you. I would never have guessed."

She looked at him fondly. "I know, baby." She rubbed her nose on his cheek.

Abby took this as her time to exit. "I should go." She pointed at the bill. "I'll send you a check." Cyrus held up the white envelope.

"Cyrus," she narrowed her eyes at him, "I could use the money."

Paula burst out laughing, sunshine restored. "Good girl. Go on, Grouchy, pay the girl. And give her a bonus." She winked at Abby. What a pair, thought Abby as she watched a sullen Cyrus shuffle into his office.

Instead of heading back toward Bantam, Abby turned east. Something had occurred to her while she was at the Leightons', and it all came back to Joey. She drove up Roy's steep road, her mind turning things over and picking through them, like someone who has found one right shoe in a sale bin and just needs to find the left one to go home satisfied.

She was relieved to see that Roy's pickup was gone. She parked the Bronco, climbed out, and banged on the front door. No answer. She heard a metallic clanging sound and followed it around the house. On the back lawn, the truck she had given Joey was up on cement blocks. She saw no sign of the boy, until she noticed a pair of legs sticking out from under the rusted body. She walked over and kicked the shredded sneakers, none too gently. She heard a bang and grunt from under the truck. It sounded as if he'd hit his head.

"Shit." His voice was muffled.

"Joey, come out."

He pulled himself out from under the truck. He was streaked with dirt and grease, but he smiled broadly when he saw her.

"Hey, Abby," he said, climbing to his feet. He grabbed a rag that was hanging from the open window of the truck and started wiping his hands.

"We need to talk," Abby said, her voice stern.

Joey withdrew visibly, stiffening. "That don't sound so good." For the first time, he reminded her of his father.

Abby found an upturned milk crate, checked it for dirt, and sat down. "You know the Callahan brothers," she said, as a statement of fact.

Joey shrugged, not understanding. "So? I go to school with B. J."

"He the little one?"

"No, one up. So what?"

"Tell me about furniture." She watched him carefully.

"Furniture? What about furniture?" She noticed he wasn't looking her straight in the eye.

"Stolen furniture. That ring any bells?"

"I don't know anything about anything stolen." He was still wiping his hands with the rag, though the action was now repetitive, limited to the palm of his left hand. Out, out damned spot. Maybe. But there was no turning back.

"Joey, there are so many damn coincidences lately. Look at this. Your poor mother is brutally shot. A girl you know and admire is beaten to death and her body left in the woods. On top of that," she went on, "I've been running into people who hire the Callahans to mow their lawns, and their furniture gets stolen. Funny, huh? But wait, there's more. These people who have been robbed are also on the hospital board, which means they probably hosted parties for the hospital. I know the Leightons did. How about the Mullendores? Everyone throwing these big old fund-raisers. The robberies were obviously committed by people who knew the houses, who had access, and who could pick and choose. So what's going on, Joey? What d'you know about this?"

Joey shook his head, threw the rag into the back of the pickup, and crossed his arms. "Sorry, I can't help you."

"Yes you can, you idiot." Abby stood up angrily. "Your mother is dead, Joey, Connie is dead, thrown in the woods like so much garbage and for all I know, it was over a few fucking hutches. I think you know something or had some part in this and I want to know what. I want the whole fucking picture, okay? People are getting killed, and I think it's all tied together."

She kept her eyes locked on his, knowing that if he looked away she would have achieved nothing. Neither of them moved until Joey took a deep, unsteady breath.

"They're going to kill me."

Abby felt a wash of relief. Okay. Good. "Why? What's going on?"

Joey scratched his head. "All I know is I borrowed my mom's keys to Mr. Leighton's house, and we went in one morning real early."

"Was it still dark?"

"Just getting light. Dawn," he added, as if he had just remembered the word. "It was during the week because we knew they'd be in the city. We went in and we took this big chest. We brought boxes and packed all the plates and stuff and took them, too."

"Who's we? Who'd you go with?"

Joey hesitated.

"Goddamn it, Joey—"

"Me, B. J., and Richie."

Abby nodded. "Ah, Richie. Is he the boss? Or is it someone else, maybe Sean Kenna?"

Joey frowned. "Sean? The plumber? No, no, it was Connie."

Abby was stunned. "Connie?"

Joey nodded, taking some satisfaction in knowing he had surprised her. "Yeah. She would check out all the houses during the parties, decide which one had the goods, do the research. She was into it."

Abby shook her head in amazement. "Jesus. Did your mother find out? Is that what happened?"

Joey walked away, then turned back and looked at her. He fidgeted. Abby thought of the children's rhyme: *liar, liar, pants on fire.* "I swear, I don't know anything about who killed my mother. Or about Connie. I don't know anything about the other furniture. I never stole anything else, just that fucking chest. I wish I had never seen it."

Abby walked over to him. "Don't try to protect anyone. There are some very serious people out there, who are only looking out for themselves, and you spend a lot of time alone on this hill." She studied the young boy in front of her. "Why d'you do it, Joey? The money?"

"I don't know. It was exciting. I guess I felt like a badass. I knew that if my mother knew, she'd go through the roof."

Yeah, that's what Abby was afraid happened. They stood for a moment in silence.

Finally, she said: "You have to go to the police. They need to know, it's important. They'll find out anyway, and you'll be in a lot worse trouble if you don't tell."

Joey nodded.

There was nothing more to say, so Abby turned to go. She was just about to round the building, when she thought of something.

"One last thing. What car did you guys use to do the job? Richie's pickup?"

Joey looked surprised at her interest. "No, someone might recognize it. We used some old blue minivan that Connie found for us. She said it was untraceable."

There it was. Dulcie's car. So maybe there never had been a lover. Maybe just a bad habit of stealing other people's property.

Joey looked at his hands, as if surprised to see the oily grime under the fingernails. "I wish I hadn't done it. All the time. I know it was because of that chest that someone killed my mother. Some weird link I don't know about."

Abby wondered if he could be lying.

He kept talking, still looking at his hands. "The things you do keep coming back at you, don't they? Maybe they change shape, but they keep lookin' for you, ready to knock you down."

Abby shook her head, not bothering to curb a rush of impatience at the boy's take on life.

"Most of us don't act alone, so don't take all the blame. But yeah, if you're saying we reap what we sow, I'd have to agree with you. Tell me, why do you think Connie wanted you in on this? Did she want to get you into trouble?"

His smile had a twist to it, his admiration for the dead girl only slightly tarnished. "I don't think so. She was a daredevil kind of person. My mother called her a troublemaker, but I think she was just looking for fun. You know, excitement?"

Abby shook her head. "Too much excitement for me, Joey." She took her car keys out of her pocket. "I've got to head back to town. Promise me you'll talk to the chief? 'Cause if you don't, I will."

The next step seemed to be to go to see Franklin. He needed to know what his client had done. He could also tell her if she was obligated to tell all this to the Leightons, considering that they had hired Betty in the first place. The fine points of law escaped her, actually the rough general ones did, too, but she did have her own sense of right and wrong. But the first thing was to give Franklin the information, in case he could do anything with it to protect Joey, or keep one step ahead of the prosecutor's office.

On the drive back to Bantam, Abby asked herself the question she had been avoiding, which was, did Betty find out, and did Joey and his mother quarrel over the stolen chest, not about books left on the kitchen table? If they had a knockdown, drag-out fight, Betty could easily have threatened to turn him in. Abby was sure that a single parent must feel overwhelmed by an angry young boy who breaks the law. Powerless. So let's say Betty threatened to report him. Abby tried to picture the scene, the anger and tears, the threat of betrayal. Maybe, in the heat of the moment, Joey picked up the shotgun and fired it, blowing a hole through his mother's chest and leaving her to bleed out on the living room floor.

By now, Abby was back on Main Street. She pulled into an empty parking space in front of the health food store. Franklin was in, and she sat opposite him in his office and told him everything. She told him about Sean's late night visit, Joey's confessing to having heard someone with his mother, the stolen furniture and the break-in at her trailer and the corpse left in her entrance way.

When she was done, Franklin took a deep breath. "Christ. You must be getting someone mad. Abby, you've got to be careful. Do you have anyone you can stay with for a while?"

She thought about it, and shook her head. No one would want her and her two dogs. And she didn't want to leave her trailer. "I'm fine. I'll keep a low profile."

"You really like sniffing around, don't you?" Franklin asked her, his head tilted to one side as if he were questioning a bug-eyed child who liked to eat her own hair. "Maybe you should join the police force, or the FBI, or something."

Abby felt extremely proud of herself when he said that. Not that she would ever join an organization like that. She'd have to go back to school and train, answer to someone and punch a time clock, get a paycheck and benefits, and finally a pension. That would be getting in way too deep. "Thanks, but I think I'll stick with being a waitress. At least I'm my own boss, you know?"

Franklin shook his head. Hopeless, his expression seemed to say. "Well, let's move on. So, a ring of furniture thieves, with Connie as their fearless leader. The Callahan boys, and maybe Sarah. Who else? Was Sean Kenna part of it?"

"I don't think so. But I think he may have known something about it, because he was friends with all those guys and he was going out with Connie."

"How do you think the two murders are connected? Or are they connected?"

Abby considered his question. "Well, they have to be, don't they? I mean, two murders. One victim is a member of the ring, and the other the housekeeper of a home that was robbed and the mother of a budding thief. I can see how Betty's murder might have happened if she threatened them with the police. I mean, people kill to avoid going to jail, right? My question is, what did Connie do to deserve being beaten to death and dumped in the woods? And which one of them did it?"

Franklin rested his head on his hand. "Maybe she had had enough. Maybe she was going to give up her life of crime and the rest of them wouldn't let her. Remember the minivan. She was smiling when you saw her, right?"

Abby had forgotten about the minivan. "You're right. Sarah is the one who told me Connie had a rich boyfriend—but I don't know if she made that up. No one else seems to be able to confirm it. Joey didn't know anything about it, and the lady at the hospital said she didn't go away at the same time as any of the staff. None of her coworkers knew of anyone. I mean, when a girl is having an affair, she'll usually tell someone."

Franklin nodded thoughtfully. After a pause he said: "I think you've done all you can do. Don't poke around anymore, Abby. Those people are obviously very dangerous, and you should let the police take care of the rest."

Strangely enough, as she walked to her car, Abby felt deflated. She should have been excited, she had helped find some bad guys. *I mean*, she thought ruefully, *nothing like nabbing those struggling farmers who are stealing from the rich to pay the taxes on their overpriced land, so as not to lose it to those same rich people who want dig it up and build obnoxious, oversized designer mansions on it.* But maybe she was giving the Lawnmower Boys too much credit. Maybe they were just thieves and murderers. Which brought her back to Connie and Betty.

# CHAPTER TWENTY-FOUR

So there she was, back on Main Street. With no particular place to go, as the song says, so she responded to the invisible bungee cord, and headed home. Though these days, her little trailer seemed less welcoming than it used to. She unlocked her new door, sniffing the air to see if she could smell blood. The dogs rushed outside. The sun was shining off the trailer's mustard walls, the honeysuckle cozily embracing its fat, stubby body. She saw her home for what it was, a tin box: frail, vulnerable, and without foundation. She didn't take her usual comfort from its adaptability, its lighthearted cheapness. It seemed as transient as everything in her life, as unreliable as all the people she cared about and as easy to open as a can of beans. Inside, it was unwelcoming and dull, the windows filmy, everything on the desk looking as if it had been sitting there too long, out of date, useless. She went into her bedroom and threw herself on her unmade bed. She thought about dead deer and teenage boys. She thought about Joey, alone, working on his truck. When he towed it Roy had left a bald, torn scar in the farm's landscape. Which reminded Abby of Sean Kenna. Her stomach tensed, and she rolled onto her side. She stared at the wall, at the Hudson River Bank calendar. The house with the porch, now a week out of date. Her mind emptied out, waiting for Jonah to seep back in, bringing with him the guilt that was strangely comforting and familiar. She waited for the memories to float easily toward her as they usually did, coating her with sensory awareness, taking her back, filling her with sadness. And as she waited, something slightly different happened. They didn't float. Instead, she realized she was actually dragging them her way. She was using muscle, trying to force her way to that sad, dark place. She was like someone who slides her feet into a worn pair of slippers, expecting warmth, but instead finds her soles in contact with the stone floor underneath. The familiar seemed suddenly worn out, used up. And the cold was shocking.

Abby lay motionless. She tried again. No, her mind wouldn't go there effortlessly, as it usually did. Tentatively, she allowed a sense of relief to fill the vacuum. She looked out the window and watched a sparrow land on the branch of a nearby tree. It was pecking at something. It hopped a few inches along, and pecked again. She wondered what it had found.

Eventually, she got up and found Sean's pager number in her wallet and called him. She lay on her bed while she waited until he called back. He did, about fifteen minutes later, and she asked if they could meet for a cup of coffee. He said he would meet her at The Bakery, on the corner of Route 46 and 103. She hung up and lay down again. The sparrow was still on the branch, busy. She watched it until it was time to go.

If Victor's Café is where the artists and nouveau locals hang out, The Bakery is where the dyed-in-the-wool inhabitants hang their baseball caps. Until the law changed, it was one of the few places you could smoke a cigarette after your coffee and bacon and eggs. Sean was nowhere in sight. She was told to take any table she wanted, so she found a corner booth and slid onto the banquette that faced the dining room. She read the menu, just to look busy.

Sean showed up about twenty minutes later. He apologized for keeping her waiting, and sat down opposite her. She found herself admiring all over again his dark, intense looks. He looked like a poet, not a plumber. He took the menu out of her hands.

"So what's up, Abby? Are we through, or moving in together?"

She was ready. "I don't think we can see each other anymore, Sean."

He looked away, then looked back. "I came on a little too strong the other night, right?"

"Yup." She thought for a moment and then continued. "I don't have what it takes to be with someone right now. I'm finally beginning to accept being on my own."

Sean rubbed his chin, and she could hear the bristle scraping against his hand. "Well, don't leave it too long. There may not be anyone out there when you decide you're ready."

She laughed out loud. "Kiss my ass, Sean." But she didn't get angry. He was allowed a little meanness, given he'd just been dumped.

"Why did you want to see me? You couldn't break up with me over the phone?"

"It seemed better to do it face-to-face. I was hoping there'd be no hard feelings. I had a great time with you."

He shook his head and let out a kind of snort. "I always have hard feelings. And I thought that was one of the things you liked about me." This was said with a halfhearted leer. Then he shook his head, and opened the menu dismissively. "I better order, I gotta get back to work."

Abby started to stand, then thought better of it and sat back down. "Sean, can I ask you a question?" she said softly. He looked up at her, his eyebrows raised in surprise, as if she were a stranger interrupting his meal. After a pause, he nodded.

She took a breath. "Why did you and Connie break up? Is it true you were seeing someone else?"

Sean put his menu down, leaned forward. "You don't get it about me, do you? I get *attached*. I was committed to Connie. I never looked at anyone else. No, she was the one, not me. *She* was fucking someone else, and told *me* to take a hike. So I did." He raised his menu like a wall between them. Abby slid out of her seat and stood next to the table.

She hesitated before leaving. One more thing to ask him.

"Do you know who it was? Who else she was seeing?"

Sean didn't look up, just ignored her. She left the restaurant. Sitting in her car in the parking lot, she glanced at the restaurant windows. She could see Sean to the far right, facing an empty banquette, the only thing in his field of vision a blank wall. He was still holding his menu but it had moved down and he was staring over the top of it.

Abby wondered if Sean had been telling her the truth. Would he lie about something like that? Rather than letting him off the hook, his story seemed to give him a good reason for killing Connie. Jealousy was a perfectly good motive, and she had seen that Sean could get physical when he felt slighted. On the other hand, grabbing her arm didn't make him the kind of person who could dump his lover's mangled body in the woods, then go out for a beer.

# CHAPTER TWENTY-FIVE

J oey must've kept his word, because over the next few days he was at the police station quite a bit, according to "church" gossip. This was confirmed by the owner of the health food store, whose sister worked for the mayor. Abby knew about the sister, so she had made a point of going in to buy a bar of Belgian chocolate, the only thing she could find worth spending her money on at the health food store. The next day, she tried calling the chief, but he snapped at her, telling her not to call him unless she had a genuine problem. Abby had been hoping to see the Lawnmower Boys being walked single file into the station, linked to each other like a chain gang. She had been especially looking forward to seeing Sarah from the drugstore making her way up those steps. But nothing happened, so she was eventually forced to turn her mind to other things.

The weekend of the Fourth of July was set for big festivities. Saturday, there was going to be a street fair on Main Street, then the parade on Sunday the

Fourth, with fireworks scheduled to start at 9:00 P.M. in the fairgrounds. People were working hard and looking forward to it. If you drove past the middle school you might see the band marching across the soccer field, the civilian T-shirts, cutoff shorts, and flip-flops in high contrast to the martial trumpeting and crashing of the instruments and the serious expressions of the marchers. Old Glory was hanging from porches, and at the restaurant the reservation book was filling up. The pages were covered in names and numbers, some of which had been erased and added to as parties grew bigger.

Early on Tuesday evening, before they opened the door to customers, Abby was on the phone taking a reservation for six for Friday night. When she hung up, Henry, standing next to her polishing forks, swiveled the book around so he could glance at it.

"How're we doing?" he asked. For busy holiday reservations, they used a map of the dining room so they could actually plan where to place people as they booked them. They knew how many seatings each table would handle, and they took reservations accordingly. When Henry saw how many little squares were filled at least once, if not twice, his ears seemed to move up half an inch when he smiled.

"Shit. We're gonna make some money. About fuckin' time." He peered more closely. "Hey, don't book 'em all at the same time." He was looking at the times she had put next to the names.

"They're staggered. As much as they can be, considering everyone wants dinner at dinnertime. Crazy people."

"We're gonna get slammed."

Abby shrugged. "Better than standing around watching the bread get stale."

Which Henry had to agree with, knowing it is bad karma in a restaurant to complain about being overbooked and busy. Much worse than running all night is to stand around, shifting your weight from one foot to the other while you wait for someone to walk in the door.

That night, Tuesday, was one of those nights. Abby had come to work early, and ended up "going to church" with the kitchen staff before opening hours. She, George, and Sandy sat on the upstairs porch drinking espresso and gossiping. Actually, she just listened. She heard who was cheating on whom, where, and how often. She found out that the motel most favored by local adulterers was Frankie's Motel, on Route 9, because the parking lot is out of sight from the road. She also heard how much they were charging for prime rib in Tribeca, and that the new French bistro in Great Barrington was using frozen French fries for their pommes frites.

That evening it felt as if everyone were staying home, building up party points for the long weekend. Abby spent a good amount of time refilling salt shakers, waiting for customers to come in. She thought of Friday night's reservations, which made her think of the expression "making hay while the sun shines," and how it applies to restaurant workers on major holidays. The hay image reminded her of the Callahan brothers, the farmers. They were making hay, and then some, she thought, and nodded, cynically. They were baling hay, they were manufacturing hay in the basement, they were spinning hay into gold, no, wait, spinning grass cuttings into gold. She couldn't get herself to stop. It was a relief when Dulcie called her name to let her know she had customers at one of her tables. She screwed on her last salt-shaker top, and went to work.

When they finally finished cleaning up for the evening, it was only 10:00 P.M. She called Mike Testarossa from the restaurant phone. The machine was on, but she talked into it, guessing that he was probably screening his calls.

"Mike, it's Abby Silvernale. I was wondering if I could stop by sometime. You can call me back. I'm at the InnBet—"

There was a click. "I'm here," he interrupted.

"Oh, hi, Mike." She hesitated, unsure of what to say.

"You want to come over now?"

"Oh, okay. Sure. Thanks. I'll be there in a few—" but he hung up before she could finish her sentence.

Abby parked in Mike's driveway. This time Connie's car was gone. She wondered if the police had taken it. She knocked on the same door she had used the only other time she had been there, the door into the kitchen. When no one answered, she opened it and peered in. The room was dim, lit only by a single fluorescent light above the stove. The light cast a bluish glow over the fixtures, and the courting couples on the walls were now nothing more than dark shapes, oversize gray masses against the lighter wall.

"Mike?"

"Come in." His voice came from the next room, so she followed the sound. The living room was even darker than the kitchen, but she could make out a human shape on the couch.

"Mike, I can't see anything. I need to turn on a light." She stood, waiting for him to do something. When he didn't, she ran her hand down the wall. She found a wall switch and flipped it. A small chandelier on the ceiling popped on, exploding the room into harsh white light.

Mike was sunk into the couch, a hand over his eyes to protect them from the glaring brightness. She looked around. The room was a formal sitting room. The floor was carpeted in deep pile, in a light shade of blue, and the couch and armchairs were upholstered in mustard yellow. A tall, amber glass lamp sat on a side table and Abby reached under the shade, fumbling for the switch. When it clicked on, she turned off the overhead light. The room became cavelike and gloomy, but at least it didn't feel like an interrogation chamber. She took a breath. "Hey, Mike. Thanks for letting me come over."

Mike dropped his hand from his face. The skin around his eyes looked puffy and his whites were bloodshot. She noticed that the phone and answering machine were on the end table next to him, blinking incessantly with unanswered calls. The coffee table in front of him had three dirty glasses on it, and a closed plastic container. Maybe the neighbors were bringing food. Other than that, the room seemed tidy, but it was stuffy, the air old. She glanced at the windows, all shut tight. The room was probably not used much. There was a small rug on the carpeted floor, red with a yellow and blue border. Glass figurines covered all surfaces. As she looked more closely, she realized that they were all hummingbirds. Audubon-style framed prints were lined up, evenly, on the walls. The subjects were more hummingbirds.

"My wife decorated this room," Mike said, looking around slowly, his voice hoarse. "Used it only on special occasions, guests, Christmas, stuff like that. Connie used to love this room, she'd sneak in here with her friends and they'd play games. We usually knew when she was in here, but we'd pretend we didn't, kept it special, you know? They'd dress up in her mother's clothes and have parties. Once or twice we made a big thing of catching her here, but it never stopped her, just made her a little sharper the next time.

"You know, maybe it's my fault, maybe I let her think lying and pretending was okay. And in the end some creep"—Mike paused, the thoughts he was having too vivid, too painful—"and now it's too late for me to help her. If I'd just raised her right, told her that some things you don't do, if I'd made her go to college. I mean, she was smart, so maybe she was just wasted here in this town, working that no-end job, getting her kicks sneaking around making fools of people."

Abby sat down on the couch next to him and reached for his hand, but ended up holding his wrist, like a nurse taking a patient's pulse. "Mike, she was a big girl. Like you said, she was a smart girl. She made her own choices. And nothing she did was that bad, but she just ran into the wrong person, and nothing can change that. It's not your fault. It's terrible, but you didn't do anything wrong, you loved her. You can't blame yourself for this, you can't."

The pain in his face was intense. It seemed to have leached the blood out of his lips and cheeks. Abby sat next to him, feeling his heart beating in his wrist. She wondered if maybe he was right, if he had let his little girl get away with too much and not taught her that once you cross the line maybe you move into some other territory. Maybe he should have rechanneled that energy and seen to it that she learned something safer, like being a tour guide in Rwanda, or racing motorcycles. Because whatever she was messing around with had turned out to be much more dangerous. But hindsight, as they say, is perfect vision. And maybe she, Abby, could have made sure that Jonah kept going to his shrink, or had him committed to a hospital where they could have helped him. Or loved and supported him more. And maybe blah, blah, blah. Hell, by tomorrow she could end up like that deer flung in her trailer, so who's to know what's the right choice?

Mike's eyes were fixed on a place she couldn't see. She knew that he had a long road ahead of him. A lot worse than hers, she sensed, because losing a child, now that must feel like the end of the line.

"Mike, I'm going to Connie's room to look for a photograph of her. Is that okay?"

He nodded. "But I need it back."

Upstairs, Connie's room was now part of an investigation. Even though some care had been taken to replace her things, there was a sense of things trampled and handled that hadn't been there before. They had obviously dusted for fingerprints and searched the room thoroughly. Abby stood in the doorway and looked around, seeing things differently than she had before. On the bookshelf she noticed two volumes on early American antiques. One was a coffee-table book, the sort with big color photographs. The other was entitled *Spot the Winner: A Beginner's Guide to Recognizing Valuable Antiques. 5th Edition.* Abby imagined that one was well used. There were no longer any photographs in view. Abby went back through the kitchen to the stairs.

Mike's room was at the top of the stairs. There were a few pictures of Connie on his dresser, but they were all of a younger girl, not the young woman whose body had been found hidden in the woods. The only grown-up photo was the nude Abby she had seen on her last visit. Mike had draped a large white handkerchief over it so his daughter was peeking out from behind it, like an amateur actress before the curtain goes up.

Mike was where she had left him. Abby held up the frame, facing the photo away from him.

"Can I take this one? I'm going to scan the picture, and make a copy of the face. I want to be able to show it around."

Mike looked at her. "Don't let anyone see, you know, the whole thing, okay?"

"Yeah. Sure."

# CHAPTER TWENTY-SIX

That night, she slept like a dead person. She woke up in the morning feeling stuffed up and groggy, as if she were harboring a cold. "This is not the time to be sick," she said out loud, looking in the bathroom mirror at her sallow skin and puffy eyes. "Not this weekend. This weekend you need to be full of beans so you can make lots of money." She brewed a mug of strong tea and washed down a couple of vitamin C tablets with it. She turned on her computer, scanner, and printer. This time, sitting at her small desk, she looked carefully at the picture. She noticed it had some green powder in the grooves of the frame. They must have dusted it for fingerprints. "You had to stir things up, right?" Abby asked the seductive girl on the couch. Connie looked back at her with a slight smile, mysterious and self-satisfied. She was beautiful, confident, and in control. The kind of girl Abby herself had always wanted to be, actually.

Abby turned the frame over, and slid open the little black tabs that held the backing in place. By pulling on the stand she removed the stiff card, tipped the frame, and let the photograph fall out. She was hoping to find something written on the photo, either on the border or on the back, but it was clean.

It took her about half an hour to scan the image, save it as a file, crop out everything but the young woman's face, and save the close-up in a second file. While she was printing this new close-up, she took the original out of the scanner. She wanted to return it as soon as possible to Mike. There was little enough left to him of his girl, and she didn't want anyone else getting hold of it.

It was then that she looked a little more carefully at the frame. It was about five by seven, and the name Constance was written on the long upper side, the script blending into the design. Abby had noticed before that it was carved, but this time she looked more closely at the carvings. They were quite intricate, leaves and birds and flowers, all intertwined and hard to distinguish one from another unless you really looked hard. And she realized it wasn't actually carved in bas-relief. It was etched, but with thin pencillike lines. She paused, trying to remember where she had seen this kind of work before, and then it came to her. Franklin. Franklin's scrimshaw. She had seen him working his little pen. He might be able to give her an insight into where someone might have bought this frame.

Pleased with herself, she turned off the computer and the printer, took the frame, and headed into town.

Franklin's secretary looked up when she ran up the stairs. "Whoa, slow down. He's with someone. Just another minute."

Abby nodded, barely suppressing the urge to barge into his office. Instead, she paced back and forth, stopping to look out the window each time she came back to it. Eventually she stopped in front of his door. She could hear murmuring behind it. To the right of the door was a framed photograph of Franklin's family when he was a boy. Franklin, his parents, and his two sisters were sitting on a rather stiff sofa. His father had his long arms along the shoulders of his entire family, draping them with his protection. Abby was just about to walk away when she noticed the frame. It was a pale wood, etched with elaborate and delicate designs of birds and plants. Across the top, in sloping cursive, was the word *Family*. Other than its size, it was just like the one she held in her hand. She stood, motionless, barely breathing.

"This is a great picture of Franklin's family," she said, finally.

"Isn't it?" his secretary agreed. "He's close to them."

"Nice frame."

"I love it. He carved that himself. I want him to make one for me."

Abby nodded, her throat dry. "Does he make a lot of frames for friends?"

Mary laughed. "No. Each one takes a long time, so if you think you're cutting ahead of me in line, think again."

Inside Franklin's office, the tone of the conversation changed, and there was a scraping of chairs. Abby pictured them standing, starting to say good-bye.

"Darn," she exclaimed—sounding stilted even to her ears, "I just remembered, I have an appointment. Will you tell him I'm sorry, it wasn't important anyway?" She turned quickly to stop any further discussion, and ran down the stairs, keeping the small frame out of Mary's line of sight.

At home she made a print for herself of the full nude, then put it in a manila envelope, along with the tight shots of Connie's face. Then she sat on her couch, studying the picture frame. The thing was, it had the dead girl's name on it, there in that curly script. Constance. So what did it mean? The obvious answer was that Franklin had made it for the young woman. However, he might have been asked by someone else to make it, without knowing who it was for. But if he had made it for Connie, that would mean that they knew each other pretty well—you don't spend hours carving something for a casual acquaintance. And if he were a friend of Mike's, wouldn't he have mentioned it? So why hadn't he said anything? She thought over everything she knew about Connie. Sarah had said that she took the car to meet a lover. They now knew she also took it to steal furniture. But, if the original premise were true, then there were certain things about the lover that seemed to be implied. The main one was that she wanted to keep his identity hidden. Abby had always taken it for granted that this was because the lover was married, the relationship illicit. But what if the affair was not adulterous, merely inappropriate, or there was some other reason she was reluctant to let people know about it? What if the man was older, or what if he was African American. Would either of these be reason enough for Connie to keep it under wraps? What about both? Abby thought about the girl's father. Mike was a local guy, a plumber. Would he be unhappy if he thought his daughter was seeing a black man, even in this day and age, and even though that black man was a respected lawyer? Or maybe he would be against it because the lawyer was twice her age. If either were the case, wouldn't this be a perfect opportunity for Connie to spit in her father's eye? Abby thought about it, and had no answer.

She was still sitting on the couch, her thumb rubbing over the carvings on the frame as if they held the answer she was looking for in Braille, when a far worse scenario drifted into her head. In hindsight, it seemed surprising it took her so long to examine it, though she supposed it had been lurking there since she first saw that frame in Franklin's office. Because if Franklin were the secret lover, then it followed that he was a prime candidate for the role of secret killer. Abby sat there, and shook her head. Impossible. He would never kill someone. But then why had he hidden the fact that he knew her well enough to make a frame for her? Did Franklin take the photograph? Finally, she curled up on the sofa, put her head on a cushion, and shut her eyes. She couldn't think clearly anymore. Maybe there was a simpler explanation. She would lie there and think for a few minutes, clear her head. Her eyes grew heavy, and she fell asleep.

She dreamed she was in the kitchen of her house, and she knew without question it was her house, though the room was unfamiliar. The back door was open, with nothing but a thin, old-fashioned screen between her and the outdoors. The land was wooded and overgrown right up to the farmhouse. Gradually she became aware of a low, deep snarling coming from the other side of the screen. She moved closer and looked out and, peering in at her, camouflaged by the dark green of the foliage, was a huge panther. Abby jumped back in terror. The panther swiped at the screen. Its massive claws moved through the fragile netting as if it were water. She became aware that there was someone next to her. A small child. Suddenly, the toddler—Abby didn't know if it was a girl or boy—ran toward the screen door, hands reaching out to the massive creature. Abby grabbed the little child just in time by its small, soft arm and pulled it back. Surprisingly strong, the child struggled to break free. By now the screening was shredded, the frame hanging on its hinges. The panther, saliva hanging in greasy loops from its fangs, was nearly through, its eyes gleaming yellow. Abby was vibrating with fear, her muscles losing their strength, her brain no longer able to fathom what was happening. She felt the child's hand, boneless in its softness, slip out of her fingers once more as it ran to the door—

The fear catapulted her upright and awake, sweating in terror, her shirt soaked, her heart doing rhythmic drum rolls. She waited for her pulse to slow and eventually she stood up and walked slowly into the bathroom and turned on the shower. She leaned on the sink, looking at her face in the mirror. She looked gray, her face drawn. Before stepping under the water, she went through the living room and locked the front door. She would've locked the back door, too, but she didn't have one.

# CHAPTER TWENTY-SEVEN

Frankie's Motel was on Route 9, between Hudson and Albany. It was in a strip-mall outpost, a lonely wart of progress surrounded by placid farmland. A taste of things to come, it was a cheap, ugly motel bordering a large cornfield. Across the road was an apple orchard, the fruit, though small and green, already visible.

The building was one story, with a flat roof. Abby wondered, as she turned off the highway, if there was a school of architects that had designed only motels and public schools, because the flat, ugly structures were often similar. Schools had a busy hivelike feeling—waiting cars, yellow buses, play-grounds, flagpoles with the Stars and Stripes snapping in the breeze. Frankie's Motel, on the other hand, had a run-down, frayed quality. Cracked asphalt showing a few too many weeds, patchwork repairs on the roof.

Sure enough, as she had learned from the "church" gossips, she had to drive behind the motel to get to the parking lot. The office and all the room doors were also to the rear, lined up evenly, one large window next to one red door. The windows were all hung with heavy beige drapes to protect their occupants from being seen from the parking lot. There were about five cars and a few pickups in the lot, parked in front of various rooms. One of the room doors was open, and a housekeeper's cart was pulled up outside. Abby parked near the office, locking the Bronco before she went inside.

There was a loud ringing as she walked through the double glass doors. The office was to the right, the counter painted bright red. Behind the desk was a board covered in hooks for red-tagged room keys. Red was obviously Frankie's home color. Abby would've thought a soothing blue would encourage rest and relaxation, but then again, she read somewhere that blue promotes depression, and no motel wants to encourage suicidal customers. There appeared to be no one in the office, though there was a small room visible behind the counter. Abby leaned against the bright red lacquer, and peered in, wondering if she should call out. Somewhere she heard the flush of a toilet.

To her surprise, the concierge who emerged from a room behind the office was a buxom woman in a sari. The sari was a bright orange rough silk draped around a fitted short-sleeved blouse. The blouse was fire-engine red. The woman was about forty, her long hair in a thick braid down her back. She was exotic and unexpected, and Abby was reminded of that moment on a gray winter's day when a male cardinal suddenly flies into view. Pleasure at the sight, and gratitude that some Greater Power took the time to create such a bird.

"May I help you?" She had the singsong accent of an Indian or Pakistani whose native tongue is not English.

"Beautiful sari."

The woman nodded, accepting Abby's praise. "Thank you. You are most kind. Are you looking for a room?"

Abby shook her head. "Are you the owner?"

The woman nodded slowly, a shadow of worry crossing her face. "My husband and I, together we own the motel."

Abby held out her hand. "I'm Abby Silvernale. I live in Bantam."

The owner held out her hand and they shook. Her grip was much softer than Abby expected.

"I am Mrs. Patel."

Abby decided to just ask. "I have a friend, a young woman, who has been coming to this motel with a boyfriend."

She saw Mrs. Patel start to frown, as if she were going to deny it. "I am not able to discuss our patrons."

"I understand. This is a little different. This girl has been murdered."

Mrs. Patel shook her head, and clicked her tongue. It was like a tut-tut, but more heartfelt. Abby took this as a positive sign, and dug in her purse. She found the print of Connie's face, and put it on the counter.

"Could you look at this picture of her, and tell me if she looks familiar?"

Still shaking her head, Mrs. Patel moved closer to the counter, and looked down at the pretty, dark-haired girl looking seductively back at her. Her head went on shaking, and now Abby didn't know if she meant she was shocked at the violence, or she had never seen her before.

Finally, she looked up at Abby. "I'm sorry, she is not one of our customers."

Abby wasn't ready to give up. "Maybe your husband—"

Mrs. Patel held up her hand. "Please. Let me explain. Mr. Patel and I bought the motel only one month ago. Therefore, she might have been a customer of the motel, but we would not recognize her."

The wind went out of Abby's sails. She had been hoping for a quick fix. "What about the old owner? Where is he?"

She shrugged. "We bought the motel from a lawyer. The owner had recently died, his heirs live in California and wished to sell immediately." When she saw how disappointed Abby looked, she added: "I am sorry. Did you know for a fact that she visited this place?"

Abby returned the photo to her purse. "No. It was a guess. Thanks anyway." She raised her hand in a gesture of good-bye, and turned away. As she went out the door, the buzzer rang aggressively.

Abby was unlocking her car when Mrs. Patel called her name. Abby looked up. She was standing at the door of the motel, the brilliant orange silk of her sari framed in the red doorway. Her skin glinted like polished copper.

"Why don't you speak to Sophie, our housekeeper? She has worked here for a good many years, and she notices quite a bit that goes on." She pointed down the row of doors to the open one, the one with the cart parked in front of it.

"That's a great idea." Abby smiled. Mrs. Patel nodded and disappeared inside. Abby relocked the car and walked on a diagonal toward the open door.

Standing in the doorway, she called out. "Hello? Sophie?"

"Yeah?" The answer was muffled, as if the owner of the voice was in a closet, or had a mask on. Abby stepped into the room.

It was a typical low-end motel room, with a double bed, head to the left wall, and facing it, a television that sat on a long, Formica dresser. The bed was made, and covered in a red and blue patterned spread, one of those stiff polyester ones that manage to spring up and touch your face in the middle of the night, filling you with horrible images of all the organisms living and breeding on it. The walls were red, a sort of crushed velvet, and the floors were carpeted in a deep brown pile. On the far end of the dresser sat a tall, ornate gold lamp, with a tasseled pink shade. The lamp gave an air of cheap bordello to the room.

There was no one in sight, but she heard the sound of running water coming from the bathroom.

Abby walked to the bathroom door. "Sophie?"

Sophie was standing at the sink, her back to her. The faucets were on and she was scrubbing the bowl. She turned at the sound of Abby's voice.

"I need some information, and Mrs. Patel told me to speak to you." Abby had to speak loudly so she could be heard over the water.

Sophie turned the faucet off. She was about thirty, small, mousy looking, her hair pulled into a brown ponytail and wire-rimmed glasses on her nose. She was wearing leggings and a loose man's shirt covered in faded palm trees. Her hands were protected by large pink rubber gloves. Abby could see she had the well-muscled legs of an athlete. Sophie put a hand on the sink, and leaned on it, casually, then looked at Abby, her eyebrows raised in question. She didn't bother to speak. The smell of commercial cleaner was suffocating, and Abby glanced at the small, high window over the sink. It was shut.

"I just have one quick question, and then I'll get out of your hair. Do you know this woman?" She took the photograph of Connie out of her pocket, and held it out to her.

Carefully, Sophie peeled off one glove and took the photograph. She looked at Abby. "Why d'you want to know?" Her voice was low and raspy, as if too many years of cleaning fluids had done some damage. Abby gave Connie's name and said that she was trying to find out the identity of the girl's boyfriend.

"Something happened to her, right?" Sophie asked, looking back down at Connie.

Abby nodded, not elaborating. Sophie handed the photo back.

"Yeah, I've seen her. She used to come with a guy."

Finally. "Did you ever see him?"

Sophie thought for a minute. "No. He would sit in the car, she would come into the office. But I think he was dark."

Abby felt cold. "Dark-skinned?"

Sophie shook her head. "Never saw him out in the open. Just got that impression."

"Do you think he was African American? I mean, could he have been Hispanic or maybe Asian?"

"I couldn't say. He was in the car, and it was night." She fitted her hand into her pink glove. Back to work.

"Did she come often? Once a week, twice?"

She shrugged. "I don't know. I only saw her a couple of times when I was working the night shift at the front desk. I only did it to cover for the boss, when he was out of town or something."

"Thanks." Abby turned to leave.

"Shame. She was married, right? With kids?" Sophie spoke to her back.

Abby looked at her, curious. "Why do you think that?"

"Her car. She was so young and pretty, I noticed the car."

"What was she driving?"

"A family car—minivan. Blue or gray."

The multipurpose minivan. Abby took Sophie's name and phone number, warning her that she would have to pass on any information she got to the police. Sophie nodded in resignation.

"Thanks." Abby turned and left the room. In the parking lot, she forgot to breathe in the fresh air. She walked to the Bronco, let herself in, and sat, staring at nothing. After a while she turned on the ignition, and drove onto Route 9.

# CHAPTER TWENTY-EIGHT

Abby changed and drove back down the hill to work, a steady buzz of facts, half-facts, and questions running through her head, a harried monologue that she could do nothing to stop so she did her best not to listen to. She looked forward to the restaurant, hoping bells, pots, plates, knives, chairs, people, and chatter would muffle the noise in her head.

The first thing she found when she went down to the bar was Dulcie, hanging pictures. Dulcie had always resisted the many requests to hang the work of local artists on her walls, saying she didn't like mixing art with food, drink, and social interaction. Or something like that. And here she was, hanging the last picture in a series of a dozen or so medium-sized canvases.

When she saw Abby come down the stairs, Dulcie stood back from the wall.

"What do you think?" she asked, watching Abby anxiously.

Abby looked at them. They were abstracts, with raw blotches of primary colors blended crudely together. They were childlike, but without the charm and individuality of child art.

"What made you decide to have a show?" she asked, not wanting to give her opinion.

"I don't know. Thought I'd try it. We're having a little opening this evening."

"Wow. Who's the artist?" Maybe it was someone Dulcie felt sorry for.

"It's a group," she replied stiffly.

"Sorry, they all look the same." To make up for her lack of discernment, Abby went from painting to painting, examining each one. "Hey, here's one by Aliara Rubin! I'd know that name anywhere, that's Malaria! It's weird, it looks"—and then it dawned on her. "Oh, my God, this is the tit class! Dulcie, I know all about this, you have to hear this! They painted these with their breasts!"

"Shh," said her boss. Abby turned and looked at Dulcie, surprised she too, wasn't amused. To her surprise, Dulcie looked uncomfortable. And self-conscious.

For the second time in less than a minute, Abby suddenly got it. "Oh, my God. You were in that class. You were in that class. Oh, Dulcie."

"It was a great class," Dulcie answered defensively.

"I can't believe it," Abby continued, shaking her head in wonder.

Dulcie suddenly thought of something. "Don't you dare tell Henry."

"I don't know if I can keep it from him," Abby said, shaking her head and breaking out into a smile. She was enjoying herself for the first time all day.

The restaurant filled quickly and stayed numbingly busy all evening, so there was little time to gossip with Henry or think about Franklin. Abby was stationed upstairs and was kept busy running down to the bar for trays of drinks, and into the kitchen to collect plates of steaming meatloaf, pasta puttanesca, and grilled salmon. Her legs grew tired, but she welcomed the distraction of aching calves.

By ten o'clock, the running was over. Most of the upstairs tables were still full as people slowly finished their desserts and wine and kept talking, not quite ready to let go of the evening. Abby's pace slowed down. She cleared plates, cleaned tables, filled salt shakers, and replaced butcher paper. Finally, by eleven, her station was empty and she was finished. As usual, she inverted chairs onto tables to make room for the floor cleaner who would come early the next morning. Then she left Mindy counting tips and went down to the bar for a drink. Sometime during the evening she had decided to work until she was exhausted, have a couple of strong drinks, drive carefully up her hill, and go straight to sleep. She would deal with the dilemma of Franklin in the morning. She would lay all her facts out on the table, then decide what to do. But first, she planned to have one strong drink. Followed by a second one.

Downstairs, the bar was still busy thanks to Dulcie's little opening, and would probably stay that way until midnight. Dulcie was bartending, which she did once in a while when no one else was available. She liked to think it kept her skills up. As she had no bartending skills, that was a questionable proposition. When she worked the bar it was a haphazard affair, reading glasses on the end of her nose, the *Bartender's Bible* propped open on the counter, and bottles collecting untidily on the counter in front of her. Henry had tried to explain the count-to-six-while-pouring rule of thumb for a shot, but she would either look away while she was pouring and fill the glass, or she would count too fast and let the liquid out in a thin trickle. A dry martini was way beyond her. She seemed relieved to hear Abby wanted a rum and orange juice.

Sitting at the bar was an odd assortment of people. Among them, Malaria, Bailey, Keith Ryder, and Josie Brown. A bar crowd from hell, as far as Abby was concerned, though everyone seemed to be enjoying themselves, even Josie, Jamison Brown's daughter. Abby was surprised at how different she looked when she smiled. Maybe having a famous father made it hard for her to relax.

Henry was clearing the tables downstairs. When Abby sat down at a small table in the corner, he called to her from across the room. "God, I love this show. I want to take the class."

Malaria, hearing talk about the show, turned on her barstool and joined in. "Abby, don't you love the paintings?"

"Yes, indeedy," Abby lied. She waited a second, picked up her glass, and headed upstairs.

The dining room was quiet and the chairs were all upturned. The room looked a little like a small field of bamboo stalks. Abby picked a table on the enclosed porch, righted a couple of the chairs, and sat down. Ah, alone at last. Recklessly, she took up a stubby piece of maroon crayon, and began doodling. She started with a circle, then put two smaller circles inside it. The problem with doodling is that eventually it allows your thoughts to float like feathers in a breeze, sinking and settling wherever they choose. Abby was tired, she took a sip of her drink, and after the bulging eyes were drawn, she found herself outlining a fat little heart, with F and C intertwined in the center. She stuck an arrow through it, blood dripping from the hole. Quickly she colored it in. She went back to drawing circles. Overlapping circles, circles that touched each other, circles that flattened out when they met. And she thought about Franklin. At the very least, he must have lied to her. He hadn't gone to law school so he could have a career making personalized picture frames to sell at street fairs. Therefore, he had to have known Connie pretty well to make a frame for her with her name on it. Abby drew a picture of the frame, writing in *Constance* at the top, and hid the name in a mass of fruits and vines until it was no longer visible. She had created one of those children's puzzles, where the challenge is to find a group of objects that have been hidden in the picture.

A burst of laughter from the stairwell made her look up. People were starting to leave. When their heads appeared over the top of the railing, she saw it was Josie and Keith. Josie was laughing. Quite the party girl tonight. Keith was shaking his head. He looked as if he had been the butt of a friendly joke, and wasn't enjoying it. Abby watched them as they left through the front door.

Relieved that they hadn't noticed her, she went back to her circles. Like her thoughts, they kept going round and round. She had no idea what to do next, but she did think she should tell the police chief what she had discovered, even if it meant nothing. There were plenty of men around who could have been with Connie at the motel. Yes, Sophie the housekeeper had noticed a "dark" man with her, but that did not mean Franklin was the man. But what about the frame, the stupid little frame? And, of course, the naked girl in the stupid little frame. Circle, circle.

When her drink was done, she stood up and went downstairs to the bar for her second rum and orange juice. She intended to stick to the schedule. Dulcie looked at her with raised eyebrows, but Abby avoided making eye contact and Dulcie handed it over.

To her dismay, Malaria was sitting at her table on the porch when she got back, a glass of white wine in front of her. Abby hadn't noticed her leave the bar.

"Abby, I sense you want to be alone. I respect that, but I need to talk to you."

Thankfully, she hadn't sat on Abby's side, where the maroon circles formed a rich beehive pattern that covered almost half of the table. The picture frame, with the hidden name, was on the upper right of the beehive, like an oversized postage stamp. Abby glanced at it to make sure the name was illegible.

"Sure. What's up?" She was still standing. She put her glass to her lips, and let the ice slide down and bump against her teeth. She felt chilled and no longer in need of the second drink. Reluctantly, she sat down in her chair, putting her glass down on the drawing of the frame, as if it were a coaster.

"I don't know why it is, but I feel you don't like me." Malaria looked at her intently.

Oh, no, not now. It was not the right time for this conversation. It would never be the right time for this conversation. But Malaria had the stubborn look of the meek, and the rum had made Abby more slow-witted than usual. There was no way out, unless a grease fire broke out in the kitchen, and she probably wouldn't hear about it on the porch until it was too late. They'd all die like roasted hogs. In the meantime Malaria was looking at her, expecting a response. Abby was too numbed by alcohol to feel much shame, but the woman was right, of course. What could she say, that she disliked her because she tried too hard, she was too needy? Could she mention her irritating hair? The little bit of shame she felt turned quickly to anger. "You know, you can't go around accusing people of not liking you. It's not going to make them like you any better."

Malaria held up both hands flat, as if to show she had nothing hidden. "No, no, trust me, I'm not trying to force you or humiliate you into being my friend. There are plenty of people who don't like me. I know they don't. And can I tell you why?"

"Why?" Abby asked, dutifully. The little voice in her head said: *Here we go, baby.* As with all rhetorical questions, she was going to hear the answer whether she wanted to or not.

Malaria sat forward, taking hold of both of Abby's wrists like synchronized dogs grabbing bones. Her hands were surprisingly warm and dry. "Because of my philosophy. I believe in Love. I believe in Giving." Abby wanted to pull her hands away, but Malaria was on a roll. "I try to live my philosophy, and I often get slapped down for it, but I have promised myself not to weaken, not to doubt myself. This is it—you want to hear it? It's very simple—I do my best to project Love in every situation I encounter, and to Give where I might otherwise want to Take." As she spoke, her eyes filled with tears. Now she sat back in her chair. Done. She seemed to be waiting for Abby to say something.

"Well." Abby couldn't think of anything much, and the sincerity in the woman's eyes was embarrassing. "Well, that's good, that's great."

Malaria seemed not to mind such a weak response. "It is, it's wonderful. That is why I want to share my feelings with you, because so often I feel that you're in pain and have no one to turn to. Am I right?"

It was strange. Abby despised Malaria. She didn't even think of her by her real name. But at that moment, when this woman looked at her as if she really cared what happened to her, Abby found her eyes filling up with tears. It was that quick.

When Malaria saw the response she had shaken out of Abby, she squeezed her wrists in encouragement. "It's okay, cry. This is a very tough world we live in, you know that? And we have to make connections with other human beings any chance we get. So don't be ashamed to cry." Now Abby couldn't stop crying. What if someone from the bar saw the two of them arm wrestling? She wanted to shield her face with her hands, but she couldn't because of the firm hold Malaria had on her wrists, so she hid her face on her forearm. The strange thing is, the familiar smell of her own skin and the warmth of it against her cheek, frozen by one and a half icy drinks, was like finding her long-lost mother, and she inhaled deeply and wept quietly, tears and mucus wetting her arm.

When it was all over, Abby blew her nose in her cocktail napkin. Rather shakily, she said: "You caught me at a bad moment."

"Is it your husband?"

Abby turned her head away. The silence collected around them. She surprised herself when she began talking.

"The last time I saw him, Jonah and I had a big fight. I drove to the city. I sat up that night with an old friend, drinking, complaining about how I had to look after him, and what a crazy fuck he was.

"The next morning I drove home. When I got to our farmhouse I pulled up in front of the house. I slammed the door nice 'n' hard so he would hear—I was still pissed at him. And then I noticed the porch light. The bulb. It was on. I could barely see it with the sun. A bright yellow wire. I mean, he could've just forgotten to turn it off, but I knew right then, looking at that bulb. I felt this terrible sense of mistake, that I had made this unfixable mistake, like some ignorant tourist in the Alps who shouts out and realizes too late he's caused an avalanche. I had done that. It took me about five or six minutes to find him—he wasn't in the house. He was a good farm boy, he knew enough to leave his mess outside. He was out back in the farm pickup. He'd used his dad's shotgun—I found it next to the rear wheels— it had been thrown out by the recoil."

Her wrists under Malaria's hands were sweating. Gently, she pulled them away. "Why do you think he did it?" Malaria asked.

Abby shook her head. "I don't know. He'd tried it before. It just wasn't working for him, I guess. Life."

"You can't always be there."

Abby nodded. "I'm sorry, I don't know where all that came from."

Malaria smiled warmly. "It's not good to keep it bottled up."

"The funny thing is, I thought I was over the worst of that."

"You might be. Maybe something else is dredging it up."

"How do you mean?"

Malaria looked at her thoughtfully. "Well, as a professional I know that sometimes other worries touch on old pain."

Abby nodded, unsure. "It could be. I was just told something that unsettled me."

Malaria looked puzzled. "To do with Jonah?"

Abby shook her head. "No. I can't talk about it specifically, but it implicates someone I care about. I'm afraid this person knows a lot more about a bad situation than he's letting on—"

Malaria interrupted. "Oh, God, he saw who killed his mother?"

Abby frowned. "His mother? No. Oh, you mean Joey. No, this is nothing to do with him. Though I think he might know who was with his mother the night she was killed." And then, kicking herself for saying too much, she added: "What do you know about Joey?"

Malaria gave her a look with raised eyebrows and a tilt to the head, as if to say Abby was being naïve. She said: "Who else could you have been talking about? This is Bantam, remember? So, have you told the police?"

Abby shook her head. "Not my call."

Malaria looked at her sternly. Abby thought she might grab her wrists again, so she moved her hands onto her lap.

"You know, they really need to know all the facts. If something happens to the boy, you'll never forgive yourself."

Abby nodded. She was relieved that Malaria had no idea she had been referring to Franklin. Either way, however, she was right. Abby had to speak to the chief of police, regardless of anything. She had to tell him about the frame, Frankie's Motel, and anything else she had come up with. She also had to make sure the chief knew that Joey had heard someone talking with his mother the night she was killed.

Malaria was watching her, unblinking, with the look of a fuzzy-haired bird. Abby was moved to show her some kindness. Make an attempt at a little Giving, a little Love.

"You know, the show is really nice. Downstairs."

Malaria looked excited, clapping her hands childishly. "I'm so glad you like it! Isn't it *wonderful?*"

Abby tried to be honest. "I think, from what you've told me, it's more about the process, right? The end result is less important, don't you think?"

"Yes, yes, but aren't they lovely? So fresh and clean? So *unworked?*"

"Yes, yes. Untouched by human hands." Abby smiled weakly.

Malaria was oblivious to any humor. "I could go on about that experience forever. In fact, I'm staying in close contact with a lot of the class members—it created a real bond between us, you know." She leaned forward, and lowered her voice. "The best part is that, the teacher and I, you know, we explored our relationship even, you know, further."

Wasn't the teacher a woman? Like it or not, Abby could see it, the paint, lots of breasts, a faceless stranger and Malaria. Mud-wrestling in acrylics.

She smiled politely. "Are you and she still seeing each other?"

Malaria frowned. "Oh, no. No, no. The teacher is a man. A very sexy one, I might add."

"Did he paint, too? What did he use for breasts?"

She giggled. "His manhood, of course."

Abby had never heard anyone nonfictional use the word "manhood." "Manhood?"

"His penis! It was the closest thing, the way it swung. Though during most of the class it didn't hang, you know." She used her finger to point up, her expression coy. She looked as if she were giving Abby a friendly warning. Abby shook her head. Amazing, what people will come up with when you give them a little free time.

"Are you still seeing him? I mean, what do you do for an encore, with a first date like that?" Abby found herself slipping in to her habitually sarcastic tone with Malaria. *Seriously*, she thought to herself, *she's an idiot. A frickin' idiot.*

If Malaria heard the sneer in her voice, she didn't acknowledge it. Instead she sighed, giving the question some thought. "You're absolutely right. In point of fact, things have slowed way down. He is pursuing other interests, and that's alright, really."

Abby watched her. She was lying. She was in love, and her lord and penis wasn't. You didn't need to be a rocket scientist to figure that one out.

"But we still see each other once in a while," Malaria continued.

Poor sucker. Before she said something she would regret, Abby stood up. Her chair made a grating noise on the wooden floor. "I'm beat, Aliara. I've got to go home."

Malaria looked at her watch. "Oh, wow. Me, too. I'll walk you out." She stood up, moving her chair carefully back.

After putting her glass in the kitchen and replacing the chairs, Abby got her purse from under the cash register and walked slowly to the front door, Malaria behind her. They stepped outside into the cool, dark night. Abby took a deep breath, as if to suck the air all the way down to her feet. She found her car keys in her purse and glanced over at Malaria.

"Just don't let this guy walk all over you. There comes a time when you have to stop Giving, you know. Start Kicking a little Ass."

Malaria smiled at her. "You're sweet." But Abby could tell her mind was on other things. She wasn't interested in her advice.

"Do you need a ride?"

Malaria shook her head, the wispy ends of her hair bobbing. "No, I'm all set."

"Goodnight, then. Thanks. And I'm sorry, about being unkind. I'll work on it." Abby left her standing on the restaurant steps.

Her car was deep in the Dollar Store parking lot. She walked over, noticing the silence of the small town. The lights above the movie theater were off, and the few streetlights gave an eerie glow to Main Street. The far end of the parking lot was dark and deeply shadowed, the dumpsters sitting like black caves next to the railroad tracks. It was a relief to get into her little vehicle. When she was safely inside she reached around and locked the doors.

Pulling out of the parking lot, she turned right in front of the building that housed the darkened police department. Abby looked back at the restaurant. Malaria was where she had left her, but now she was sitting on the top step with her arms wrapped around herself as if she were cold. Abby headed out River Street, and just as she did, a car came down over the tracks from Route 107. Abby was surprised to see Keith Ryder driving. He was alone. Abby slowed down and watched him in her rearview mirror. He drove around the circle to the InnBetween and pulled up in front of the steps. Abby slowed to a crawl. She watched Malaria stand and walk briskly down the stairs. When Keith's car drove away, she was no longer there.

# CHAPTER TWENTY-NINE

Abby pulled over, wondering what she had seen. Was Keith just giving Malaria a ride home? He and his fiancée, Josie, had spent the evening at the InnBetween with her and the other barflies. That was when he had probably offered to take her home. Maybe her car was in the shop, its transmission blown, so she needed a ride. But it was late, so why hadn't she left with Keith and Josie earlier? What Abby had just seen looked different, smelled different to her. She thought of Malaria all bright and giggly as she talked about the "exploration" with her teacher. Maybe Keith was her teacher—after all, he was an artist, so he would have the credentials to set up an art class. Did you need credentials for that kind of a class? And weren't affairs usually carried on with younger women? Malaria seemed a strange choice for an affair: older and even more peculiar than Josie. Abby had to assume that Malaria had something else to offer; their relationship had had a kinky christening, so maybe that was the pull.

It was a dark, oppressive night, the stars hidden behind a blanket of cloud cover. On impulse, Abby did a U-turn on the empty street and followed Keith's car down Main Street. Their lights were tiny pinpricks ahead of her. The Bronco seemed noisy, the exhaust echoing on the deserted street. She crossed the railroad tracks. In the distance she heard the lone whistle of a train. She drove past the Blue Seal feed plant to the light at Route 103. Keith's car crossed the intersection while the light was green, but it changed to yellow when Abby approached, and she stopped as it turned red. She watched Keith's car slow down on Hudson Avenue, then turn right into one of the long driveways. When the light changed, Abby followed slowly behind. The comfortable Victorians that lined the avenue sat way back on the far side of the earlier, disused train tracks, hidden by trees and distrustful of passersby. Abby drove by, and saw Keith and Malaria get out of his car and go into a large, two-story building with a front porch that led up to double matching front doors. It had either been built as a multiple dwelling, or carved into one a good while ago. She slowed down long enough to see lights come on in a lower right apartment. Turning around at the end of the avenue, she parked in the darkened service station across the street. She had an unobstructed view of Malaria's apartment and Keith's car. She turned off the ignition and made herself comfortable by reclining her seat. Then she waited.

Abby woke up to pitch blackness, disoriented. She was cold and sore from sitting too long on the Bronco's old bench seat. She started the car, doing her best to remember what she should have done, why her subconscious had been kicking her in her sleep, telling her to get up, get up, before it was too late. And strangely enough, in the dark, it came to her.

That nagging little detail of the apartment on Malden Street. Someone had told Malaria about that apartment before Connie was known to be missing, and certainly before she was found dead. If she was having an affair with Keith, and if Keith had told her about the apartment, then that would mean Keith had known Connie was no longer going to be needing the apartment. And the only person who could have known, at that point, that Connie wasn't coming home, was the person who killed her. And, if he was the killer, then anyone who knew about his involvement was in danger. Which could mean Malaria.

Across the street, Keith's car was no longer there. The lights in Malaria's apartment were off. Abby crossed the road, hoping she wouldn't set off anyone's dog. She walked toward the porch, and with each step the gravel crunched noisily. Carefully she climbed the three steps, and read the names on the mailboxes. Sure enough, Rubin, the black letters freshly pasted on, was number two, downstairs right. Abby moved over to the right-hand door, and pushed the doorbell. A faint buzz. She waited, and then pushed the bell again, this time holding it down until it was sure to wake the dead. No movement from inside.

She rattled the door, hoping to find it unlocked. When she didn't, she left the porch, and started to walk around the apartment, trying to see in one of the windows. About ten feet back from the front of the house was a large bay window, the shades pulled down low. Abby peered through the slit at the bottom, but the room inside was dark, and she could make out nothing but the black outlines of furniture.

She kept walking along the side of the house, her anxiety increasing. Mature rhododendron bushes flanked the building once she got past the bay window, and they made movement difficult. Abby was afraid that someone in an upstairs apartment would hear her crashing through the bushes and shoot at her, or call the police, so she tried to move as surreptitiously as possible. The next window she came to was a tall single window. She crouched down and tried to look under the shade, but it was pulled all the way to the sill. The side of the shade, however, was bowed out, so she could see in. One eye up to the opening, she strained to see into the darkened room. The shape she saw seemed to be flat and wide. Most likely a bed. Abby rapped on the window. Was there a person on the bed, or was it a trick of the dark shadows? She banged again, this time a little harder. No answer.

At the rear of the building she discovered another porch. It seemed far more decayed and slanted than the front one, but it had two doors opening onto it. She walked carefully up the sagging steps and tried to find names, but there was nothing. She assumed these were the back entrances to the lower apartments. Screens covered the cheap aluminum doors, and she pulled the left one gently and tried the door itself. The handle turned.

The door pushed inward, and she followed it. Inside, she felt for a light on a wall. The switch was low, as if it had been put in to suit a child. She pushed it up, and fluorescent ceiling lights flickered on. She was in a kitchen. The walls were papered in an electric yellow design with large orange flowers. The counters were a speckled beige Formica, and brown linoleum covered the floor. There was a small kitchen table made of wood, flanked by two wooden chairs. The room looked neat, a couple of dishes and glasses in the drying rack.

She took a moment to remember Malaria's real name. "Aliara?" she called out. "Aliara, are you here?"

No answer. No sound from the dark doorway on the other side of the kitchen. She moved toward it, and followed it down a short narrow corridor. She figured that the bedroom she was looking for was to her left, so she paused at the first door and looked in. Sure enough, the same room she had seen from the outside. Large bed, figure on it. She felt for a switch, and found it on her right. A standing lamp to her right filled the room with a low, yellow light.

Malaria lay on her bed, a light sheet covering her naked body. She was twisted at an unnatural angle. Her eyes were closed, her mouth open, and her arms spread out. Abby walked over to her, horrified at what she had discovered, but not surprised. She knew she was too late to help her.

Abby stood looking down at her, paralyzed, overwhelmed by anger at herself for not having called the police, not having come sooner, not having done something. "I'm so sorry, Malaria," she whispered, tears filling her eyes.

Suddenly, the corpse on the bed heaved a deep breath, smacked her jaw shut, and turned over, the sheet wrapping around her legs and uncovering her behind. Abby's heart, already moving at a good pace, backfired, like some old car when the light turns green. She literally jumped a few inches off the ground.

"Aliara, goddamn it, wake up!" Abby reached for her upper arm, and shook it. "Wake up, I thought you were dead!"

For someone back from the dead, Malaria woke up quickly once Abby grabbed her. Her eyes shot open, and she stared blindly at the woman standing over her bed. Abby suddenly remembered that Malaria lived alone, and might find the whole situation a little unsettling.

"Wha—wha—wha—" was all the woman on the bed managed to say.

"It's okay, it's me, it's Abby, everything is okay," Abby repeated. She did her best to sound soothing, repeating the woman's name, telling her no one was going to hurt her. Finally, Malaria started to focus. She stared groggily at Abby. Finally, along with consciousness, came anger.

"Get out, get out, get out!" Her voice started out soft and got louder and louder. Abby saw strands of saliva bridge the space between her upper and lower teeth.

Abby backed out of the room. She went into the kitchen, and sat on one of the wooden chairs. She rested her forehead on the table, and rolled her head from side to side.

A few minutes later, Malaria came out of her room. She was wearing pajamas and a robe, her hair held back with a large tortoiseshell clip. She pulled out the other chair, sat down, and looked at Abby with a hard, glassy stare. Her eyes were puffy from sleep. She held out something for her inspection. It looked like a small cylinder.

"Ear plugs, Abby. My upstairs neighbors stay up very late, so I wear ear plugs." She slipped it into the pocket of her robe. "I also have trouble sleeping, so I take something to help me."

A heavy silence hung in the small, bright room.

"So, why break into my house at two, no, three-thirty in the morning, creep into my room and attack me?"

This new, angry Malaria was a revelation to Abby. "I'm sorry, I— When you didn't answer the doorbell, I thought—" She tried to defend herself. "I'm really sorry, Mal—Aliara, but I didn't actually attack you, I had to see you and you didn't answer the door, so I had no choice. I mean, for God's sake, I saw you lying there, I was sure you were dead."

Malaria looked at her coldly. "Why would I be dead? Why wouldn't I be sleeping, at this time of night? Why assume I'm *dead?*"

Abby scratched her eyebrow, stalling for time. She looked away from the puffy-eyed woman across from her, suddenly feeling foolish. "I thought Keith Ryder had murdered you."

Malaria laughed, not a real laugh, but a loud "hah!" snort of derision.

Abby frowned. "You can laugh, but I was afraid for you. I saw him pick you up tonight, so I figured he taught your class, he's your guy, and if he's your guy, then he's a two-timing liar and a cheat."

"Yeah? So? Does that make him a murderer? Anyway, I'm comfortable with the arrangement," Malaria claimed defiantly.

Abby waited for her to look at her. "Aliara," now that she knew her name, she couldn't seem to stop using it, "here's something I need to know. I asked you once before, but you wouldn't tell me. Who told you about the empty apartment on Malden Street? You knew about it so quickly, before anyone else. Remember? You mentioned it to me at the café, when you were still house hunting."

It was Malaria's turn to look uncomfortable. Her eyes darted to the side, as if she were going to make a dash for the counter and hide in a cabinet. Why would she look so uncomfortable, if the same questions hadn't crossed her mind?

"It's really important that you tell me."

At that the older woman looked annoyed. "I don't have to tell you anything. Remember, you just broke into my house."

"Look, I said I was sorry. But the person who told you could be dangerous. I really need to know. Please, for your sake, for the sake of the boy."

"You're crazy, you know that? Get some help, Abby."

Abby stood up. "I'm tired. I'm going home."

She stood. When Malaria didn't say anything, she walked out of the room. It had been a long night. She sure as hell wasn't going to creep around the yard again in the dark so she let herself out the front door. By the bottom step she remembered something else that had been bothering her. She caught the door before it closed, and went back in the apartment. She walked noisily into the kitchen so Malaria would know she was coming. "One more thing," she said.

Malaria hadn't moved from the kitchen table. She raised her eyebrows in question.

"When he picked you up tonight and drove you home, wasn't he planning to, you know, spend time with you?"

Malaria's smile had a bitter twist to it. "I thought so."

"So what happened? Did you fight?"

"No. He just said he had things to do, tonight was a bad night after all." She sounded a little skeptical.

"Was this when you first got in the car?"

Malaria thought about it for a moment. "This is none of your business, but no. It was when we got here. I admit I was disappointed."

"On the way over, did you mention the conversation we had at the restaurant?"

Malaria looked offended. "You mean, about your husband? Please, I'm a therapist. I consider that confidential. Anyway, why would he care?"

Abby grabbed the edge of the table and shook it. "No, about Joey—"

Malaria shot a quick look at the cabinets again. *Yup*, Abby thought, *she told him*. Malaria glanced at Abby and realized she'd been caught. "I didn't think you'd mind. He's a caring person and he knows the boy."

Abby picked up the edge of the table and slammed it down. Malaria jumped. "Where's your phone?"

Reluctantly, Malaria took her into the living room, switching on lights as she went. A portable phone sat on a desk by the bay window. Roy Goodrich, Joey's father, answered on the second ring.

"Yeah?"

"Roy, this is Abby Silvernale. Is Joey there?"

"What the hell's going on, anyway?"

"I need to talk to him."

"You playing some sort of game?"

"What do you mean?" Abby's bad feeling was getting worse.

"You can't talk to him, can you, because he ain't here. You know, he likes you, feels he owes you."

"Roy, what's up? Where is he?"

"You tell me."

"Hey, Roy, I don't know what you're talking about. Where'd he go?"

There was a silence on the other end. "Look, missy, he went to meet you. Took my truck. Said you needed some kinda help."

It took her a minute to understand what he meant. "I don't need help. Where was he going?"

"He said somebody called with a message from you and he should meet you in Bantam, at the InnBetween. I figured, he's a big boy, he's got his license now—"

"Roy, I gotta go," she interrupted, disconnected the call, and handed the phone to Malaria. "He's got Joey. I'm going to the restaurant. Call the police, tell them what's happening."

Malaria frowned. "Abby, I don't know what's happening."

But Abby was already pulling open the aluminum door. "Call them, tell them that Joey Merchant is in trouble, I think Keith Ryder wants to hurt him, and tell them to meet me at the InnBetween," she shouted, and ran out the door.

Abby drove as fast as she could back to Main Street, did the circle on what felt like two wheels, and pulled up on Findlay Street, down from the side entrance to the restaurant. She got out and ran back to the door. She looked at her watch, trying to make out the time. It looked like 4:10. Or 1:20. She tried the door handle. It was open, propped with the brick. It would be so easy for someone to get in and all they would have to do was hide in the building while Dan the Man was working. She stepped inside as quietly as she could. She stood for a minute in the darkened foyer, listening. The smell of old cooking grease wrapped its arms around her, the odor crawling up her nose, bitter and pungent. The door to the upper floor was open. There was no sound coming from upstairs, so, as quietly as she could, she pushed open the swing door to the kitchen area. A streetlight, shining through one of the kitchen windows, cast a yellow glow over the clean linoleum floors now stripped of their black rubber work mats, on the polished stainless-steel workstations and the tall, sleeping shape of the commercial dishwasher. Here, the smell of grease backed down to give way to the poisonously clean smell of bleach. Abby listened carefully before moving as carefully and lightly as she could into the kitchen itself. She felt her way around the long, tall stainless-steel counter that divided the stoves from the rest of the room, and made her way into the cooking area. The pilot lights from the massive iron stoves burned watchfully. Turning her back to the stoves, she felt for the drawer handles on the counter. Carefully, she pulled open the drawer closest to her, and tried to decipher what she was seeing in the pale light of the streetlamp. It seemed to be filled with the usual kitchen junk—string, meat thermometers, and measuring spoons. She closed it gently, pulled out the drawer to the left, and found the motherlode. George's knives. Not just any knives, restaurant knives, professionally sharpened once a week to make sure they stayed dangerous. This was going to be a little tricky. She picked out a lethal-looking carving knife with a six-inch blade as carefully as if she were playing pick-up-sticks, doing her best to stop the other knives from hitting each other. The childhood tune went nervously through her head:

> *She cut off their tails with a carving knife*
> *Did you ever see such a sight in your life*
> *As three blind mice—*

Abby swallowed anxiously, and slid the drawer shut. She held the large weapon in her right hand, and left the kitchen. When she reached the top of the dark and narrow back stair that led down to the bar, she stopped and listened.

Something or someone was moving around downstairs. Footsteps approached the foot of the staircase. She backed away from the stairs and moved quickly and quietly back into the kitchen and crouched down behind the counter. Sure enough, someone was coming up the stairs. Heavy footsteps, but fast. Abby could see the top of the stairs through a space in the stainless-steel shelving under the plate warmer. For a moment the footsteps stopped, and she made out Keith Ryder standing a few steps below the landing. He seemed to be listening and looking into the kitchen.

She was sure he would be able to see her feet, but he continued his climb and made his way stealthily through the prep room and out to the foyer. She thought she heard the back door open but she couldn't be sure. She waited and listened for more footsteps going upstairs, but she heard nothing. Her heart was drumming, pounding so hard, she felt as if it were trying to break its way out. It seemed amazing to her that Keith hadn't heard it.

Abby wondered if she was too late to help Joey. She held the knife in her left hand, away from her body, hoping she wouldn't fall and stab herself. She moved as quickly as she could down the back stairs, her right hand guiding her, running against the damp stone of the foundation wall.

Downstairs, the blackness was total. She turned on the least obtrusive light, the strips under the bar that lit up the sinks. They cast a greenish glow in the room. She walked around the bar, and nearly tripped over Joey. He was on the floor, lying on his back. She couldn't see any blood, though his face was ashen, so pale it looked an eggshell blue in the fluorescent light. She squatted next to him and touched a hand. It was cold, but she could feel a slow, dull pulse in his wrist. He stank of booze. A bottle of rum lay empty on the floor near him, its little copper pouring spout neatly next to it. No glass. Not far from the bottle was a small container, something a pharmacy might dispense. She picked it up and looked at the label but it had been picked off and the container was empty. "Shit," she whispered.

She listened carefully. Still breathing. She knew she should try to keep him awake, though it would not be easy, as he was already out cold. She took his shoulders and shook him.

"Joey, Joey, wake up!" she hissed. His head lolled on his neck. She thought she saw a flicker of an eyelid, but otherwise no response. She rolled him onto his stomach. Standing over him, she put her arms under him and heaved him up, trying to get him into a kneeling position. But his muscles wouldn't engage and he kept flopping down like a rag doll filled with liquid cement.

"Throw up, you stupid little shit, throw up," she whispered to him, but he did nothing. She ran to the sink, grabbed a cocktail shaker, and filled it with water. Spilling some of it on the way, she brought it back to him. She turned him over, raised his head and shoulders, and slid her lap underneath him. She was sweating, her muscles trembling. She tried to make him drink the water. At first it just poured out the sides of his mouth, soaking his face and her jeans. Finally, he seemed to swallow. He coughed, and she worried momentarily that she was drowning him. "Stupid, stupid boy, wake up, you stupid boy," she muttered, trying to force the liquid down his throat.

Suddenly, he lurched sideways and vomited a fountain of rancid, dark liquid, his body heaving with each wave. The smell filled the room, and the vomit pooled on the wood floor. He groaned. "Good boy, good boy," she said, wiping his hair off his forehead. The trembling in her body increased, and she realized her face was wet with tears and sweat. Shouldn't the cops be here by now? The restaurant above them was as silent as a tomb, the intermittent drone of the ice machine sounding loud in the dark, heavy silence. She slid out from under him, making sure to leave him lying on his side so he could empty himself without choking. She went to the bar and picked up the phone receiver. She held it to her ear, but it was dead. She put the receiver back in its cradle, giving the machine a chance to behave, then picked it up again and held it to her ear. Still dead.

Just as she was replacing the phone, she heard something upstairs. She walked softly to the foot of the back stairs and stood still, listening.

And then she heard it again, the creak of a footstep on the floor above her. With a fresh burst of strength brought on by fear, she ran back to Joey and grabbed him under the arms. She dragged him across the room toward the bar. She stopped and listened. This time she didn't hear anything. She got the boy out the doorway into the passage behind the bar. Her arms felt like old, stretched-out rubber bands that had reached the snapping point. She reached the back door, and pushed the panic bar with the small of her back, expecting it to give and release the door. The panic bar gave, but the door itself held firm. She let the boy down, and turned to the door, putting both hands on the bar and pushing hard. Nothing. It was locked, or jammed. They couldn't get out.

Abby heard more noise upstairs, and looked around, desperate for another avenue of escape. To her right was the vegetable-cooler. She didn't think she could drag Joey much further so she grabbed the handle of the vegetable-cooler door and pulled it toward her. It slid smoothly on its rails, and when she let go of it, started to slide slowly shut. Taking the boy under his arms, she swiveled him around. She managed to wedge her backside in the door, just before it slid shut. She ducked her head and backed into the cooler, pulling the heavy teenager in with her.

Inside the cooler the ceiling was low and she had to bend over so she wouldn't hit her head. She backed up as far as the rear wall, the boy's legs still sticking out the door, propping it open. She had to climb over him, and bend his legs at the knees. When the door was finally clear, she closed it as quietly as she could. Then she felt around in the dark until her hand crossed paths with the thin chain that hung from the basic porcelain light fixture. She pulled it and, thankfully, the light popped on. The bare bulb was encased in a wire cage, and cast a strange light on the reclining boy, carving dark shadows on his pale, sunken face. The shelves above his head were filled with crates of broccoli, red-leaf lettuces, potatoes, and onions. The air in the little room was cold, a get-in-your bones, dank cold. She looked for the thermostat, but couldn't find it. She pulled off her sweatshirt and draped it over the boy's chest like a large bib. She hated to leave him like this, but she pulled the light switch, plunging the cooler into darkness. If he woke up, he'd think he had been buried alive, but she had no choice. If someone opened the door, there was a small chance he wouldn't be seen if the cooler was dark. She had to get help. As quietly as she could, she slid open the cooler door, listening. Nothing. She stepped out, and slid the door shut behind her. Goodnight, sweet prince.

The *thunk* of the closing door seemed as loud as a head hitting a stone wall. Abby moved silently down the hall. At the bottom of the stairs, she waited. Another creak, and then a whisper from the top of the stairs, out of her field of vision.

"Abby, is that you?" Oh, God, Malaria. What was she doing here?

"Yeah," she whispered back. "Where are the police?"

"They're on their way. I had trouble getting them to believe me. Are you alone?"

"No, Joey's down here. He's in bad shape."

She heard motion and she looked up the stairs. Malaria was standing on the top step, her face hidden by the dark, and her frizzy hair backlit by the pale light from the kitchen.

"Come on up," she whispered. "Keith's left, but he'll be back. Hurry. We'll come back for Joey."

Abby nodded, relieved, and started quickly climbing the back stairs. Her arms were still shaking from the strain of dragging the boy. The cops would call the paramedics, and they could haul the poor kid out of the cooler. A few more minutes and it would all be over.

Abby made it to the landing at the top of the stairs and turned the corner. She looked at Malaria, who, to her astonishment, was in the middle of swinging a cast-iron skillet at Abby's head. By some piece of luck, the momentum that brought Abby up the stairs allowed her to raise her arm and begin to turn away, and when the heavy pan hit her it was off-center. She lost her balance, skidding on the linoleum floor. Her head hit the small utility sink on her way down. Once she was down, she tried to sit up, but her muscles didn't seem able to support her and she collapsed. She sank into a gray, speckled unconsciousness.

# CHAPTER THIRTY

The pain woke her. She came to slowly, aware only that the front of her head was pounding. She lifted her hand, intending to touch her forehead, but her arms wouldn't move. She tried again and failed. She panicked and tried to wrench them apart but they wouldn't separate. The adrenaline rush helped to clear her head and when she became fully conscious she realized her wrists were tied in front of her. When she tried to move her legs she discovered that someone had used the same kitchen twine to tie her ankles together. Abby rolled carefully over onto her side. A wave of nausea passed through her. Finally, slowly, pushing off with her wrists, she sat up. Her head pulsed violently where she had hit it against the sink, and her right shoulder was throbbing. She edged herself back to the wall and leaned against it. She couldn't quite remember what she was doing there, sitting on the linoleum floor of the restaurant. Slowly, the last half hour came back to her. She remembered putting Joey in the cooler, then coming upstairs to get help. She couldn't quite remember why. But she remembered Malaria waiting for her, and coming at her with a frying pan. Her shoulder surged in pain, as if to confirm her thoughts.

She had to get out of there.

She looked around for something sharp. The light in the little prep area was so poor she couldn't see. She remembered the beautiful carving knife she had found in George's drawer, but she must have left it downstairs, on the bar. She lowered herself to the floor again and looked under the counter across from her, her head pulsing harder the lower she went. She could see a couple of discarded crusts of bread, a napkin, plenty of dirt, but nothing she could use. She looked under the dishwasher. More dirt, an unrecognizable clump of god-knows-what. If she made out alive, she was going to have a talk with Dan-the-Man.

Abby heard a drawer open and then slam shut in the kitchen. She studied her wrists. The knots were tight and small, a number of them on top of each other. Someone wanted to make sure she wouldn't go anywhere. She listened to the sounds coming from the kitchen as she tried to reach her fingers around and pick apart the tight little knots, but her fingers were unsteady and the rope wouldn't give.

She heard the rustle of movement from the kitchen, and Malaria appeared in the doorway. She was wearing an apron. "I have so much respect for you."

Abby felt a surge of rage. "You hit me over the fucking head with a pan!"

Malaria flinched at Abby's outburst. "I tried to keep you out of this. I did. I tried to protect you." She turned and went back into the kitchen.

"Wait, wait, Aliara! Protect me? Goddamn you, come back here!" When no one appeared, Abby started screaming. "Hey! Help! Help! I'm tied up!" Malaria reappeared, a bucket of water in her hands. She heaved the contents at Abby, hitting her square in the face. The cold and force of it knocked the wind out of her and filled her mouth and nose with water. While she gasped and sputtered, Malaria leaned in to her, speaking intently. "You have to shut up, okay? We didn't want your face all taped up, but he said you'd shout and told me to have the water ready. As usual, he was right." With that, she picked up the bucket and left the room.

Abby was soaked, and the chill in the room and her fear made her shudder. However, the cold helped to clear the last foggy areas in her head. She groaned. God, she had handled everything so badly. She hadn't realized the enormity of what she was doing when she casually crossed into this world where there were no boundaries, where people would do anything, believing they had everything to lose. Now it was too late to back quietly away. She was tied up on the floor of the place where she worked. She visualized herself walking across this floor. She had done it countless times, on automatic, not thinking about anything but the desserts she needed, or the check for B6, or when she could go home. Who would have guessed eight hours earlier that she would end up in this same room, tied up like a roast, knowing that she might die. Because her options seemed to be running out, she felt sure.

She started to cry, partly as a ruse, but mostly because, feeling the way she did, it came easy. She projected the mewling sound as much as she could. Finally, Malaria looked out the doorway. Abby put all the pathos into her face that she could muster. "Aliara, he's dangerous. He killed Connie, I'm sure. That's how he knew about the empty apartment, that's how he knew so quickly that she was gone. He left her dead in the woods, and he'll do the same to you."

"Oh, Abby, you don't know him at all. He's not like that. He's not a violent person, he'd never hurt me."

Abby started to plead. "I swear, he was with her. Ask him, make him tell you, you'll see. He's coming back here, isn't he?"

"God, yes. And I have to keep going. I've got things to do."

"Wait, please. Tell me about Keith. Why this is happening. I deserve to know."

Malaria smiled pityingly at her. "It's hard to explain."

"Tell me about Connie—"

"That girl, what a piece of work." She shuddered. "I mean, I've seen a lot of predators in my line of work, but she was something."

"How?" Abby pictured the dark-haired girl at the wheel of the minivan, smiling.

"From the minute she set her eyes on Keith, she knew she wanted him and there was nothing he could do to get away from her."

"Oh, come on." She wiped the moisture from her eyes with her tied hands. "You don't really believe that, do you?"

"Okay. Shut up. I won't talk to you anymore."

"He's taking you for a fool, Aliara. You're in love with a guy who is engaged to someone else, and who fucks around on you both. And you're defending him."

"Look," Malaria said, her armor undented. "So he couldn't resist a manipulative woman, who used her sexuality to get what she wanted. Big deal. But he was always honest with her, always told her he was committed to someone else, that he could never stay with her—"

"Committed to Josie, right?"

Malaria didn't answer, but her mouth twisted.

"So why kill her? Why not just break up with her?"

Malaria looked at her as if she were missing the obvious. "Because she wouldn't let him! She said she was going to go to Josie!"

"So what did he do, just take her out in the woods?"

"No, no, he's not like that. He would never have done that. He tried to work it out with her. He's not a violent person! He brought her to me!"

Abby was stunned. "To you? What do you mean?"

"I'm the therapist. He did the right thing. He brought her to me. He knew that if anyone could convince her to let him go, it was me."

Abby nodded. There was a down-the-rabbit-hole logic to it. "Go on."

"So, they made an appointment and came to see me. It was all highly professional. I listened to them, I led the discussion, I helped them weigh the issues. I did everything in my power to make her see his point of view. And at the end of the hour, she seemed to understand his needs. And then, just as they were getting ready to leave, she went"—acting out Connie's gesture, Malaria slapped the sides of her face and dropped her jaw, a caricature of someone who had just learned something astonishing—" 'Oh, my God—I get it! You're fucking him, too!' " Two angry red spots appeared on Malaria's cheeks. "God, she was lower than dirt!"

"And? What did you say?" Abby prompted.

"She was an ignorant rude slut, and I told her so. Keith told me to calm down, which was ridiculous, I was calm and professional. But I had to shake my head, I mean, it was funny. I said to her: 'He'll never give up Josie for you, you can be sure of that.' And she laughed! She looked thrilled and she laughed in my face and said: 'Come on, Doc, we're not talking about Josie, are we? But he'll never stay with you, no matter what he's told you. He's using you to help him hide all his little affairs, clean up his little messes. Not only that, you're old. So here's a News Flash—' she talked like that, like a cheap character on a sitcom— 'so here's a News Flash—I'm gonna keep him. For now. But you, you can go on giving him the occasional blow job in the backseat of his car, I don't give a shit!' Ahh, can you believe anyone would talk to a fellow human being like that?" She looked at Abby. "Can you?" Malaria's words had become louder, more deliberate, crisper. She went on with her story, unasked. She probably couldn't have stopped if she'd wanted to. "The little bitch turned away, so pleased with herself. On my desk I have this beautiful rock, a big smooth gray rock Keith gave me. He found it on a beach in Maine and I use it as a paperweight. When she turned away, I felt the blood rush into my eyes and without thinking about it I picked up this big rock. And as hard as I could, I hit her on the head with it."

Abby moved her head away in disbelief. "You? You killed her?"

Malaria frowned and blinked. "I didn't mean to, but it was like she was asking for it, she wouldn't stop."

"You hit her over and over with a rock."

"Abby, you don't get it. All Keith's future, his plans with Josie's father, Jamison Brown, everything would have gone up in smoke. He and Jamison are actually going to work together on a major show. It's all decided."

"But you killed her because you were jealous of her."

Malaria didn't answer, just turned her head away.

"You know he's not going to stay with you—he's going to marry Josie."

"So he says. But I'm patient."

"You're wrong. Josie has everything going for her. He'd never leave her for you—"

"You're the one who's wrong. Look at Prince Charles and his mistress. He always loved her, even when he was married to Diana, who was so like Josie, in fact, both of them with chronic eating disorders—"

"Yeah, but Charles had to marry Diana, it had to do with being in line for the throne—" Abby couldn't believe she was getting drawn into a discussion on the British royal family.

"Abby, shut up, you talk as if I'm delusional. I know Keith isn't the king, but everyone has forces greater than love and sex at work on them—"

Speak of the devil. Just then, the back door swung open and Keith came in. He pulled the brick out and shut it firmly behind him. "Aliara, you ready?" he called out, in a cozy, honey-I'm-home kind of voice.

"What took you so long? I've been talking with Abby," Aliara called out.

"I couldn't get away." Keith came into the prep kitchen, his eyes dancing around the room, as if he were on speed. He was wearing a one-piece work suit. "Come on, come on, we got to get out of here, it's going to be morning soon. I got to get back. You ready?" His gaze passed over Abby without stopping, as if she were a piece of furniture. The fact that he wasn't acknowledging her as a human being frightened her more than anything that had happened before.

"Nearly," answered Malaria. "I've packed up the steaks, even though they look a little grisly. And there's a lot of salmon. Shall I take it?"

Abby swallowed hard. "You're stealing food from the kitchen?"

Keith looked at her for the first time. "Why waste it? I love salmon,.Aliara, pack it up. Come on, let's go."

Malaria, moving briskly like a housewife getting ready for a party, disappeared into the kitchen. Abby took a deep breath. "Wait, please, Keith, tell me. If she killed Connie, why didn't you just call the cops? You didn't do it."

Keith watched Malaria through the doorway. "Because no one would believe that I wasn't involved. And either way, all the dirt would come out, wouldn't it? The affair. Josie would dump me, and I know Jamison would cancel our joint project. I'm an artist. I can't lose that."

Abby was awed by his sense of self-importance. "And Betty? You killed Betty? What did she do to you?"

"Honestly, who cares? Even her kid hated her." He shook his head. "One of the parties, she caught Connie and me together. She hated Connie, was always trying to get her in trouble. If they discovered Connie's body, eventually she'd have thought of me and gone to the cops. She backed me into a corner." He tilted his head at Abby, and raised his eyebrows. "Ready?"

"Ready for what?"

"We're going to burn this building down, with you and the boy in it."

# CHAPTER THIRTY-ONE

In the kitchen, Abby could hear Keith and Malaria opening and closing drawers and discussing food options like a pair of Sunday shoppers at the local Price Chopper. Back against the wall, she tried to think calmly about what was waiting for her and the boy, as soon as the two killers were done bickering over cuts of beef. But her head was filled with white noise and confusion and she couldn't seem to put aside the panic long enough to think of a way out. She knew he meant what he said and there didn't seem to be anything she could do about it. All she could think of doing was to delay them, make them talk. Maybe the police would show up after all. Maybe lightning would strike.

She cleared her throat and croaked: "Keith! Keith! I need to talk to you!"

Impatiently, he looked out of the kitchen. "What d'you want?"

"Please, you owe me. I need to know. How did you get Connie to pack her bags, and leave a note for her father?"

Keith grinned, confident in his infinite ability to charm. "Good question."

He walked over and squatted next to her. He dropped his voice. His proximity scared and disgusted her, but she needed to keep him engaged. She tried not to flinch.

"I'll tell you a little secret. But don't tell Aliara. Before we went for our 'couples therapy,' I had already decided what was going to happen to Connie. And I had a feeling about Aliara, that she would help me. I didn't think she'd do all my work for me, but I thought she'd help me. So I asked Connie to run away with me, to bring a bag, and leave a note for her father. She was so excited. And then I said we should play along with Aliara, who was an old 'friend' of mine."

"So you were going to kill her, no matter what."

Keith looked pleased to be able to show off his smarts. He nodded. "You are not only beautiful but sharp." He touched her lip with his thumb. She had to resist the urge to grab it with her teeth and bite down.

Malaria emerged from the kitchen. She was holding up a filleting knife. The blade was sharp and glistening, as if wet. A look of anger passed over her face when she saw Keith so close to her. Like it or not, Abby thought she might be able to take advantage of it. She pretended not to notice Malaria and giggled softly at Keith. Or did her best imitation given the circumstances.

"Keith, you and I have some unresolved issues," she murmured.

"What are you up to?" Malaria snapped suspiciously.

Keith bounced onto his feet and started to laugh. "Oh, Abby, you don't want to do that. You don't want to piss her off—she is a monster with a heavy object—" and he put his arm around Malaria, pulling her toward him.

"You bastard." She held the knife up to him, and, to Abby's amazement, the woman's eyes filled with tears. "I can't leave you alone for a second—"

Keith pushed her knife hand away and kissed her, and for a moment she resisted, then responded hungrily, biting his lower lip.

Abby's stomach churned with fear. "Before you two get down to it, tell me, how did you get Connie into the woods?"

Malaria pulled her mouth away from Keith but kept looking at him. "Keith drove her car, I drove mine."

Abby persisted. "What did you do with her stuff? Her bag?"

Malaria looked at her. "Gave it to the Salvation Army. Keith, ticktock, ticktock."

Keith nodded and went into the kitchen. Abby knew there was very little time left. She felt her throat tightening until it hurt. "Cut me loose, come on, Aliara," she whispered, trying to make eye contact.

Malaria shook her head. "Not possible."

She played her last card. "Aliara, you know what Keith just told me? He told me he set you up to kill Connie. He manipulated your feelings for him. He made you jealous, knowing you'd lash out at her."

Malaria looked at her, and there was something like resignation in her eyes. "Well, I guessed that. But you know what they say, if you really love someone, you love them for their weaknesses as well as their strengths."

"Aliara," Abby said in desperation, "what happened to the Giving? The Not Taking? All that Love, for Chrissake?" She looked at the woman in front of her, who was getting ready to kill her. "What about Joey's mother? Betty? You both killed her, too, as a team?"

"That was a mess."

"What happened?" Abby's only hope was to keep her talking.

"She called Keith and he asked me to go with him to see her. She had some weird idea that he had been working with the girl, Connie, *stealing furniture*. She was crazy."

While Malaria was talking, Abby noticed a flicker of movement behind her. Leaning on the doorjamb, as if he were having trouble standing upright, was Joey. His skin was a gray tone, his eyes sunken and dark in their sockets, and he was wearing her sweatshirt. In his right hand he was holding a pricey bottle of Glenfiddich. Abby could hear Keith moving around in the kitchen. Terrified she would give Joey away, she tried to keep Malaria talking. "Then what happened?"

Malaria looked down at the knife, twirling it. "Keith tried to get her to listen, but she was relentless. She kept jabbing her finger at him, telling him to tell the girl to keep away from her son. All she could talk about was her son. She was raving. Poor Keith didn't know anything about the kid. He kept saying, 'I don't know what you're talking about, Mrs. Merchant.' But she said she was going to go to the cops, tell them everything about him and Connie and the furniture. Stupid cow, she kept saying she knew everything. She did know that Connie had seduced Keith. I don't know how." Malaria gave a snort. "Anyway, out of nowhere she pulled out a shotgun! Insane! The woman was dangerous. When we finally talked her into putting it down, and she was looking the other way, I picked it up and shot her. I got all this spray on me. Yuck, what a mess. The boy was there, wasn't he?"

Joey had listened to this casual retelling of his mother's slaughter. His face was motionless and his eyes on the back of Malaria's head were glazed with pain. He pushed himself off the doorframe, and started to raise the bottle.

Suddenly, Malaria wrinkled her nose and said with a sneer: "What is that awful smell? Vomit, it smells like vomit—" She started to turn toward the boy. Too slow, he swung the bottle of whiskey at her head. He made contact, but not hard. The bottle, unbroken, slipped from his hand and skidded away across the floor. Malaria raised her knife. The boy gave a hoarse war cry and propelled himself at her, knocking her down. Though he was taller than her, he was obviously weakened by the pills and alcohol in his system. He tried to pin her down. Malaria let out a howl and fought him, bucking and slashing. To her horror, Abby saw a red line open up on his arm. Keith ran in from the kitchen, and stood next to them, trying to grab some part of Joey while trying to keep his hands out of the way of the moving knife. Abby crawled to the Glenfiddich, praying that Keith wouldn't notice the movement. Just then, Joey rolled onto Malaria's chest and managed to get a knee on Malaria's knife arm, holding it down. He grabbed her neck. Abby picked up the bottle of Scotch by its short neck. It crossed her mind that he should have gone for some top-shelf brandy instead. Carefully, wobbling, she got to her knees and then, pulling herself up on the sink, she stood.

Malaria bit Joey, twisting, trying to throw him off. The boy kept shouting incoherently. His hands were still around her neck. Finally, Keith managed to get a grip on Joey. He got him around the neck with his arm and started to twist and pull. He was strong and fit and very quickly Joey looked as if he was starting to lose it. Abby shuffled forward, her ankles tied, holding the bottle like a baseball bat in her two tied hands. She reached back, took careful aim, and swung at Keith's head with all her might. There was an awesome crack. The bottle exploded, raining golden single malt onto them all. For a second Malaria, Joey, and Abby all stopped moving. Keith let go of Joey and, like a cartoon character, tottered one way and then the other. Finally, his knees buckled and he fell heavily down onto the floor. As if by mutual consent, the woman and the boy started fighting again. Abby moved toward them, still hobbled by the rope, and managed to grab the knife hand that was pinned down by Joey's knee. Doing her best to avoid the sharp blade, she twisted Malaria's wrist. The woman held on with a steel-like grip. Abby grabbed a finger and bent it back hard until, with a cry of pain, Malaria released the knife. Snatching it up, Abby tried to stop the trembling in her hands long enough to use the knife to cut the twine between her ankles. She looked up to see that Joey had his hands around Malaria's neck and she was making a grating sound. In the ashen face of the teenage boy kneeling over her, Abby read stony determination. He was going to kill her.

"Joey! Stop!" Abby yelled, trying to get through. Without undoing her hands, Abby dropped the knife. She threw herself at the boy, knocking him off the woman. He kept fighting to regain his position, though his grip had weakened.

His hands finally relinquished their hold. Malaria didn't move. Joey curled up on the floor, a small, keening wail coming from him. Moving very slowly, her muscles trembling, Abby stood. Her balance was off and her shoulder was throbbing. She leaned against the counter, dizzy, waiting until the worst of it passed. She found the knife on the floor. Out of the corner of her eye, she saw Keith move. She used the blade, pointed toward her chest, to saw apart her wrists. Quick, quick. On the floor at her feet lay the neck of the broken bottle of Glenfiddich. She picked it up.

Turning to the back door, she took a breath, then ran at it, kicking it. It was locked tight and all she managed to do was slam her foot and send the shock up her spine. Her arm, shoulder, and head throbbed in sympathy.

Turning, she ran unsteadily up the uneven flight of stairs to the second floor. In the office, she picked up the phone receiver. No dial tone. She hurried across the hall and opened the door to the long porch. Church. The staff chairs were still in place, waiting. A dirty espresso cup sat on the wooden deck, a reminder of a different time. Abby stood there and screamed for help at the dark and deserted Bantam Circle. Her voice came out threadbare, as if she'd been shouting all night long.

"Help! Someone . . . help!" There was a police car parked in front of the Lacey Memorial across the large square, but it was empty. No one came running. She waited, and called again. Nothing. She went back to the landing, tears of frustration and fear running down her face. The madwoman would soon wake up. Joey was in danger. And Keith—he might already be on his feet. She listened for someone on the stairs. In the office, she tried the phone again. Nothing. Outside the office, she noticed the window that led out onto the rooftop, where the air conditioners were, was propped open, often the case when it was too hot inside. Making a decision, Abby dropped the broken bottleneck and picked up the useless phone. Holding onto the cord, she pulled it out of the wall. She climbed out of the open window, carrying the phone awkwardly under her arm. She ran over to the railing.

This side of the restaurant faced Route 46. Small, shabby buildings, long since broken up into apartments, were lined up across the street from where she stood. Abby shouted. No one answered. She yelled again. Nothing. She took a deep breath, and, holding the old, heavy phone by the recessed hold under the receiver, she pulled her right arm back, and, like a discus thrower with her left arm out for balance, she flung the black phone across the street. It soared over the narrow canyon of Route 46, the phone separating from the receiver, which followed like the tail of a kite. She expected it to hit the side of the building. Instead, the body of the phone sailed right through the center of an eight-paned window, exploding it into a shower of glass. The receiver tried to follow but didn't make it and bounced against the brick facing, cracking in two on impact. What was left of it came to rest hanging from the cord. Abby stood on the rooftop, her hands covering her mouth, wondering if she had just brained someone in their sleep.

And then she heard a bellow, the kind she would imagine a bull would make when stuck with a small but sharp sword. "Hey!" trumpeted an angry male voice, gritty with sleep. Abby waited, and sure enough, a bright red face appeared at the edge of the broken window, tentatively, in case another missile followed the first. Abby waved.

"What the hell—" called out Red Face.

"Call the police, quick," she called out. "I'm trapped in here with two murderers. And hurry, please, they're waking up."

It turned out that, after all, she wasn't the only person awake in Bantam that morning after all. Roy Goodrich had not rolled over and gone back to sleep after her call. As he told her later, he spent some time waiting for the phone to ring. When it didn't, he got dressed and walked to a neighbor's house, which was a half mile away. Joey had taken Roy's truck, so he had no wheels. He borrowed his neighbor's car and drove into town. Finding the restaurant shut down and the lights off, he looked for his pickup. He found it not far from Abby's Bronco, parked down the street from the restaurant. This was about the time she was throwing the phone across Route 46. So Abby figured they would have been saved, even if she hadn't woken up Red Face. She hoped. She hated to think of two lives hanging on her phone-tossing skills.

The police discovered a can of gasoline in the kitchen. It looked as if that was going to be Keith and Malaria's solution to the little problem of Joey and Abby. The sprinkler system in the basement had been deactivated, in preparation. It would look like a murder followed by suicide through self-immolation. The plan might have worked, simply because no one knew about Malaria and Keith.

Joey was in bad shape. He had to have his stomach pumped at the hospital and twelve stitches in his arm. Malaria was alive, though her throat would be bruised for a few days. Two shopping bags were found in the kitchen of the restaurant, ready to go, filled with an assortment of food—salmon, steaks, polenta, arugula, shrimp, beef stock, fudge sauce, and Sandy's profiteroles.

On the sidewalk outside the restaurant, as the sun was starting to lighten the sky, the chief of police pointed a meaty finger at her. "You're a piece of work, Abigail. You should've come to me first. I can't decide whether to lock you up, or buy you a beer." And he gave her a light cuff on the side of the head, which seemed to express his feelings perfectly. She promised him that, as soon as she had taken care of the dogs and caught a few hours of sleep, she would come to the station and go over every single detail of the past month.

When she finally got home it was a little after six in the morning. The dogs were waiting anxiously and as a reward she took them to the back pasture and let them sniff the cowpats. The sky was beginning to brighten, exposing the quiet fields where they had lain hidden during the dark night. It was a reassuring sight, this earth like a huge, patchwork turtle, and she, a small speck, riding on its back in the early dawn.

# CHAPTER THIRTY-TWO

•

Abby took the next week off from work, read a lot, cleaned the trailer, and walked the dogs. She left her machine on and didn't return any calls. The first morning, she drove down Route 46 and visited Joey at the hospital. The medication he had in his system had been from Malaria's stash, the pills she took to help her sleep. She had ground it up and added it to the booze Keith had forced the boy to drink. One of his doctors told Abby the temperature in the cooler might have helped Joey by keeping his body from sinking too deeply into sleep. Like most teenagers, he recovered quickly once he was in the hospital, but they wanted to keep him an extra day for observation. He seemed to enjoy her visit. Roy was there when she arrived, and the three of them played Gin Rummy.

As Roy was dealing out the cards for a second round, he said to his son: "I think you have something to tell this young lady."

Abby, expecting some kind of parent-fed speech of thanks or acknowl- edgment, said: "Come on, Roy, Joey and I are even. He saved my life."

But Roy shook his head and raised an eyebrow at Joey.

Joey picked up his cards, then put them down again. He looked at Abby. Shifted uncomfortably. Cleared his throat. Spoke. "I knew about the dead deer. Before they did it. I'm really sorry I didn't warn you, but she said if I did, it would be worse for you."

"Who's 'she'?" Abby asked.

"Sarah. She and Richie came up to the house."

Abby shook her head, disgusted at the sheer meanness of it. "Of course. Who else, right?"

"I didn't know what to do. I'm sorry, it really sucked. You're probably really pissed off now. That's okay." Joey, tense and unhappy, watched her.

Abby thought for a moment before she spoke. When she did, she looked the boy in the eye. "Joey, I know you," she said, "you did your best in a bad situation. And I know your best will get better all the time. Thanks for telling me, though, it really means a lot to me."

Joey nodded and lay back against the pillows.

"On the other hand," Abby added as she picked up her cards, "that deer might not have been quite so forgiving."

The afternoon of the second day, she printed up a good clean picture of Connie's face, a close-up taken from the full, reclining nude. The young woman looked beautiful and pleased with herself, and once more Abby couldn't help but admire her confidence. She slid it into the carved frame, and put the original nude behind it, out of sight. She closed up the back of the frame and wrapped the whole thing in tissue paper.

The day was clear and breezy when she knocked on the screen door of the ranch house on Malden Street. The wooden door was open, so she could see through the dark mesh into the kitchen. No one answered her knock. "Mike! Mike, you there?"

After a few minutes, she heard footsteps. Mike appeared in the hallway and walked across the kitchen to the door. He didn't open the screen, nor did he invite her in. She noticed his clothes seemed to hang on him, as if he had lost weight. He looked stooped.

"Hi, Mike. I brought you something."

"Oh, yeah." He stepped outside, pulling the screen closed behind him. He blinked in the sunlight.

"I brought you this." She held out the wrapped frame for him, and he took it. Without curiosity, he held it.

"How's it going?" She wasn't sure what else to say.

"Oh, okay. You know, I'll be fine." He looked at her, nodding his head. She noticed the dark, bruised-looking shadows under his eyes.

Abby put out her hand, and took one of his. She didn't know what to say so she stood there, holding onto his thick, rough paw. Finally, he used his free hand to pat her cheek. He was dismissing her. She started to let go but changed her mind.

"Mike, I need your help."

He paused before answering. "I don't know. What's up?"

"You're going to think this is stupid, but I need to learn how to bowl."

For a moment, she thought he was going to tell her to get lost. Instead he smiled. A small thing, but it touched his eyes. "Why's that?"

"I'm thirty-two years old, it's time. I hear you're good. And we've got a bowling alley in town."

He shook his head. "You're trying to make me feel good. Get the old man out. Bowling therapy, or something."

Abby nodded. "You're right, bowling therapy. That's exactly it. You need it, too. That's funny, because people around me are telling me it's time I get out more, get a hobby. So, I thought, bowling. Last time I tried was in fifth grade. What do you think, Mike? Just the basics, okay? The part where you run up to the line and throw it, one leg behind you." She showed him, letting an imaginary bowling ball fly up into the air. She covered her head to protect herself.

He gave an involuntary laugh.

Taking this as encouragement, Abby fished her date book out of her bag. "Next Friday?"

They heard the crunch of wheels on the driveway and before he could answer, a pickup pulled in behind her Bronco. Abby and Mike watched as

Sean climbed out of the driver's seat. Abby closed her date book and shoved it back into her purse. "Mike, I'll call you soon, okay?"

Mike didn't answer. Sean walked up to them. Abby glanced at him. He looked especially good. Maybe it was his walk, or the white shirt he was wearing.

"What are you doing here?" Abby asked, sounding sour even to her own ears.

Sean raised his eyebrows at her. "Mike's my boss. I come here all the time. What're you doing here?"

Before she could answer, Mike said: "She wants me to teach her how to bowl. She says she needs to get out more. Needs a life."

"That's a fact," Sean said with a nod. "You gonna do it?"

Mike shrugged. "I was thinking about it, but suddenly she's gotta leave."

"Shame." Sean turned to Abby. "It's a good idea. Yeah."

Mike looked at her, too.

Abby blushed. "Look, Mike, I'm late. I'll call you, okay?" She walked around Sean toward her car.

"I never took you for a quitter, Abby." Mike frowned.

"I'm not, I—"

"I'm a pretty good bowler, myself," Sean said. "I could help out. You know, with the finer points."

Mike shook his head. "Arrogant bastard." He looked at Abby. "Maybe you're right. It'll be good for both of us. I'm in if you're in."

Sean leaned back on the hood of the Bronco. "Hey, we could even start a league. Testarossa Plumbing. Embroidered shirts. What d'you say, Abby?"

The fourth day, she stopped in Bantam on her way home from the hospital and went up to Franklin's office. He happened to be in, and alone. He was sitting at his desk going through some papers, and looked up when she walked in.

"Hi, Franklin. How's your head?"

He smiled. "Much better, thank you. I've been keeping to my own car, and using the trash can for trash. Can't ask for much more. How are you?"

Abby shrugged, not sure of the answer. He looked at her, as if expecting her to say something more, but she'd used up her small talk.

"Can I sit down?" she asked, gesturing to a chair.

"Would you shut the door, first?"

Abby nodded and did as he asked, feeling the burden of privacy once the heavy wooden door closed them in. She sat down.

Franklin spoke first. "Did you hear about the Callahan boys?"

She shook her head. "No, I've been hiding out for the last few days. What happened?"

"Chief Sheriff has been working on this for a while, I gather. There've been a steady trickle of thefts reported, each of them unsettling, but none big enough to make the police blotter in the *Bantam Reporter*. He's had Richie Callahan in his sights for some time. Since he arrested him two days ago, he's had a rash of people call in, reporting past thefts of furniture. He's going to have to wade through them all now."

Abby shook her head. "Strange, two murders on one hand, and all these thefts on the other, and they're not connected. Keith and Malaria had nothing to do with the Callahans." Her theory, for what it was worth, was being shaken. She had been sure that anything that appeared coincidental in her small town could not be, that it would prove to be connected.

"I know," said Franklin. "But you're wrong. They are connected. Through Connie. She was involved in the robberies. Callahan claims it was her idea, said she would feed him names of potential victims. She was the link."

A connection by personality. Weak, but better than nothing. Abby hesitated. "What about Sean Kenna? Was he tied in with them?"

Franklin started tidying up some papers on his desk. "Doesn't look that way. He was friends with them, but he says, and the Callahans concur, that he knew nothing about the thefts."

He stopped talking, and beyond the rustling of papers, the quiet in the room grew heavy. Abby knew it was her turn to break the silence.

She cleared her throat. "Tell me about the picture frame."

If he had told her it was none of her business, she would have left his office, and that would have been that. Instead, he looked away, and shook his head.

"Where to start? I met Connie at one of those parties. Just like Keith Ryder did. I don't go often, because they don't interest me, but I'm an asset, you know, local, black and a lawyer. Anyway, Connie was doing what she did, flitting around, talking to all the men, looking good."

Abby waited, and watched his face as he spoke. The words came slowly, as if it hurt to speak them.

"At some point she noticed me. I don't know if she knew I was a lawyer, but she found out quickly. She quoted Shakespeare to me, that line from *Richard III*: "first, kill all the lawyers." I can't tell you how many times people have done that, and it's usually mildly obnoxious, but from her it was different. She was sexy, funny. I've wondered what it was about her—she knew how to make you feel she was really interested. Like she was drawn to you, intrigued. She made me feel young, sexy, fascinating."

He sighed, and shifted in his chair. She thought he might want to jump up and move around, but he seemed sunken into the furniture, his hands splayed out on the desk, covering his papers. She wondered again how old he was.

"I'm forty-one years old," he continued, as if she had spoken out aloud. "Not so old, but too old for a girl her age. But she said that wasn't so, she was much too mature for most men her age. They bored her. I believed her because I wanted to, and we started seeing each other. It was always away from Bantam, though. Albany. Great Barrington. Once we met in Manhattan. She claimed it was more fun, but I started to feel it was because she didn't want to be seen with me. Because I'm black? Maybe. Truth is, she was the kind of girl who liked to keep secrets. She enjoyed knowing things other people didn't. It gave her control.

"And that was it. One day she cancelled a date. Told me she'd call me, but she never did. I tried her a few times, but she never returned my calls. And I never saw her again. I mean, I'd see her occasionally around town, but we never spoke. The next thing I heard, she was dead."

He inhaled deeply then let his breath out in a long, slow stream.

"What about the frame?" Abby asked softly.

"A present. I wanted to give her something that mattered to me."

She could've asked him about Frankie's Motel, but she didn't. "Why didn't you tell me about your relationship with her?"

"I don't know. I didn't feel I had any information that would be helpful to anyone. I don't know. I just didn't want to."

And that was that. Again, not completely satisfactory, but as good as it was going to get. Abby took a deep breath.

"Want to get lunch? I'll buy, as long as it costs less than seven dollars. For both of us."

Franklin gave it serious consideration, then nodded. "You're on."

They walked out of the building, and stood for a moment on Main Street, enjoying the sunshine, the brilliant blue sky.

"Doesn't it seem strange it's only the beginning of July?" she asked him, and Franklin looked at her for a moment.

"It does," he said, and they started walking to the café.

# ABOUT THE AUTHOR

Julia Pomeroy spent her childhood in Libya and Somalia, and her teens in Italy. She lived in NYC, where she worked as an interpreter and an actress. She eventually moved upstate, where she and her husband opened a restaurant. Julia Pomeroy lives in Columbia County, New York.